Sanjida O'Connell was born in 1970 in Pakistan of Bangladeshi/Irish parents. She studied zoology at Bristol University and is now a TV producer/director. She has written one previous novel, *Theory of Mind*, also published by Black Swan and one work of non-fiction, *Mindreading: How we learn to love and lie*. She lives in Bristol.

Also by Sanjida O'Connell

Fiction

THEORY OF MIND

and published by Black Swan

Non-fiction

MINDREADING: HOW WE LEARN
TO LOVE AND LIE

ANGEL BIRD

Sanjida O'Connell

BLACK SWAN

ANGEL BIRD
A BLACK SWAN BOOK : 0 552 99712 9

First publication in Great Britain

PRINTING HISTORY
Black Swan edition published 1998

Set in 11/13pt Bembo Schoolbook by
Phoenix Typesetting, Ilkley, West Yorkshire.

Black Swan Books are published by Transworld Publishers Ltd,
61–63 Uxbridge Road, London W5 5SA,
in Australia by Transworld Publishers (Australia) Pty Ltd,
15–25 Helles Avenue, Moorebank, NSW 2170
and in New Zealand by Transworld Publishers (NZ) Ltd,
3 William Pickering Drive, Albany, Auckland.

Reproduced, printed and bound in Great Britain by
Cox & Wyman Ltd, Reading, Berks.

To my mother, Rosemary O'Connell, who taught
me how to name the wild things.

I would like to thank the following for taking the time to share their expertise with me:

Gert Beyens for unravelling magpie behaviour, Lloyd Buck for his thoughts on rearing magpies, Nick Davies for his insights into the mating habits of dunnocks, Sandra Bell and Cecilia Yang for expounding on the intricacies of orchid growing, and for disclosing their culinary secrets, the chefs of Mezzo and The Apprentice.

One of the main source materials on magpie biology was T.R. Birkhead's *The Magpies* (T. & A.D. Poyser, 1991).

Henry Keys kindly took care of me in Ireland, and I'm grateful to Colin Cameron, Guy Cowlishaw, Richard Dale, and my parents, Rosemary and James O'Connell, for their comments. I'd also like to thank Joanna Goldsworthy for her thoughtful editing.

All errors are my own .

One for sorrow
Two for mirth
Three for a wedding
Four for a birth
Five for a christening
Six for a death
Seven's heaven
Eight is hell
Nine's the devil's own self.

— *Anon*

I was born a zoologist, as was my father, Charles Edwards, and his father, Robert Eamonn Edwards, before him. We lived in a schizophrenic house in Kew. Upstairs the light, filtering through dense swathes of ivy, was snagged by the dark spaces gouged out of masks from Papua New Guinea, caught by the edges of pottery vessels fired black, and trapped in the sharp glass eyes of stuffed animals. The library had spears above the door and a man of woven grass in the corner. Most of the books were old, leather-bound and embossed with gold lettering, their pages fly-specked and yellowing. Piles of notebooks written in copperplate, the edges of the paper marbled with coloured ink, spilt from the shelves. My grandfather wrote them on his many voyages and my father had been slowly and painstakingly transcribing them. He had already transferred his own journals onto the hard-drive of his computer, but he felt that his words were not as poetic as my grandfather's. I've read all my father's published works. They're written in the dry neutered style required by science journals, but here and there a little of his love seeps through.

Downstairs was where my mother reigned. In her domain the light had clarity and there was an absence of dust. Piles of magazines – *House and Home*, *Country Gardens* and *Elle Decoration* – were stacked at one end of the pine pew she'd upholstered in gingham. The rooms looked as if they were kitted out by a designer from Habitat who had had a nervous breakdown in Harrods. She left gourds, misshapen orange and green fruit, on the kitchen table, artfully arranged in disarray until they began to decompose, and her vases from Purves & Purves were always full of flowers. But not orchids. There were to be no orchids in the house. Is it not enough, she said, that we should have a greenhouse full of them, and that your father has the run of seven at Kew? That in his youth he trapped and stuffed small mammals from Peru until he fell in love with a strange and beautiful flower that drinks the blood of flies, and stinks like rotting flesh, an orchid known as *Dracula bella*? That since that day he has dedicated his life to this vampiric genus?

My mother's friends all had moon orchids, white, brash and easy to grow, wrapped in moss, drooping gently on their occasional tables. My mother had gerberas, bright cartoons of flowers in clouded glass jars, lined up in rows on the kitchen window sill. When I saw her small, pale, anxious face appear between the floral equivalent of postmodern, it seemed like a warning, somehow.

'You will be careful, won't you?' she asked, and I nodded.

I drank ethical coffee and ate Andean biscuits from the charity shop where she works. They tasted disgusting. She tried to fit health-food chocolate bars – the kind that are always bitter and covered with a white bloom – and apples into my already overcrowded rucksack. She'd rather have given me a bullet-proof vest.

'Mother,' I said, 'I'm sure they'll sell fruit,' but she looked dubious.

She stood up and scrutinized me, pushing a strand of blond hair behind her ear.

'Why you have to go there I don't know. You could

have stayed in Cambridge. David offered you the money, and he'll miss you, you know.'

'It's not as if I'm going to Patagonia, for God's sake. There are telephones. I'll visit.'

She nodded. 'Say goodbye to your father.'

As always it took me a few seconds to adjust to the profusion of leaves and flowers: a visual overload that was initially like sensory deprivation. My father was at the back of the greenhouse. Orchids are high maintenance plants, but he often came here just to be alone, and to think. Neither of us said anything; we looked at the plant together.

'*Zygostates*,' he muttered, though he knew I knew what it was.

'I'm off then,' I said.

'*Ophrys apifera* – the bee orchid. Grows on coastal dunes.'

I nodded. 'I'll keep an eye out.'

The humid air from the greenhouse had melted a patch of frost around the door. I looked back once and could vaguely see his misty shape through the condensation. He was still holding the plant as he watched me leave.

It had been hard to explain to David too. He glanced down at the proposal I'd written, leant back in his chair and stretched. When he looked at me, his smile was wry.

'Well, of course I'll endorse it,' he said. 'It seems a little odd though.' He frowned slightly. 'I do expect some help when you're back here writing up.'

'Sure,' I said. 'Be glad to.'

David was over six foot and had a crew cut. He was in his early thirties and always wore blue Ronhills and hooded tops with 'Northface' or 'Stone Monkey' embossed on the front. He was a behavioural ecology lecturer at Cambridge University and had supervised my PhD and postdoctoral work. We had an unspoken agreement, David and I. Every couple of months or so, he bought me a pint at our local and pressed two keys in my hand. I pocketed them without a word. One opened a safe containing his will, and the other unlocked the hard-drive of his computer. If David did not return after his weekend, I was to give the will to his girlfriend and write up any papers he was working on. He was an enthusiastic rock climber, the sort that goes up E1s and hangs in a sleeping bag overnight several thousand feet off the ground. So far he'd always returned strangely relaxed with a Clint Eastwood glint in his eye. At Cambridge he studied wrens.

There was a curious quality to David, a kind of inner tranquillity. He was capable of standing in a wood for hours without moving a muscle, yet his lean, rangy body could slide instantly into swift and sudden action. I was constantly surprised by just how tiny the wrens looked when he caught them and held them in the palm of his rock climber's hands. When we went out for a drink together people sometimes commented: we were both so still save for our restless eyes.

'I don't get it. Why Northern Ireland? It's not as if there aren't plenty of magpies over here.'

I started to give him the spiel – no-one's ever studied magpies in Ireland, no-one's ever looked at a bird designed for the plains of Eurasia but which is now happily living along the seashore and in towns and cities, no-one has . . . but he cut me short – he'd read the proposal already. How could I tell him that I'd woken from an impossible dream and gone for a weekend without saying anything to anyone, that when I was there, I felt I had to stay, that flocks of magpies cried through my nights and in the mornings I rose with the taste of salt on my tongue? He was my mate, after all.

I shrugged. 'What other behavioural ecologist has seriously studied magpies recently? Especially urban ones — they're like avian rats, highly intelligent, and able to exploit us and the landscape we've created with a degree of success almost unparalleled by other birds. Besides, I've got to make my name somehow. And Ireland is foreign enough to be alluring to the guys awarding the grants, and near enough not to be expensive.'

He grinned. 'Least you're finally thinking straight.'

'Buy you a beer?' I said, and he nodded.

'You better bloody well come back and count nests with me, you old bastard.'

Gathering

There are more magpies in Dublin than anywhere else in the world. Belfast must be second on the list. I could see them lined up on the giant arm of Goliath, the biggest crane in the western world; they flew in flocks over Napoleon's nose, a craggy lump of nasal rock sprouting from a mountain worn to resemble the great man's face glowering over the city. It was January. I stepped onto a concrete harbour surrounded by a khaki sea, magpies arrowing across the sky, stepped onto foreign soil and felt as if I were home.

I'd come to stay in Ballynanane, a small village on the east coast of Northern Ireland. It was little more than a single street called Main Street, as were most of the major roads in these tiny towns. It had a harbour, a municipal park, a pub – the Sandpiper with mustard-coloured plaster walls and windows as thick as the bottoms of beer glasses – a Spar shop and an insurance broker's called John Lloyd's that had a toy scene in the window with miniature cows and plastic trains. There was a café called the Pink Geranium which I was to discover had a tiny cinema screen in a back room, and a church in solid grey granite. The house I had rented was at the far end of the village. It was an end terrace house, two up, two down, with a handkerchief of a garden front and back and a date palm tree by the gate that had seen better days. The house looked out onto the sea and the wind howled round the gable end and frayed the palm leaves into thongs.

I'd bought a bicycle in a junk shop before I left, and the first thing I did when I arrived that January day was ride through the village. At the far end was a wood bisected by a mud road potholed with puddles. The grey stone walls surrounding it were high, a good couple of metres, and topped with battlements. Blocking the entrance was a rusty iron gate with great spikes set between two stone turrets. The gates were chained together but the padlock had a flower of pure, shiny silver round the keyhole.

I cycled past the entrance to the wood, and at the point where the road curved away to the south and left the wood behind someone had painted 'For the love of the blue skies of Ireland we will not surrender to the Republic' in ragged white letters on the walls. There was little hope of that. The sky was dark grey, it was drizzling and the skeletal trees were black with rain. Tattered remnants of leaves clung like sodden garments to some of the branches, and great cables of ivy wound round their limbs, burying finger-thin suckers knuckle-deep in the bark. I could just make out part of a large house deep within the wood. It was painted pale olive green; the reflections of black storm clouds swum viscously in the lifeless windows. And then they came. I heard the beat of their wings first for they were utterly silent. The base of my spine started to tingle, and I felt a chill draught creep along my scalp. There must have been about two hundred of them, shoaling through the sky, black and cruciform, blocking out what little light was left. It took at least a minute for them all to pass over my head and slide as one sinuous body over the wall, and through the wood. They alighted on some oaks and clustered in dense groups along the branches as if the trees were growing ill-formed and shifting galls. From the heart of the wood came the strangled cry of a crow, and now for the first time they called, a rattling clamour that issued from their hoarse throats.

Cabaire breac in Gaelic, *maggot pie* from the French, my first sight of a communal roost of Irish magpies. I stood in the rain and watched them as they stirred and seethed along the damp limbs of the trees. It looked like an optical illusion, the dark trees crowned with black and white birds – it was difficult to see where one bird ended and another began. My eyes watered, and the noise hurt my ears, but somehow it seemed right that I should be welcomed in this way.

I stopped at the Sandpiper on my way home. I stood in the entrance and dripped gently as my eyes adjusted to the gloom. No-one spoke. I walked a little unsteadily towards the bar and ordered a Guinness. When in Rome . . . The burr of talk began to build back up. The place was full of a dense fug of smoke, the floor and the bar were made of dark wood, and the seats were upholstered in mulberry imitation leather. I liked the timing of the drink, the no-rush attitude while the barman propped his chin in his hands and waited for the froth to settle. A few youths were playing pool in one corner, and in the other a couple of old men were huddled over their pints by a hissing gas fire. There were no women. Someone once told me you could get all the nourishment you needed if you existed on a diet of Guinness and peanuts. I sipped my drink, and watched the pool with one eye and the motor racing on Eurosport with the other. The sound had been turned down and the cars veered, swerved and collided in perfect silence.

'Will you not join us?'

I looked over. One of the old men was leaning on his stick with one hand and gesturing towards me with the other.

'C'mon over,' he said. His face was lined and his hair was wild and white. Even in the yellow light filtered through the beer-glass windows I could see his eyes were bright blue. 'New to town are you?' he asked as I sat down.

'I arrived today,' I said.

'And where were you saying you're from?'

'You're not Irish be any chance?' said the other. 'Every bloody Englishman thinks he's Irish. There's more Irish over the water than there are here.' He was small and round with a pink face and sunken, bleary eyes. His hair was reduced to sandy wisps and he only had one front tooth.

'Definitely English,' I said, 'I live in Cambridge and my parents have a house in Kew.'

'You're the student then, the one in the O'Malleys' house,' said the blue-eyed one.

'Kind of,' I replied.

'Kind of staying in the O'Malleys' house or a kind of student? Och, aren't all students kind of studying?' He chuckled and held out his hand. 'George,' he said. His grip was surprisingly strong, his knuckles large and misshapen. 'And this is Cyril.' He nodded at his plump companion. 'Runs the cinema across the road, so he does. Not that you would be interested, you young folk, all you want is to be Terminated or Robotcop or some other nonsense. Cyril here shows old films. Black and whites.'

I shook Cyril's soft white hand. 'My favourite kind,' I said and his eyes lit up.

'And what will you be studying?' asked George.

'Magpies.'

He stiffened and fixed me with his piercing gaze. 'Magpies is it? That's a queer thing to be learning. Mark my words,' he leant forward and gripped my hand, 'they're the devil's bird and they've a drop of his own good blood under their tongue.'

I recoiled from his beer-laden breath.

He suddenly laughed, a wheezing sound emanating from the depths of his chest, and I was no longer sure whether he had been teasing me or not.

'Magpies indeed. Well good luck to you.'

The two old men clinked their glasses together and Cyril gave a gap-toothed grin.

I nodded at them and stood up to go. As I was putting on my still damp coat George called out to me, 'What did you say your name was, son?'

'It's Niall,' I said. 'My name's Niall.'

In 1909 the Reverend W. Darwin Fox wrote about the Great Magpie Marriage. He was describing ceremonial gatherings which aren't marriages, but more like teenagers dating, flirting and fighting, although, as he says, 'The whole affair was evidently considered by the birds as of the highest importance.' I saw a ceremonial gathering the following morning. Maybe it was just luck; I certainly took it as a good omen.

I spent the morning cycling round the winding roads that led out of Ballynanane trying to familiarize myself with the landscape. The sky was white and the visibility low, fog obscuring the tips of the trees. I stopped at a sheep-bitten piece of scrubland by the edge of the sea. Where the grass ended and the cliff began there was a drop into nothingness; the caw of seagulls, wheeling in as if from nowhere, was muted. The chill air was sharp with the scent of gorse, and there were tatters of wool beaded with dew on the scraggy hawthorn bushes. I left my bike propped up against a wall and walked across the grass. About a hundred metres away from the cliff edge the gorse and the hawthorn grew denser and taller. I pushed my way through and in the centre was a natural clearing. A stream ran round the edge, its banks overflowing muddily onto the sodden earth. A couple of magpies were crouched in the puddles, shaking water through their feathers. As soon as they saw me they flew through the trees. I crouched down behind a gorse bush amongst khaki-coloured needles and waited.

It wasn't long before the pair returned and started to poke about in the short grass for worms and beetles. I was so engrossed watching them that I didn't notice the others arrive. There must have been about ten of them, sitting almost motionless in a small hawthorn above the foraging pair. Against the overcast sky, their white plumage did not show up and they seemed to be irregular birds, painted with a Picasso touch. Suddenly one of the males hopped down onto the grass and bounded towards the female. The resident male stopped in his tracks and bounced in an exaggerated fashion over to the female too. She continued pecking and prodding the ground as if deliberately ignoring them. The males started to circle her, hopping faster and faster after each other, uttering shrill cries. The first male flew directly at the interloper and the three of them headed for the hawthorn. The other magpies burst in a cloud from its branches, chattering harshly. Like disturbed butterflies, they drifted back down, but almost immediately, one aimed a peck at another. The fight escalated until the whole tree shook with the beat of their wings, and the heavy air reverberated with their caws. As the noise increased, the birds broke into two groups and began to chase each other round the small bushes in the clearing. Other young birds, drawn by the spectacle, started to fly in, in pairs and threesomes, swooping low over the branches and seeding themselves like strange fruit in the stunted trees. The overspill landed back in the centre of the clearing. They appeared to be pecking for grubs, watched by the new arrivals, but I saw a pair of birds flirting on the outskirts. The male had fluffed his white feathers up, and angled his tail towards the female, a sure sign of his amorous intentions. She was pretending to feed, but was, in fact, edging closer and closer to him in small hops. The male that had prior claims on the female darted in and the usurper chattered excitedly and flew at him. And then the whole clearing seemed to erupt in screaming, fighting, flapping magpies. It felt as if there were about fifty of them now, a pack of juveniles without homes or mates, testosterone-fuelled and high on the thin, fine air. They flew above my head flashing their piebald wings and my ears rang with the noise. They tangled in the bushes and fought in the clearing, and then crested the tips of the trees and disappeared into the mist-thick field.

I burst from the gorse bush, snagging my coat on the thorns and scattering needles. My legs ached with cramp, and my steps were jagged. I slipped on the slick grass, righted myself and tore through the hawthorns in the direction of the young birds. But they were nowhere to be seen. They had vanished as quickly and as silently as they had come. The clearing was probably prime territory belonging to a resident pair, and they had been challenged by the youngsters. The others had watched and joined in the skirmish as a way of probing the limits of the resident pair's endurance, and in the hope of quick sex. Too young, I thought. They had yet to learn that this sort of thing was best conducted in privacy lest you lose your woman.

I wandered around for a while, my trainers and trousers getting increasingly wet and muddy, then cycled a little way on. There was not a magpie to be seen. It was now mid-afternoon and a bad time to try to find them anyway. I rode back into town and stopped at the Sandpiper. I bought a couple of Guinnesses and carried them, froth peeling away in the wind, to the Pink Geranium. The thickly plastered walls were a livid shade of fuchsia, and the roof was thatched, a thin stream of peat-laden smoke guttering from the chimney. A door from the café led into the cinema. Cyril was perched on a high chair next to the projector at the back of the room, a film flickering on the opposite wall. I handed him a pint.

'Well, bless you, bless you, lad, an' you haven't spilt a drop,' he said, and his face cracked open in a gummy grin. 'I'll wind the film back to the start. We can't have you missing any of it.'

As I was the only customer, there were no objections. I slumped into one of the dusty, dried-blood-red chairs, put my feet on the back of the one in front of me and spent the rest of the afternoon drinking and watching *Passport to Pimlico* in glorious, scratchy monochrome.

'Next week,' said Cyril in a stage whisper as the credits rolled, 'we'll be showing *Sunset Boulevard*.'

On my way back through the village I stopped at Spar. It was run by Mrs O'Malley whom I rented the house from. The shop played a game of musical lights – there didn't seem to be enough electricity to go round so only one light was ever on at a time. Shrivelled carrots and limp cabbage wilted in the darkness. Mother was right, there was almost no fruit. Mrs O'Malley swapped the lights round so I could find the tin can section. A young man stepped out of the shadows and peered over my shoulder as I was trying to decide whether to go for Custard Creams or Jaffa Cakes.

'Oh, don't mind William,' called out Mrs O'Malley. 'Come away from there,' she said, to William, I presumed, as if he were a dog that had been poking its nose in something unsavoury. 'William's harmless,' she added, steering him into the corner of the shop and pushing him into a chair. 'He's just a wee bit soft in the head.'

It was difficult to tell, but I thought he must have been in his early twenties. His black hair was unkempt and slightly greasy and he curled his arms around himself as he sat hunched over in the hard-backed chair. He watched me surreptitiously from large vacant eyes and dribbled a little. I bought several tins of sardines and baked beans, a loaf of Mother's Pride, a jar of Marmite, a packet of Jammy Dodgers and some Cheese Triangles.

''Tis a shame about the weather but,' said Mrs O'Malley as she reached me down a six-pack. She had one of those perms where the curl doesn't quite meet the scalp.

I looked outside. It was still raining. 'I imagine I'll get used to it,' I said, as much to myself as her.

The sofa at home was green and lumpy with the springs poking out uncomfortably. There was a threadbare mat on the floor and a cast-iron fireplace. I turned the sofa to face the window and sat looking at the sea eating sardines on toast. Between the coal grey of the water and the darkening of the sky was a thin line of light. I watched it narrow as the wind whined round the house and whistled through the chimney.

After a week of baked beans and sardines, the odd bag of chips from the Sandpiper, and sticky cakes from the Pink

Geranium, I thought I should have a proper meal. David had bought me a copy of *The Rough Guide to Ireland* – I think it was his idea of a joke – but it said there was a restaurant out past the lough. It was vegetarian, but you can't have everything.

It was already dark when I left for the Greenaun and the wind felt like a force field that I had to fight my way through. In the heart of the wood a couple of lights were shining. I cycled past and out of the village into the darkness beyond. The wind was particularly vicious as it knifed over the tops of the low stone walls. In the distance I could hear cows lowing. It took me a good half-hour to get to the restaurant though the lough was only about a couple of miles as the crow flies from Ballynanane. The light from the occasional car froze the waves approaching the shore in a snapshot of movement. At the most northerly end was a large reed-bed alive with roosting sparrows. As the reeds hissed and seethed in the wind, small clumps of birds fell from the stalks and fluttered into the dark beyond the beam of my bike light. I thought that I was disturbing them so I turned off my light. Above the whispering of the reeds, I could hear the cheep of the birds and the trembling of tiny wings. Then there was a single shrill cry and the flock winged away en masse to another part of the marsh. I wondered what could be hunting them. I put my light back on. A few metres away, a couple of magpies flew up from the road giving alarm calls and disappeared over the nearest wall. I stopped the bike and bent down to look. The mutilated body of a sparrow was lying on the road, its neck broken and its chest skewered open. I immediately decided to come back when it was lighter. Magpies killing sparrows – I'd never heard of such a thing before. Did they hunt the sparrows in groups? Was this an example of a magpie 'tradition' found only on the east coast of Ireland? Or was it an isolated incident born of necessity because the winter was so bleak? I left them to their meal and rode on.

The restaurant was upstairs in a Georgian-style house overlooking the lough. The tables and chairs were of solid pine and heavy folds of calico hung at the windows. Walls, the colour of baked pumpkin, had been covered in pale yellow stencils and spider plants hung from the ceiling. It was pretty full. I took a small table in the corner. Below me I could see part of the reed-bed and a floodlit pier extending into the lake.

I ordered half a carafe of house white which came with a glass tumbler like the ones you have at school and a beet-root and sour cream risotto with chargrilled courgettes. It certainly wasn't green – the courgettes had brilliant yellow skin – but probably contained a few more vitamins than my normal fodder.

There was a slight commotion on the table in front of me – one of the party was demanding to see the manager. Apparently there'd been some mix-up with the order. The waitress was beginning to look uncomfortable.

'Our manager never comes in, so he doesn't,' she said.

'Well, who runs the place then?' asked the elderly man who'd been making the complaint.

'I suppose it's Eddie really, our head chef.'

'Well then, send him up. I'd like a wee word with him.'

I turned away at that point – I thought I saw an owl sliding past the oil-black water. When I looked back at the party, they seemed to be smiling up at the chef, soothed no doubt by the newly uncorked bottle of wine he'd brought up for them. He had his back to me, but even so he was like no chef I'd ever seen. He was about my height and thin, and was wearing a tight black T-shirt, purple suede

26

trainers and navy Levi's. His hair was short and black, and round his waist hung a set of kitchen knives hooked together on a thin chain.

He started to walk away from the table, but the elderly gentleman called him back. 'Since you've been so kind as to give us the wine, we'll be so kind as to pay for it,' he said, but I scarcely paid him any attention. As the chef turned to face the man, his belt of knives swung out, scattering beams of metal light across the walls and ceiling. Even more noticeable, the chef was a woman, no, a young girl, of about nineteen.

A little later, on my way back from the gents, I passed her leaning out of the landing window, smoking.

'I'd complain about the food too if it wasn't so good,' I said ruefully.

She turned to me and blew out a plume of smoke. 'Then what would you want to be doing that for?' she asked sharply.

'Well, just trying to work out how to get a free bottle of wine,' I said and cringed inwardly at how lame my attempt at humour had been.

'I'll see what I can do,' she said, turning away from me.

I slunk back to my table. Half an hour later she slid into the chair opposite me. She had brought a tumbler with her, and immediately poured herself a glass of wine and refilled my glass, emptying the carafe.

'Fetch us another, would you, Siobhan,' she called to the waitress and turned back to me. 'Eddie,' she said, extending her hand.

'Niall,' I replied.

She began to roll a cigarette, a very thin one made of liquorice-coloured paper, and I noticed that her big, strong hands were laced with tiny white scars. Her eyes were large and blue, and although she was good-looking her nose was too big and her lips too thin for her ever to be called beautiful. She said nothing until she had finished rolling her cigarette, lit it, and taken a drag and a gulp of wine. By this stage I'd recovered from the fact that he was a she, but there was something terribly familiar about her face — though for the life of me I couldn't think where I might have seen her before.

'So what,' she said, 'brings you here?'

'Magpies,' I said.

She nodded. 'I was having a smoke outside and I saw you on the road. Was it a sparrow you found? They're allus killing them in winter.'

I noticed that she had extraordinarily clear skin, almost translucent. I remembered I was supposed to respond at this point but I couldn't stop staring at her. I said 'You look too young to be a head chef.'

She shrugged. 'Everyone allus says that. I'm twenty-one. When you're young you've more ideas, you're not so set in your ways as they are round here. So you liked your risotto then?' She looked down at my plate which I'd scraped clean, leaving only thin lines of pink beetroot juice. It had reminded me of a savoury version of the rice pudding they served in the college at Cambridge, but that was fine by me.

'Yes, it was great. I didn't even know you could get yellow courgettes.'

'In the back of beyond. Surprising what you can find. Anyway,' she stubbed her cigarette out resolutely, 'I must get back. Come again.' She got up, clinking slightly. She had such a long neck. I thought of how it would feel if I cupped it in the palm of my hand. Eddie strode across the room and disappeared down the stairs to the kitchens.

*   *   *

I settled into a regular pattern. I spent the afternoons in the cinema or in the Sandpiper, and once a week I cycled over to the Greenaun for a meal that was bizarrely gourmet for the north of Ireland. Eddie was usually weird but spot on; occasionally she missed. Peanut butter, cottage cheese and mandarin pizza followed by tomato ice cream was definitely wide of the mark for me, and as far as I know she never repeated it.

I set up an office in the house in the back bedroom which was little more than a boxroom. Mrs O'Malley lent me a rickety table that I had to prop up with chips of wood. I made myself a filing cabinet out of a cardboard box for my papers on magpies, and customized my Psion so that I could collect data from it in the field and download it to the laptop at night. It took me two days to match the spread-sheets from the Psion with those of the computer. The frustrating thing was that there was no phone line so I couldn't even have e-mail. Ironically the lab in Cambridge did have a satellite phone that hooked up to the computer, but I'd never even considered that I might need it.

I spent three weeks mist-netting entire tracts of the coast-line and the outskirts of the wood in a vain attempt at catching magpies. Hanging a net in one place ensured that you could never return to trap them there again; they were far too cunning. For those three weeks I was up by six in the morning, staggering through the dark and crashing about in the undergrowth, becoming entangled in my own nets, growing sodden and cold. I thought of my father in tweeds (though even he, surely, would have worn some-thing sensible in khaki) wandering through the Peruvian jungles inspecting traps for small mammals, and his brief excitement when he found them full. At that time he would have killed them and stuffed the specimens. The place had probably been crawling with four-inch cockroaches and jungle rats, but it seemed a far more sedate occupation than waiting in the freezing cold for a wily white and black bird which, if caught, would attempt to lacerate your hands with its beak and scratch your eyes out with its claws, not to mention having to release the quivering songbirds that I also inadvertently trapped. But eventually I managed to catch and ring a sufficient number of the birds and felt I could now begin to start collecting data.

The day I began my research properly two magpies (unringed) alighted on the harbour wall as I was wheeling my bike out of the house. A lucky twosome, and, indeed, I was fortunate that day. Dawn was just breaking, the village was bathed in a steel-grey glow and there was no-one around. I'd chosen a section of land past the wood as my study site. A field of long grass led to a coppice of pine trees bordered by a high stone wall which was festooned with ivy. Beyond that was a scrub wood of hawthorn and elderberry with dense tracts of bramble and dead bracken that gave way to short, rabbit-cropped grass. The grass bordered a bay that was a good two miles long. At one end the wood by the village swept right down to the shore; the other side of the bay grew increasingly stony rising to a dark black cliff with a disused lighthouse. About half a mile out to sea was a rocky outcrop, barren save for nesting seabirds. It was called Skull Island.

My site seemed to be ideal magpie habitat because there was short grass for them to feed on, and a choice of tall trees as well as the denser hawthorns to nest in. What I hadn't realized was that I'd walked onto a battlefield. As I crossed the first field with its lush grass, dark shapes fell out of the pines and flew agitatedly amongst the trees, cawing bitterly. In the half-light as they swooped about me and their calls tore the air I could just make out the grey cape on their shoulders: hooded crows, after people the magpies' most hated enemies.

I walked along the seafront as the day broke, scanning the land for birds with my binoculars. The tide was on its way out and had left a flotsam of cuttlefish cases and kelp, the stalks as bleak as bones, the holdfast shrivelled hands whose fingers had been ripped from rocks. The sea was calm today, the colour of pewter. And then I saw a male magpie. He was tree-topping, standing on the tip of an elder whose branches were glazed green with algae, bobbing and lifting his tail in the air, the proud gestures of a bird asserting his territorial rights. I focused the binoculars on the tree. The female was there too, crouched in the thicket of branches, her brash black and white plumage almost perfect camouflage as it broke up the outline of her body and melded into the shadows. To my intense relief, I had already ringed both of them.

Pacing up and down my study site, I discovered that there were four territories each with a pair of magpies along the scrub by the beach; I decided that they would be the main focus of my study, although I needed to survey other birds in the rest of the area which, if the winter roosts were anything to go by, was densely populated. It wasn't long before I came across an old tumbledown cottage at one end of the site – the roof had been thatched but was mostly caved in, and behind it was a small greenhouse; miraculously some of the panes of glass were still intact. It was only marginally warmer inside than out; a chill wind seeped through the shattered glass. I stood on the stone lintel and thought of my father. One of the first things he'd done when we moved to our house in Kew was to build a greenhouse in the garden. He was home from work by six and spent the rest of the evening and all his weekends assembling it. Meanwhile cuttings and tubers accumulated bit by bit along every window sill in the house. I carried bits of wood and passed him nails, screws, putty, orchids. I thought I was indispensable, but I'm sure I just got in the way. I was only eight at the time, but I remember seeing my mother standing at the back door with her hands on her hips watching him, an apron wrapped around her middle. She'd been going to tell him that his tea was on the table, but the words were stillborn, and even at that age I could feel her despair though then I found it incomprehensible.

'It's not your usual day,' said Eddie, sliding my plate in front of me.

'And that's not your usual job,' I said.

She sat down opposite me, chin in her hand, and said, 'It's not so busy. I can take a few minutes off.'

She reached across to an empty table for a glass and poured herself a small measure of my wine before she started to roll one of her thin cigarettes.

'Well, d'you like it?'

I'd only taken a couple of mouthfuls, but I'd learnt that the response had to be immediate if I didn't want to offend her. She was sitting hunched forward, her eyes screwed up against the smoke, her whole body tense. For once she was wearing her chef's trousers, but with a CK T-shirt and Nike trainers she still managed to make them look like a fashion accessory.

I nodded with my mouth full, but realized I wasn't going to be let off that lightly. She'd baked flat-cap mushrooms, their lids lined with basil leaves, soaked in white wine and garlic. There were also roast potatoes and parsnips coated in apple jelly. It was delicious. I told her so, and felt as if I were back home again. It wasn't so bad when my mother cooked – she felt it was expected of her and we were rarely obliged to comment, but whenever my father made anything, his burnt, hard, or largely inedible food was the main topic of conversation. He, like me, could quite happily live on baked beans on toast and bread and jam but for my mother's sake he occasionally tried to cook. Once when my mother was away for the day we baked a cake together and took it out of the oven too early – on purpose. The bottom was a glorious blend of molten strawberry jam and runny golden cake mixture. We ate it straight out of the tin. The only thing that spoilt it was my mother coming home and finding every surface in the kitchen smothered in flour and smeared with margarine, dishes scattered from the sink to the table. She'd dropped her Liberty bags on the floor and burst into tears.

Eddie didn't smile, but her eyes glowed briefly when I praised her cooking. She finished her wine and got up to go.

'Do you ever get any time off?' I asked. I'd been prac-tising all day. It was meant to sound nonchalant, and had by the fifteenth time down on the seashore as I waved the mug of my thermos flask in the air. Now it came out as a hoarse croak, my voice regressing to a pre-pubescent squeak at the end.

'Sure I do. I'll come over to Ballynanane some time.'

I watched her walk away from me, weaving past the potted plants, her knives clattering by her sides, and I thought of her hands with their smooth almond-shaped nails and the myriad scars. That was too easy, I thought. There had to be a catch.

★ ★ ★

The following day was a complete disaster in terms of my fieldwork, but that, I suppose, is the pattern of these things. As usual it was dark when I got up and there was a dense fog that clung to my clothes. It was so thick I could barely see more than a metre in front of me; like the drapes of a curtain being shaken, the shifting mass of cloud released the sharp smell of salt, fish and oil. On the beach I could hear the water breaking gently as if from afar, and when the dawn broke, it was with a thin blue light that seeped through the mist.

I wandered up and down the beach, but the visibility was so poor I could see nothing. It was slightly frustrating, but comforting in a way — for some reason it reminded me of my childhood. Just after seven in the morning, the mist started to clear and I was aware of the brooding mass of the sea. I was holding a shell at the time — I must have picked it up in an idle moment. It was a top hat — a sleek cone, pale grey-blue wound with opal and purple like an ornate turban — and when I turned to look down the beach in the direction of the wood I saw a horse and rider emerging from the mist. The horse was galloping but its hooves made no sound on the sand; its legs rose and fell as regularly as pistons, the muscles bunching and sliding under its skin with smooth, oiled precision. The animal appeared to be moving in slow motion: for one long moment neither horse nor rider seemed to draw any nearer to me. The rider on the dark bay was clothed in red from head to foot. And then the two were upon me and for one brief moment I looked up at the great sweating animal and saw that its rider, clad in what I now perceived to be a cloak, was sitting side-saddle, the brilliant scarlet material billowing out behind her. They passed me and were once more engulfed by the fog, and I was left only with the stark image of them indelibly impressed on my mind.

I did not see a single magpie that day.

When I was at Cambridge I studied dunnocks. Sometimes they're called hedge sparrows because they're small and brown, scurry wren-like in hedges and look like fatter versions of their namesakes. Dunnocks have a rather strange social life: one female mates with two, sometimes three, males and they all help to rear her chicks. Like every-thing in life there's no equality; it's not a caring, sharing household. One male is dominant, and he gets to mate with the female most of the time. But the female actively solicits sex with her other 'husbands' and will sneak into the bushes with them when she thinks the top male isn't looking. The reasons for this are twofold (they, of course, have nothing to do with love). The female gets a good mix of genes from different males – it's the old adage of not putting all your eggs in one basket. Mating with one male would mean all her chicks inherited his deficiencies, but at least some out of a bunch of nestlings with different fathers will survive – the ones with the best genes. And the other reason is that it's not exactly in the males' interest to look after chicks that don't belong to them. The problem is that they can't tell which fledglings are theirs so they've compromised: all the males feed all the fledglings, but they only feed them in proportion to the amount of sex they've had. If the female copulates with all the males, they all think they've produced lots of chicks, and will fetch numerous caterpillars. It seems like a reasonable strategy, but personally I thought the males didn't need to work quite so hard: they couldn't yet understand that the number of times one has sex doesn't necessarily correlate with the number of offspring one produces.

I worked in the high-walled botanical garden which was quiet and sheltered and trapped the sun in odd corners. It was by chance that I discovered the scientific proof for multiple parenthood of the dunnock chicks. I was watching a female hiding in a flower bed with one of the subordinate males, and as she was about to mate with him she ejected a little white pellet. After the birds had done their business, I collected this pellet and took it back to the lab. It proved to be full of sperm – from different males. The males were not just competing against each other on a day to day level, playing a game of subterfuge as they hid amongst the winter jasmine, they were also filling the female full of as much sperm as they could, and their sperm were continuing the battle inside her – may the best sperm win, and all that. But the female had defeated them all and was chucking the stuff out every time she wanted to mate. I concentrated on collecting and analysing these sperm samples but, unsurprisingly, I didn't find many. One morning a female I was watching expelled a sperm parcel which landed on a leaf. I waited until she had flown away, and went to collect it, slide at the ready. But as I got to the bush, the pellet slid off the leaf. I started crawling round in the undergrowth looking for the tiny white blob. I was lying face down in a flower bed covered in mud and twigs when I saw a pair of shiny black sensible shoes. I looked up and there was a nun standing in front of me. She bent down and peered at me through her glasses.

'Young man,' she said, 'what on earth are you doing?'

'Ugh! And you told her you were looking for bird sperm?'

Eddie, I thought, had no sense of irony. We were at my

house and I'd just finished telling her about my dunnock research. It was about a week since I'd last seen her and I'd got back from the Pink Geranium in that warm and befuddled state that comes from drinking pints in the dark whilst watching an old B-movie and finding, on your entrance back into the real world, that although you have squandered your afternoon, remnants of the day still remain. She was sitting in her car outside my house, hanging her cigarette out of the window. I didn't ask how she knew where I lived; in Ireland everyone knows everything about everybody. She was looking in the wing mirror and as soon as she saw me approaching she stubbed the cigarette out on the side of the car, and started bustling me and all her provisions into the house. She'd bought boxes of food, crockery and cooking pots plus all her knives.

'I didn't think you'd have anything decent to cook in,' she said, giving me a cast-iron wok to carry. She was right, but she was disgusted at how right she was. 'Is this all you have?' she asked incredulously, opening one of the cupboard doors. 'How d'you manage?'

I looked inside the cupboard which contained an ill assortment of chipped china and old Pyrex. 'You only need a plate and a knife for sardines on toast. Maybe a spoon as well.' I changed my mind. 'In fact, the beauty of this dish is that you don't need a thing — not even a tin opener.'

Eddie curled her lip at me.

She inspected my fridge too, and was about to close the door, her face screwed up at its lack of anything edible save for two loaves of Mother's Pride and some half-used margarine, when she pounced on a silver-foil-wrapped parcel.

'What have you here?' she asked, pulling it out.

'My sandwiches.'

'You've a brave few in here. Are you on some kind of weight-gain diet?' She balanced the sandwiches in one hand.

'No, they're for the week.'

She looked at me quizzically.

'It saves time. You do them all at the start of the week, and I can just grab them as I'm going out the door. I have to get up early, you know,' I protested.

She shook her head at me and giggled. 'You kill me, so you do.'

She'd been wearing a knee-length camel-coloured fake fur coat that looked as if it had been made out of a bathroom mat; underneath she had on a black T-shirt with a green plastic alien sealed into a clear pocket on the front.

'What on earth is that?' I asked, trying to put on a deeply plummy accent, peering as closely as I could at her chest.

'Get away with you,' she said, shoving me hard.

She was incredible: she'd brought two sorts of wine, an ice bucket and some ice. I didn't even know you could buy ice – it reminded me of the days when men cut slabs from fjords in Norway and shipped them back to London, the clippers racing each other and the melting ice wrapped in sackcloth. Back on the Thames they unloaded the ice onto the dock and it glittered cold and blue and alien as traders haggled for slices of frozen Norwegian rain. This stuff was in a plastic bag shaped into cubes with hollow centres. The wine we were supposed to start with as an aperitif was pink and from somewhere called Blossom Hill. I thought it was a bit of a girlie drink, but it was surprisingly nice and not sweet at all.

I watched as Eddie chopped up the food, slicing her blade down as if it were a guillotine. Seconds later an onion would still look like an onion, but when she swept it into a pan it fragmented into myriad minute cubes. She mistook my close scrutiny and said, 'It's not what you think, you know. I started playing about with knives when I was wee. I used to watch the chefs on telly and try to chop things as fast as them. I practised on old turnips and bits of stick, anything that was around, and the knife slipped a bit sometimes.'

I realized she was talking about the scars on her hands. She started telling me why she was vegetarian. I stopped listening after a while and just looked at her instead. As she bent over the chopping board, the light caught the line of each fragile bone in her neck. I imagined running my fingers down her vertebrae and with difficulty prevented myself from mentally peeling off her alien T-shirt.

Eddie rolled out pastry and cut it to fit the shape of a deep tin, two circles for the top and bottom, a rectangle for the side. She worked deftly, the blade of her knife flashing, and with almost no measuring at all she created a perfectly lined tin with none of those bits of awkward pastry that normally dangle over the side, or the edges that won't quite meet so you have to do a cut and paste job. The only time I ever made pastry was at school in home economics lessons and my flan case looked like a patchwork quilt embroidered to imitate the dark side of the moon. Eddie rubbed her eyes and left a smear of flour on her temple. Once everything was in the oven, she washed her hands, rolled a cigarette and flung open the kitchen door.

'C'mon, it'll be a wee while before it's ready.'

We walked across the road and leant on the railings overlooking the sea. They were ice cold and burnt my stomach. Below us the sea heaved. Street lights catching the dark water chiselled it into fine-cut waves; occasionally spray arced towards us. Far out at sea came the deep boom of a foghorn. I thought how amazing it was that the sea could be the same and yet different, the waves rolling in following a pattern programmed by the tide, and then, for some indefinable reason, a rogue wave would smash against the concrete shore and shower us with sub-zero sea water.

Eddie had baked sweet potatoes in their skins and mashed them with yoghurt, ginger and green peppercorns; the pastry turned out to be for a deep mushroom pie which she cut into perfect slices, and there were roasted pink onions, split open like flowers, tender and caramelized in balsamic vinegar. She poured us red wine that tasted of cinnamon and earth. We took the kitchen table into the sitting room and sat in the dark with one candle between us and the night, the palm tree flailing at the window and the sea moaning barely metres away.

She was slightly flushed from the wine and from cooking and I noticed that she ate very little, but made many small movements, darting at her plate with her knife and fork. She told me that she had grown up in the next village along the coast and had lived there all her life. She couldn't wait to leave 'this poky wee island'. She said she was Catholic, third in a family of five: there were two older brothers, a baby boy, and her sister was five. She talked about how difficult it was with the baby at home, always crying, and her sister who pinched the child when she thought no-one was looking, how her brothers came home drunk from time to time and her father was away at sea for months at a stretch. She glossed over the religious differences between her family and the rest of the village, saying only that she never went to church. When I asked, she said her name was an old Irish one, Eithne, and in the way that abbreviations become diminutives, she was Et, and then Ed, before her brothers began to call her Eddie.

We washed all her pots and packed up the leftover food and then she drove home. I stood in the sitting room which smelt of wine and thought how stupid I was. Stupid to allow her to drive away half drunk along these dark and winding roads. Stupid because I didn't kiss her. When she stood at the doorway and looked at me, I suddenly realized with a lurch why she seemed so familiar. She was standing in the shadows, and although she was slouching she was almost as tall as me. I stared at her deep blue eyes and short dark hair as if seeing her face for the first time. It was like looking at an old friend. I knew then that she was what I would look like were I a woman and the thought made me mildly uncomfortable. But that isn't why: I didn't kiss her because I could have done. I thought if I could, then so could other men; probably other men did. The fact that she had come and cooked this meal for me and me alone I dismissed because, after all, that was her job, cooking was what she did.

She had hesitated, then brushed her lips against my cheek and left. She waved once without looking back.

Courting

The next time I saw her was a few days later and I was watching magpies on the seashore. It was early in the morning, but the sky was a clear blue. In the bright sunlight, the soft sand near the grass glowed blue like snow and each individual pebble had its own sharp shadow. By the water's edge the sand had been smoothed by the sea; the reflections of gulls and oystercatchers sped across its slick and glassy surface. Each wave hung for one perfect moment, the salt water glistening bottle green before breaking on the beach.

This time I saw her come out of the wood and begin to gallop towards me, a tiny red pinprick set against the granite walls. Slowly horse and rider approached, shimmering like a mirage that coalesced into definition. I watched her with my binoculars until she would have seen me and then stepped back onto the short grass by the beach. The sun glinted on the horse's tight, hard muscles, so well defined they could have been sculpted from molten bronze, and his breath hung in a frozen cloud about his muzzle. Just as they reached me, the hood of her scarlet cloak blew down and her hair tumbled out, long and jet black. For one fleeting moment she turned to look at me.

The good thing about buying Cyril a drink on the days I went to the Pink Geranium was that if I were late, and

even if there were other customers, he would wind the film
back to the beginning. Also, I no longer had to pay the
paltry admission fee: the girl serving in the café would wave
me through and, often as not, press a few leftover cakes
into my hands as I was leaving. Maybe she, like Eddie,
thought I needed feeding.

We wandered over to the Sandpiper afterwards and
joined George who was sitting with his back straight as a
die, both hands resting on his cane, his pint squarely in front
of him.

'Who,' I started to ask, realizing I was going to sound
stupid, 'is the girl in red?'

George chuckled. 'You best watch out, son, she'll have
you for breakfast.'

Cyril grinned gummily into his drink.

'Yes, but who is she? Where does she come from?' And
why, I thought, does she wear scarlet and ride side-saddle?

'She lives at the big house,' said George.

'Nadia, her name's Nadia,' piped up Cyril.

'Big house?'

'Aye, the one in the wood. Sure you'll have seen it on
your travels.'

I nodded.

'It's owned by the Ismails, so it is, and Nadia runs a riding
school over on the lough way.'

I thought of her frozen in that split second, her black hair
flying around her face, her cloak caught on the wind,
turning her small, dark face towards me. Nadia Ismail.

'Now don't you be getting any wild ideas,' said George
dourly.

On Eddie's day off we drove to see the Butcher of Sligo.
I'd had a meal at the Greenaun the night before and she

wanted to take me for a cup of tea at the Butcher's place. But Eddie didn't finish work until around two a.m. and I was normally up by five so we arranged to meet the following day after I'd finished magpie-watching.

'The Butcher of Sligo,' I mused. 'He's a bit lost then.'

Eddie gave me a caustic look. 'You said that yesterday, so you did.'

'The truth is,' I said, 'I'm a little nervous about meeting a friend of yours who's also into sharp knives.'

It was dull and overcast, rain just beginning to spot the windscreen, and the lake was murky and dark as a piece of scrap metal. I rarely saw it during the day and was disappointed that the banks were so muddy, the grass beige and lifeless. A couple of bedraggled swans were hunched by the side of the reed-bed, their undersides caked in dirt. One of them flexed its wings, opening them to their full extent, and hissed at the car as we drove past.

The village where the Butcher lived was only one street long and his shop was in the middle flush with the road. There were pheasants and rabbits hanging in the window and a whole pig's head flanked by salmon and mullet on ice. It felt as if the whole slab was full of eyes staring up at me. The rank odour of blood tempered by sawdust wafted through the open door. I was just about to go in when Eddie grabbed my arm.

'He doesn't work there any more, you eejit.'

She pulled me down a dark alleyway next to the shop which opened up into a large courtyard. The wall at the far end was the gable of a ruined cottage; pots of crocus spears and snowdrops had been placed in the eyeless windows. The yard was full of light and the sweet smell of severed wood. The Butcher himself was there caressing a massive log with a chainsaw. Chips of wood fountained from the saw as he methodically skinned the log. He killed the chainsaw and, turning towards us, lifted his visor. He kissed Eddie full on the mouth, speckling her with wood, and shook my hand so hard it hurt.

'Pleased t'meet you. My name's John.'

'Niall,' I muttered.

'C'mon in will you. Have some tea and cake.'

He made us strong tea in a chipped brown pot and cut thick slices of barm brack. There was something about the generous doorsteps of fruit loaf so ineptly spread that the butter stayed in solid lumps, I started to warm to him in spite of myself. Like the butcher's shop, his cottage was flush with the street, but it was warm and cosy – there was a real fire, huge, overstuffed sofas and armchairs adorned with several dozing cats, and, by the front door, a sculpture of a fish leaping, its tail still welded into the original log.

The Butcher was a little like David, tall and rangy with short hair, but John was broader, his face rounder and his eyes were dark and soft. I could imagine women falling for him on the strength of those eyes alone. He and Eddie sat on the sofa, unconsciously echoing each other's posture, legs apart, scarred hands resting on their laps.

'Magpies, that's what he's studying.'

'One for sorrow . . .' said John, and I thought, Not again, I must have heard it a dozen times by now.

'. . .two for mirth, three for a wedding, four for a birth, five for rich, six for poor, seven for a bitch, eight for a whore, nine for a burying, ten for a dance, eleven for England, twelve for France.'

They were both staring at me. I had to admit this particular version was new to me.

John grinned and slouched back in the sofa. 'Help yourself to more cake.'

'So, er, you used to work in the butcher's shop?'

'I still own it, but I was spending all my spare time sculpting. I put my pieces in the shop and people were starting to come from all over to buy them – with a wee bit of meat as well – so I thought I might as well do it full time. I just make big things now. Come and look in my workshop.'

I followed John into the next room. Stacked to one side of his workshop were logs of wood, in the middle was a table, his tools hung on the opposite wall, and his sculptures were ranged across the far side.

'Take a look at this.' He pointed to a misshapen lump of wood. It was gnarled and twisted and very nearly black. The surface had been planed and was as smooth as ebony.

'Bog oak. Could be two thousand years old. Once the whole of Ireland was forested – when the trees died they were preserved in the peat bogs. See here, you can just make out the rings, one for each year. Bad years when there's no light and no nourishment, the rings become so thin you can hardly see them – it's a record of when a volcano erupted, or a comet went past. The dust they released blacked out the sun; no light could get through and the cold was queer and fierce. For a few years the trees could hardly grow at all. If you were to chart the rings from all the trees that had been dug from all the bogs, you could chronicle the history of Ireland going back seven thousand years.'

I touched the smooth black surface.

'Bugger to work with but. If you dry it out too quick, the wood splits apart, and it's so old it's as hard as bloody rock – splinters and fragments, there's precious little give in it.'

His sculptures were mainly natural forms – flowers, fish and birds – which seemed to grow from the wood, breaking free of its restraints, yet retaining an essence of what that tree had once been like.

'Spalting,' said John.

'What?'

John nodded at the lizard I was looking at. It was beautifully patterned in green, the lines like an abstraction of scales set against its pale cream-coloured flesh.

'It's where two fungi grow within the wood, and where they meet there's a chemical reaction – they're both trying to frighten each other away – and it causes these patterns. C'mon,' he said suddenly, slapping me on the back, 'Eddie will be getting bored, she's the attention span of a gnat.'

John ushered me into the sitting room and disappeared into the kitchen. He returned with two cans of Guinness which he cracked open. He handed one to me.

'What would madam care for?'

Eddie was looking down at the cigarette she was rolling. 'Do you have any wine?' she asked without looking up.

John winked at me. 'From the Butcher of Sligo's cellars, we can offer Chateau de la Ballynanane, or a classic Bordeaux from the fair hills and vales surrounding Lough Erne, or . . .'

'Piss off will you.'

He grinned and tousled her hair, and she attempted to slap him.

'Will this do you?' He held up a bottle for her to inspect.

'Will I like it?' she asked, wrinkling her nose and drawing on her cigarette.

'Well heaven help us, Eddie, how am I to know? You're as changeable as the wind so you are.'

'I'll have some. I'm used to drinking any old shite with you.'

'Ungrateful wench.'

'Is it cold?'

'I'd be taking my life in my hands to offer you warm white wine.' He uncorked the bottle and poured her a glass. He waited for her to taste it, and when she did, she nodded up at him and he smiled.

'Can I pour you a wee drop too?'

'Yeah, I'll try some.'

I only took a little – I still had my can – but it was delicious. It was a Cabernet Sauvignon from New Zealand so pale it was nearly clear; it tasted of green-gold gooseberries and grass.

Eddie drove back hunched over the wheel peering intently into the night. She pulled up outside my house and turned to face me.

'Are you going to invite me to stay or not?'

'Well, yes, if you like,' I said and then cursed myself for my lack of warmth.

I made her a cup of tea. I thought about the things I wanted to know and knew I shouldn't ask. I asked. 'Did you and John, ever, you know . . .?'

'Oh, we've slept together a few times, you know how it is. I've known him for years.'

For Eddie, years probably meant about three. She came and sat on the sofa next to me, leant over and kissed me. I had that same uncomfortable feeling – that she was almost indifferent – that I could have been anyone, any man. Why I should have felt this I don't know – maybe it was because she was so open about what she wanted, and what she wanted was sex. It unnerved me – I was always used to making the first move, trying to coax girls into bed with me. As she undid the buttons on my shirt I thought that had she been more reticent I would probably

48

have tried to sleep with her long before now.

My self-restraint did not last long.

Afterwards she lay cradled in my arms, for once still and relaxed. The sound of the sea was distant and soothing as the murmur of blood when you hold a shell to your ear.

'Tell me,' she said, 'what's the first thing you can remember in your whole life?'

I had that sinking feeling – first the sex, and then the exchange of little intimacies. But I should have known Eddie better. Almost before she'd finished the sentence she started to put her clothes back on. 'It's bloody freezing in here,' she said in response to my reproachful look. She knelt on the floor and started to roll a cigarette. 'Well?' she said, glancing briefly at me.

I looked at her long fingers and strong white hands dexterously rolling the liquorice-coloured papers and thought of how her skin had looked just now in the moonlight, flushed with the same inner luminance as an orchid.

'Sea horses,' I said, 'I remember keeping sea horses. You know the male and the female mate for life. They dance every morning when they see each other.'

She snorted. 'Don't be expecting me to be doing any dancing if you're getting up so bloody early.'

'My male sea horse had babies – I remember them coming out of a hole in his stomach – they were so tiny, and they were transparent, you could see their hearts beating.'

'Are you sure your mammy wasn't spinning you a wee tale?'

'No, all the males have babies,' I laughed.

'And they come out of a hole in his tummy? Was this your first sex education lesson by any chance?'

'No, really. The female implants her eggs in the male's stomach and then a bit later he gives birth. But what I loved best about them was their tails. They would cling to bits of seaweed with them and just hang there. They'd hold on to you if you put your hand in.'

'Strange thing to have as your first pet. How old were you?'

'Seven, I think.'

'What? Can you not remember anything before that?'

I thought for a minute and then said slowly, 'No, no I don't think I can. I've never really given it much thought. It's as if my life began at seven. But can you imagine,' I said, turning to her, 'holding hands with a fish?'

Eddie didn't stir, much less dance, when I left the following morning. But at one point in the night I woke to find her holding my hand.

My magpies were in fine fettle. As the sun rose, the pair that were nearest to me began to stake their claim to their territory. The male stood on the uppermost branches of a hawthorn and tree-topped – he bowed and flicked his tail. The female crouched below. I was close enough to see that the harsh black and white of their plumage was much more ornate than one would think at first: their wings were gilded peacock blue and gold and their tail feathers were burnished purple. As I watched, a rival male came sailing out of the sky, the light glowing through the white of his wings. He settled in an elder nearby. The resident male tree-topped even more vigorously than before and uttered a harsh chattering call. He was so irate that he looked like a round ball – he'd puffed out the white patches above his wings to make himself look bigger and tougher. In contrast, the incoming male, though every bit as loud, was much sleeker – younger and more frightened, I presumed.

The resident male flew at the intruder and chased him from bush to bush through the scrub until he'd seen him right off his territory.

He returned to his female with a little triumphant flick of his tail. She flew down to the short grass along the shore, scattering a couple of rabbits, and started to feed. But the male had other things in mind. He began to hop around her, inclining his tail towards her and uttering a call I had never heard before, a soft, babbling sound. She continued to stab the earth with her beak, but gradually started to respond to his advances, twitching her tail up and down rapidly and crooning back to him. They spent the rest of the day building nests – they would build several – the male fetching twigs and the female arranging them in a misshapen mass in the low-growing thorny bushes. In between their frantic nest-building, they would carefully preen one another, yet another step in the courtship ritual, the female winking at him with her white eyelid.

By mid-afternoon they'd stopped doing anything other than rest and I wandered aimlessly along the seashore. The character of the beach altered a lot during that two-mile stretch. The part I liked the best was where the flat dark rocks began. They pointed jaggedly out to sea and seemed naturally of a piece with Skull Island. Near the shore thrift and yellow lichen like fragments of gold leaf clung to the rocks; further out they became encrusted with barnacles and baby mussels growing in dense seed-pearl clusters. Where the tide had receded the dark rocks had trapped pools of water hidden by curtains of brown bladderwrack. I parted the seaweed and looked down into the pools. Each was like a miniature world, complete unto itself, with dense forests of seaweed, stiff skeletons of pink coral weed, translucent shrimp and sand gobies. Herds of periwinkles grazed the stony slopes and hermit crabs withdrew pincers as daintily as ballet slippers into stolen shells.

There were anemones everywhere, glistening and drooping on the rocks, spreading their tentacles within the pools. This common species, *Actinia*, has two types, a red kind and a blue. They fight viciously for the only thing that matters in their asexual existence: space. The one lethal weapon they possess is formed of flesh – they blow up a section of skin just below their ring of tentacles. Using this inflated beach ball, they touch one another with it, firing mini poison-laden harpoons into their opponent; the barbs blister and tear the soft tissue. I learnt all this at university, I think, but it seemed as if my scientific knowledge was just a thin veneer; underneath I knew the story of these rock pools instinctively. I could rattle off the Latin for periwinkle, could label the myriad types of seaweed, was able to distinguish a shag from a cormorant, but from somewhere deeper was a knowledge of the kind that you didn't have to learn – how to hunt for olive-brown baby crabs hidden in the bladderwrack, where to collect pocketfuls of shells, how to touch sea anemones until they were no longer frightened and would unfurl their tentacles beneath my fingers. A wave of misplaced nostalgia swept over me for a childhood I never had, for days spent as a prisoner of the tides; as far as I could remember, my parents hadn't even taken me to the beach.

I stood up suddenly and a wave of dizziness rushed over me. I had an image of a cove filled with shells as big as the palms of my hands. The sea was pink with moon jellyfish. I slipped on the rocks, managed to right myself and opened my eyes to the grey afternoon, the gulls cawing with hunger as they waited for the fishing boats to sail home. On the beach a woman and a white dog were watching me. When she saw me turn towards her, she walked away. I'd seen her before. Sometimes she walked along the sand in the early morning accompanied by the white dog; she always wore green boots, a Barbour, and a pale cream headscarf tied tightly round her hair. I was cold and hungry, and at that moment nothing seemed more inviting than the prospect of the Sandpiper's electric fire and their plates of large, fat chips.

About three weeks later I came home to find the house smelt very different. The smell seemed to be coming from the bathroom. I put my bike in the hall and went upstairs. The scent of perfume became stronger and there was the sound of splashing.

'Niall? Is that you?'

'Yeah. What are you doing?'

'I'm having a bath so I am, what do you think I'm doing?'

I smiled, and wondered how she'd got in. I guessed Mrs O'Malley must have given her a key. I went into the bedroom and stopped short. There was an open suitcase on the floor overflowing with clothes, but that wasn't what was so startling. My room, like everything else in the house, was exceedingly bare – just a bed with an iron bedstead, an old wooden chest of drawers and a wardrobe. The wallpaper had a faded floral motif and was peeling in places. Now the room had been utterly transformed. My first impression was one of gold and light until I had time to assimilate the changes. It was full of angels. There were gold cherub candleholders on the walls and the chest of drawers, a bronze angel with anorexia looking like a Giacometti by the wardrobe, a wooden one twisted as a gnarled branch of bog oak that had John's initials burned into one foot; the bed was covered with a blue throw emblazoned with sunflower-yellow angels and on the walls were posters – a Tintoretto of fat flushed cherubs swathed in orange damask, a William Blake, all fiery lines and harsh lights, and others by artists unknown to me – of angels with flaming swords and burnished wings hovering in the ether.

'I thought the place needed brightening up a bit.'

Eddie had come in, still damp from her bath and wrapped in a towel. The candles were giving off some strange, sharp scent.

'It smells as if you're about to make a sacrificial offering.'

'It's only for a wee while. It's a bit tense at home.'

I wondered vaguely whether she was trying to trap me, get a free ride back to England when I left, and then thought that (a) I was flattering myself, (b) Eddie was as likely to get bored and go off with someone else as hang around waiting for me to take her to London and (c) – (c) was lost when she dropped her towel on the floor and walked towards me.

Laying

There is a legend that when the world was young the magpie was the only bird who did not know how to build a nest. The rest of the feathered community kindly said they would help her. But to all their instructions the magpie said 'I knew that afore', so in the end the birds lost patience with her and said 'Well, if you knew that afore, then you can do it yourself', or something along those lines, and ever since then the magpie has never been able to complete a nest.

That is, of course, anthropocentric rubbish. The reason many nests are unfinished is because each pair builds two or three before choosing one which they will complete by lining it with mud and grass. They look misshapen – large balls of twigs untidily gathered together – but they serve their purpose. They even build roofs, and I was to find out the reason why.

By now it was mid-March and courtship and copulation had begun in earnest. In the scrubland the ground was speared with dark blades of daffodils, the embryonic flowers still crumpled inside the buds, and the newly minted bracken fronds were coiled as tight as snail shells, bright green and primitive.

Now that the nests were finished, I didn't think it would be long before the females started to lay. I watched my second pair, who had built a nest in one of the tall pine trees on the fringe of the scrub. That morning the male had spent much longer than usual perched on the uppermost branches of the pine, feathers sleeked down, bowing and tipping his tail. He uttered a single harsh call over and over again, occasionally making a lower, softer sound directed at the female below. She began to beg for sex, giving little plaintive pee-wit calls, and she crouched down, flicking her wings at him. He mounted and was finished in seconds. After that he never left her for a minute, and although she was foraging he guarded her so closely that he hardly ate anything.

About mid-morning he settled on the low stone wall at the edge of the scrub while she poked and scratched in the undergrowth below. Presently I noticed that he had fallen asleep, his head drooped and his eyes closed. I wasn't the only one that had noticed. Although I hadn't seen the young male in the stunted elder perched amongst the blood-purple clusters of Jew's ear fungus, the female had. He flew down and landed beside her, his tail angled towards her. Instead of threatening him and chasing him off their territory, she crouched and her wings quivered. She opened her beak as if to give the begging call, but did not utter a sound. Their mating was swift and silent and took place barely a metre away from her partner. He opened his eyes and jerked awake just as the youngster was hopping down from the female. So much for monogamy. The male called sharply and chased the interloper away, but it was a half-hearted attempt. The deed was done, and the male gave up, nervously returning to the female as quickly as possible.

She calmly continued to search for food as if nothing had happened.

I wondered how long the male could hold out, fasting as he was, but I needn't have worried. He found a crust of bread on the grass by the beach which the gulls had over-looked and hid it in a crack in the stone wall. Every time the female went back to the nest to add more grass or rearrange the twigs, he snuck his bread out and ate a few crumbs before hastily flying back to his errant female. I felt for the poor bastard, I really did.

Skull Island was an indistinct blur, and the sea itself was several shades of indigo with pale patches of pearl-coloured water that glowed as if lit from within. Water flowing from a little stream through the scrub fanned out and spread across the beach, corrugating the sand into the scales of some prehistoric creature. I breathed in deeply. The salt smell of the sea and bitter tang of rotting seaweed were as familiar to me now as the harsh calls of the gulls and the magpies that still chattered in my sleep. The woman and the white dog were standing looking out to sea. I climbed over the stone wall and walked down to meet her. Just as I reached her she said, 'They used to kill basking sharks here, you know. They caught them at sea and towed them to Ballynanane harbour where they were dismembered. They wanted their livers for oil. You wouldn't think it would you, such gentle creatures, and now there's not a stain of blood on the sand, nothing, nothing to remember their deaths.'

Her voice was very English. When she turned towards me I saw her eyes were pale grey-green with a faint web of crow's feet around them. She must have been in her mid-thirties. A few strands of platinum-blond

57

hair escaped from under her headscarf.

'Niall,' she said, holding out her hand, 'I wondered when I'd get the pleasure. I've heard all about you.'

'I suppose,' I said, 'there's worse things done to whales.'

'No doubt you're right, but somehow, when it happens at sea, it leaves no taint. It doesn't seem personal. But this town was built on the blood of those sharks, it grew rich on the fat of the sea. I suppose there wasn't anything else to take their place when the sharks died out or went away, and now the town is nothing but a grey concrete collection of run-down houses and run-down people.'

'On the contrary,' I said, 'the Pink Geranium film theatre is a hive of activity.'

'Ah yes, I heard you spent your afternoons in there.'

'Is nothing secret here?'

'I'm afraid not. Come back and have some tea. You start work so frightfully early, you must be in need of some refreshment.'

We started walking towards Nadia Ismail's wood.

'I don't know your name,' I said.

'You don't spend enough time with Mrs O'Malley or you'd know the business of everyone still living. But I suppose you have little call to buy quite so many tins of sardines now that your girlfriend has moved in.'

I swallowed uncomfortably.

'Ruth,' she said and we walked in silence for a little way. The white dog kept running ahead of us, sniffing amongst the rocks and the seaweed, before returning, drawn inexorably back as if on an invisible leash.

I lived in the first house in the village, Ruth lived in the last. It was slightly separate from the rest of the town, and it had its own small plot of land adjoining it containing a vegetable garden, two white nanny goats with kids, and

58

some white bantam hens. I felt as if I were in some strange fairy tale. The house itself was large and airy, one long room running from the front to the French doors at the back which overlooked the sea. The kitchen was off to the right and a white iron spiral staircase rose up to the second storey. The floor was made of bare wooden boards covered with a couple of thick white rugs, and hanging from the walls and arranged around the room were flotsam and jetsam from the beach – driftwood worn into smooth sculptures, bits of cloud-green glass sanded by the sea, glass floats tangled in drift nets, a packing crate with 'Venezuela' burnt on one slat filled full of shells and desiccated sea urchins, an elegantly thin anchor, red with rust, and a ship's lantern with a candle inside. There was a half-partition across the middle of the room made of small cubes of glass and on one side of it was a desk and a computer.

'Make yourself at home,' said Ruth. 'I'll get you some tea.'

Below me I could see the sea silently breaking on the shore. Ruth had an old boat tied to a palm tree and a garden of sorts. I say of sorts, not because it wasn't well cared for, but because it looked as if it had been made by a beachcomber who practised Zen. It was composed of beige gravel, with egg-shaped white pebbles arranged in circles and spirals; more driftwood and bits of iron were stuck into the ground. The few plants that grew in that garden were wild – marram grass, sea holly, thrift.

Ruth handed me a white china cup without a saucer or a handle; the liquid within was almost clear save for a couple of leaves floating at the bottom as if I were being given a very minimalist message to read.

'Chinese green tea,' she said.

I must have looked as if I were going to ask for milk. She'd taken off her Barbour and her boots and scarf. Underneath she was wearing a thin dress of fine grey wool and her blond hair was cut into a sleek bob. She was like something soft yet fragile – a snowdrop perhaps – that was just past its bloom. Ruth said she worked from home, translating Russian into English.

'How long have you been here?' I asked.

'Nearly ten years. But even if it were twice that long, they'd still treat me as an outsider. It can be so deceptive – the friendliness of strangers.' She looked out to sea and the white light burned her eyes.

I woke up that night to see Eddie sitting on the window sill, her silhouette sharply defined in the clear moonlight. She was drinking from a small bottle of sweet dessert wine the colour of honey and smoking a joint. I had no idea where she'd been, whether she'd just come back from work, or if she'd been out. And I thought about what Ruth had said as I watched her drink and smoke and look out to sea.

Finally she got into bed, and I felt her take me in her mouth, hold me there for one long moment before she started to suck and I swelled and grew, pushed out of her mouth into the chill night. She kissed me in a trail across my stomach and my back arched involuntarily. She bent towards me, and as I slid inside her she inhaled sharply and her breath, which tasted of grapes and resin, was sweet and smoky.

'There's no point in going to sleep,' she said, 'I've got to go to market in about an hour. Will you come?'

'What?' I asked blearily.

'I've to get fresh vegetables for the restaurant from

60

the wholesale market at Balmoral, just outside Belfast. It'll be much more fun if the two of us go.'

The thought of driving to Belfast at four in the morning to buy vegetables did not sound even remotely like fun.

Eddie drove fast and recklessly through the night and as she drove, she talked about her angels. She told me how when the world was created Satan presumed to challenge God. At that time, Satan was his right hand man, so to speak, but he didn't feel he'd been given enough power. He and a band of rebel angels challenged God's rule and God threw them all from heaven. Where they landed was a place of utter darkness called Chaos.

'Satan fell through a burning lake with his rebel angels, and he said,

> '"Farewell happy fields
> Where joy for ever dwells: Hail horrors, hail
> Infernal world, and thou profoundest Hell
> Receive thy new possessor: one who brings
> A mind not to be changed by place or time.
> The mind is its own place, and in itself
> Can make a Heav'n of Hell, a Hell of Heav'n"

'And so he decided to stay in hell and rule there – he said,

> '"To reign is worth ambition though in hell:
> Better to reign in hell, than serve in heav'n."'

I looked at Eddie in surprise. Here was this twenty-one-year-old kid with no education quoting Milton at me on the way to a wholesale fruit and vegetable market at some ungodly hour of the morning. I realized that I hadn't taken enough trouble to get to know her: her blunt manner could easily be misinterpreted as openness. She told me about the seraphim and the cherubim, the first two of the nine orders of angels that surrounded our Lord. But what interested her was not the idea of cute cherubs with rosy cheeks or guardian angels, one at each end of the bed to guide your way, no, what had captured her imagination was Michael, Gabriel, Raphael, the angels of God who lit the way with their flaming swords, who sought justice and avenged the Lord with cold, bright steel. I wondered whether it was the Catholic in her and it made me remember the bad joke about whether you had any Irish in you.

'You've seen too many pictures of Jesus with his heart on his coat and a little candle burning inside.'

She gave me a withering look.

'Either that or you've been inhaling incense again.'

'I haven't been to church for years,' she retorted.

'So how many angels can fit on the head of a pin, then?'

'Scholars have been debating that for years, so they have.'

'And the answer's forty-two,' I said, referring to the meaning of life, the universe and everything as deciphered by a computer in *The Hitchhiker's Guide to the Galaxy*. My attempt at wit was utterly wasted on Eddie.

She took a bend so sharply I had to grip the armrest.

'If they're spiritual creatures, then an infinite number of them can dance on the pin. But if angels have bodies, then you can only fit so many on a pin. When Adam and Eve fell from grace, Michael talked about sex as if he knew what it was, so they must have had bodies.'

'There was far too much falling in the old days. Hadn't God invented gravity?'

'Michael said to Adam that angels enjoyed themselves, and that,

"If spirits embrace,
Total they mix, union of pure with pure
Desiring; nor restrained conveyance need
As flesh to mix with flesh, or soul with soul."'

I was about to make some flippant remark, but she made me uncomfortable by adding, 'Not that that's much like sex, but at least they had an idea what people do so they must have had a bodily form.'

So Eddie didn't think that sex with me was like mixing soul with soul? Of course it was nothing like that, but I didn't like the idea of Eddie treating sex as a purely physical act. I tried not to run through those questions that bubbled at the back of my mind: how many, and how often, when and with whom?

'We're here now.'

She pulled into a large floodlit car park. Next to it were open-sided buildings like football stands without seats running across the middle of the market and freight lorries lined up in front of them. I had never seen so many vegetables in my life. There were freezer containers of mushrooms, piles of round white cabbages glistening in the artificial light like alien spoor, mountains of potatoes coated in a thin film of earth, racks of leeks whose white bulbs had the gleam of old ivory. Eddie left the car parked at an angle and strode across the tarmac. I trailed behind half-heartedly. She walked awkwardly, with the kind of gaucheness of a young giraffe, and her thin boyish figure cast a long shadow. She was wearing her fluffy coat, and as she argued and haggled with the traders they reached out and slapped her on the shoulder as if she were a horse. It reminded me of my father: although we were close we were never emotional. At times of stress, or general companionship, we would sit either side of TK, our golden retriever, and pat her roughly. When she died we didn't know what to do with our hands.

There were vegetables here I didn't even know the names of – things with ridges and spines, fine veins and leathered skin. I heard Eddie tell a small, balding man that she'd be a fockin' eejit to pay that price and in response he took her arm and bent her closer to a pile of aubergines that lay like small beached whales on the concrete as if being nearer to their enamelled hides would make her change her mind. I wandered over to the truckers' caff on the corner and ordered baked beans, fried onions, fried eggs and toast, and because Eddie wasn't there, black pudding and sausages, and because I was in an industrial estate on the edge of Belfast at five a.m., a Guinness. The guy serving behind the counter winked and cracked open a warm can for me. The sun was just breaking the lead from the sky when Eddie joined me. She poured two sachets of sugar into her tea and started rolling a cigarette.

'All done,' she said, 'no thanks to you.'

'I wouldn't know one end of a vegetable from another.'

'Sure if it doesn't come out of a tin, you're queer and stuck,' she said, and turned away from me to light her cigarette.

What I remember most from my childhood are afternoons in the Orchid House polishing leaves and cleaning roots. To get to the Orchid House you had to walk through a large dry greenhouse – it was supposed to be for desert plants and it was light and airy. I imagined I was in

Arizona, walking past seguaro cacti and aloe vera with a John Wayne swagger. There were beige-coloured pebbles strewn over the ground, perfect camouflage for a family of quails who darted beneath the metal trestles of flesh and spines and peeped incessantly. The female scattered eggs as carelessly as confetti; the gardeners gathered them up, and occasionally some hatched: the babies scurried through the stones, desperately trying to keep up with their flighty mother.

My father's greenhouse had its own inhabitants. A black-bird had made its nest at the back of the greenhouse; the male would fly through the fine mist of water we sprayed to keep the humidity high. He brought the female worms and leatherjackets as regularly as clockwork. Once my father lifted me up to see the eggs: they were a shocking blue in the deep green of the Orchid House.

In spring my father would repot every orchid in all the greenhouses and I had to help him. We would take them out of their pots and brush away the dirt from their roots which were thick as coagulated gelatine, and then I would smear them with Virkon which smelt of disinfectant and nail polish. I would pack them into their old pots with fresh soil and return them to the greenhouse. I also spent every holiday sitting on one of the wooden shelves in the pale, underwater light painting every leaf of every orchid with the same Virkon solution and pruning away the dead leaves with nail scissors.

I suppose it must have disciplined me in some way: made me realize the virtue of being methodical. The whole of scientific enterprise is like that; every time I record what the magpies are doing – with whom, where, and what time of day – I am painting another orchid leaf, and at the end of it there will be a profusion of flowers. Of course, as soon as any of our orchids bloomed, they were whisked away to be displayed in the public greenhouses. Sometimes my father took me to see them and I knew that were it not for our constant attention to detail (even as a young child I said 'we' when I talked about my father's orchids) – the disinfecting, the trimming and the removal of bugs with the sharp end of the scissors – there would be no monstrous show of petals for the public.

I guess this linear progression and attention to detail left me unprepared for John. His workshop was a homage to the unfinished. It must have held about ten largish sculptures and several smaller ones – some were barely more than raw wood, although to my untrained eye most of them looked perfect.

'Och no, I still want to alter this wee bit here,' he said, pointing to a lizard's foot. 'It needs to curve round here, and then I'll make long, fine claws that'll wind into the gnarled part, and I'm not so sure about the sunflower, I think that'll have to go.'

It was a little over a week since I'd gone to Balmoral market, and John had unexpectedly asked Eddie to invite me over to his workshop. 'Don't you sell any of your work?' I asked, looking around.

'Oh, some. Most of my commissions are large pieces and I have to carve them on the site. I've been known to go back later, though. I made this one piece – of barnacle geese – they were thought to be born from barnacles attached to the timbered wrecks of ships sunk to the bottom of the sea and they were more fish than fowl so the Irish would eat them during Lent. My sculpture showed the birth of these fish-like birds but I wasn't happy with it. It was for a National Trust park and once it was installed I went back one evening, climbed over the fence and finished it off. Took me a couple of nights – I stayed in a tent in the field opposite. I'm still not quite happy.

'You see, Niall, every piece has to tell a story. You might know the story you want to tell, but you have to find the right bit of wood – the shape of it, the colour, the kind. Yew will give you a pale pink, Japanese cherry is a dark burgundy, sycamore has more of a cream tone. You have to ask yourself, what is the colour of my story? You have to see it lurking within the wood, and set it free.'

His workshop smelled of sweet peat burning, freshly cut wood and the oil he used to grease his tools.

'I've another story for you. There was once a man who lived not far from the shores of Lough Erne and he had a small plot of land. He started to notice that his corn was disappearing during the night. Now, he wasn't a rich man, and couldn't afford to lose his corn, so he stayed up all night to see who it was that was taking it. But he was up at the crack of dawn every day and by evening he was always worn out, and night after night he fell asleep, and every morning a bit more of his precious corn would have disappeared. So his mother gave him a strong potion to ward off sleep, and that night he saw two magpies eating his corn. As the first rays of sun touched the grain, they turned into two beautiful raven-haired maidens whose skin was white as the driven snow. They got into a horse-drawn chariot and rode into the middle of the lake and disappeared.

'The next night he says, "Mother, will you be giving me more o' that potion."

'But she says, "No, son, it's queer and powerful and it'll not do you a blind bit o' good if you keep taking it."

'So your man persuaded her that it'll only be fer the one

night, and she agrees and gives him the potion. This time he waits by the shores of the loch, and when the dawn comes, he sees the beautiful twins driving back in the chariot towards him. Just as they plunge into the lake, he grabs one of the girls and asks her to be his wife. I'm telling you, things were a damn sight easier then than they are now. Anyway, she says yes she will marry him, on two conditions, the one being that he must never call her by her name, and the second being that he must never strike her.

'Well, his mother's very pleased he's got himself a beautiful wife, though she thinks she's a little queer in the head, and everything goes well for the next twenty years. Then one day his wife asks her husband to pass her the horse's bridle. He throws the bridle over to her and it strikes her on the cheek.

'"Now look what you've done," she says, and she runs back to the lake. Who should be waiting for her on the shore but her twin sister. She plunges into the water and drowns, and her sister, who is immortal, turns into a magpie and flies away, cawing bitterly, destined to remain in the body of a magpie for all eternity.'

As he finished speaking, he pulled a soft piece of flannel from a sculpture that was about a foot high. It was of a magpie rising from a contortion of wood that could have been a wave, its wings outstretched. My mind filled with images of magpies flying across the sky, the sun flaming through their wings, diamonds for tails. We looked at the sculpture in silence and then he said, 'It's for you, Niall.'

I didn't know what to say, how to thank him.

He shrugged and said, 'Actually, there's a bit I'm not so sure about, round the tail. Do you see it now? This part here?'

★　　★　　★

That night when Eddie came home I got up and lit a candle. I made my hands into fists and held them out. 'Which one?'

She chose the left hand. I opened my hand, empty palm upwards, then opened the other. Nothing in either hand.

'You daft get,' she said.

I grinned and gave her a tiny parcel wrapped in a twist of tissue paper torn from a wine bottle wrapper.

'For me?' she said, and ripped the paper open swiftly and messily.

I'd taken advantage of John's invitation to visit him, and borrowed some of his tools when I was there. I'd found the top hat shell I'd picked up on the beach in one of my trouser pockets and I used John's lathe to saw a sliver from each side of the shell. I was left with a small but perfect spiral. I held it in the palm of my hand, light as a feather. It's funny, I thought, how the laws of mathematics are reflected in natural forms; a logarithmic equation can describe the unfolding of a shell, predict the fractal pattern of a fern, determine when and how a zebra will get its stripes. Some scientists think that one day we will be able to describe the world in formulae, chart our destiny in numbers: biology will bow to physics in a Theory of Everything. But to me the maths did not yet seem precise enough; even in one shell there was infinite variation which a log of the curvature of the spiral smoothed away as sea erodes stones.

John watched me quizzically but didn't say anything. I drilled a hole in the top of the shell and threaded it onto a fine strip of leather.

Now Eddie held the necklace to the candle and looked at it carefully. She pressed it against her throat and turned round for me to fasten it for her. When she turned back she laid the length of her body against mine, wrapped her arms around me, and kissed me on the lips.

'Thank you,' she said softly, and the candle flame gleamed in her eyes.

I thought about showing her the magpie John had made for me, and decided to wait until later.

As well as detailed observations of my four pairs of magpies, I recorded territories all around the coastal area, counted nests and numbers of courting pairs, noted their sex, and followed bachelor gangs and flocks of adolescent females. Many of them disappeared into the wood and so one morning in the middle of March, I ventured into the home of Nadia Ismail. The narrow Gothic arch in the wall she used to get to the beach was barred. I followed the wall down to the sea where the sand turned to stone. The sea was a pale, clear grey stained black where rafts of seaweed had been skewered by the jagged pinnacles of rock around Skull Island. The stones along the shore were large and dusky pink. Someone had lit a fire down here, and when I poked one of the rocks with my foot it split apart cleanly, black on the outside, the colour of roast pumpkin inside. I thought they were some kind of sandstone that would flake apart: you would be able to prise away the leaves of rock like tearing off sheets of gilt to find fossilized seaweeds and the footprints of shells. Poisonous yellow ragwort grew along the wall and tiny ferns hid in the crevices, black and green and suckered as the tentacles of squid. There were a couple of runways down to the sea and recesses for boats were built into the wall with thin doorways and curved ceilings as if they'd been designed to hold wine, or even smuggled goods. In one of these recesses was a sailboard, the sail tightly scrolled round its mast, another was empty but dripped rancid water from the ceiling; there were several more but they were larger and had heavy wooden doors sealing the entrances. Next to the runway a white boat was moored in a small concrete harbour. The arms of the harbour all but enclosed the boat which was trussed up by a web of rope as if it were a wild animal. I could see part of the large Georgian house glowing magpie-egg green. I kept going, picking my way along the shore. The wall became much lower now and I scrambled over. I looked back once. Behind me the sea was perfectly calm with one single line of current contrary to the rest of the tide gleaming like a silver stretch mark.

The ground was marshy and there were dank pools of bronze water impaled by the dead skeletons of bulrushes, trees with brittle bone disease and giant rhododendrons whose corrosive juices had killed all the wild flowers. I pushed my way through and emerged onto a sandy, potholed path. To my left were a couple of outhouses and I could hear a girl's voice. As I turned the corner, both she and the large bay horse she was grooming looked up. The horse was huge and she was so small, she barely reached his withers. She was wearing black jodhpurs and her long straight hair was held back in a loose bunch. Her skin was very dark, and her eyes were such an intense blue they took my breath away. Nadia Ismail. In the flesh. She looked at me in a bored fashion, then resumed grooming the horse.

'I presume you're looking fer magpies.' She had a strong Northern Irish accent. 'Our gamekeeper kills them. They're a bloody nuisance.'

The horse nickered softly and nudged her shoulder with his soft black muzzle.

'Nice horse,' I said, nodding at the animal. She didn't reply. I tried again. 'You run a riding school?'

She nodded. 'Up by the lake. I just stable Gabriel here – and Toby.'

A small white Shetland was tied up by the stable door.

'Keeps him company. Gabriel's too valuable to be left with the others. He was a racehorse – my father bought him after he sprained a tendon.'

Her eyes never once left the animal and I watched as she smoothed his fine hair. She went into one of the outhouses and came back with a side-saddle. After she'd tacked him up, she disappeared for a couple more minutes, and when she returned she'd brushed her hair so that its ebony sheen matched the bright gleam of the horse's coat, and she was wearing the red cloak. Nadia led Gabriel to a mounting block, and swung into the saddle.

As she passed me she said, 'A word of warning. If you're going to be snooping round here looking for magpies, watch out for Brendan.'

I was so transfixed by her incredible eyes that it wasn't until she had ridden round the corner of the stables that I thought to run after her and call, 'Who's Brendan?'

'The gamekeeper,' she said without turning round, and spurred the horse into a trot. I watched until her scarlet back disappeared between the dark green of the rhododendrons.

After that I often came looking for magpies in the wood, and I tried to pass the stables when I knew she would be tacking up Gabriel. Sometimes I managed to see her, and she always looked bored – it was the way her eyelids seemed to droop heavily over her fine almond-shaped eyes. She didn't speak much and I felt like an awkward schoolboy in her presence, but once she told me that her father originally came over from Pakistan in 1961 and started selling clothes door to door. He was the first person to open a shop in the heart of Belfast after the city had been bombed almost to a standstill, and now he owned a chain of boutiques and the two largest hotels in Belfast.

One day I asked her why she always rode side-saddle.

'Because,' she said, grimacing slightly as she attempted to tug a brush through a knot in Gabriel's mane, 'my daddy wants me to be a good little Muslim girl and marry the man he chooses for me. And for that, of course, I need to have an intact hymen. We wouldn't want it to get broken accidentally, now would we?'

She suddenly looked up at me as if seeing me for the first time. She held out her hand. 'Come with me.'

I followed her into the stable feeling slightly stupid. She spread her cloak on one of the bales of hay at the back and patted the place next to her. It took a few moments before my eyes adjusted to the semi-darkness. The air was heavy with the sweet smell of straw; particles of dust turned lazily in the stream of light filtering beneath the wooden door. My heart swelled in my throat. When I sat next to her, she cupped my face in her hands and kissed me. She smelt of sandalwood, and leather, horses and hay. She moved my hands swiftly to her waist and I slid them beneath her jumper. Her skin was soft and yielded to my touch, her limbs were rounded. I held the heavy weightiness of her breasts in my hand and felt her nipples harden, puckering in my palms. We made love lying on our sides, one of her legs between mine, and as I thrust into her she tilted her head back and closed her eyes. I held the arch of her back in one hand and bent my lips to her breast. I thought of mornings on the beach watching her ride towards me, moving with the horse, the horse galloping in slow motion, a choreography of muscles sliding beneath the smooth skin, his nostrils flared, his breath echoing the heavy folds of fog that swirled around them.

When Konrad Lorenz, the founding father of the study of animal behaviour, discovered that his geese – who he'd always thought mated for life – sometimes committed adultery, he was devastated. His assistant sought to comfort him by saying, 'Don't worry, doctor, geese are only human.'

About ninety per cent of birds are monogamous, but genetic tests of the fledglings show that most have affairs or EPCs – extra-pair copulations as the jargon goes. It's all to do with genes. You need to pass them on, and the bird looking after your eggs may not have the prize ones. Best to mate as often as the opportunity arises, spreading seed far and wide, planting broods in nests for other males to rear. Luckily the desire to mate has a genetic basis.

There is a bird called the stone wheatear which is programmed to find a female, as is every male, but the poor bugger collects stones for his sins. He carries pebbles in his beak and builds a heap of them on a ledge in his cave. The stones aren't used to build a nest, they're solely to impress the female with. Back and forth he flies with his bloody pebbles until his pile is big enough to attract her. She rewards his stones with sex.

I was standing on the beach looking towards the shore, absentmindedly picking up pebbles and keeping an eye on one of my pairs of magpies. During the night thick swathes of seaweed had been washed up and they were picking through it for any crustaceans and sand lice caught in the stinking fronds. The surface of the seaweed seemed to be heaving. I looked through my binoculars and realized it was alive with small brown starlings, their gold wing spots

74

glittering in the harsh light. I jangled my pebbles in my palm like foreign currency and wondered if I should give something to Eddie, some token. I didn't quite know what, or for what, but somehow I couldn't see myself ferrying rocks about for extra sex. Just then my magpies uttered their chattering alarm cry and flew towards me before veering away and disappearing into the bushes further down the coast. Eddie was standing by a gap in the old tumbledown wall waving at me. She was wearing khaki army pants, Fils sandals and a tight striped jumper which looked as if it had come from a second-hand shop but was actually from somewhere expensive called BV8 in Belfast. I walked over.

'I thought I'd come and see what you get up to all day. I'm starting work late this afternoon.'

'Well, you've certainly managed to scare off my subjects.' I rattled the pebbles and then said, 'Come with me, I've got something to show you.'

'What?'

'Surprise.'

'Tell me. Will I like it?'

'You'll love it,' I said, 'I promise.'

We crossed over a small stream and Eddie said, 'There's an angel for everything, every living thing, you know. Anpiel is in charge of protecting all the birds, Shakziel is angel of the water insects, and Trgiaob is angel of wild fowl and creeping things.'

'Creeping things?'

'Yeah, that's his official title. There might even be a magpie angel but I doubt it – they've already got Anpiel and Trgiaob. Any more would be greedy.'

About halfway down the beach the bracken and the brambles coarsened and we turned in towards the fields. I took her hand and led her through the trees, past the old tumbledown cottage to the greenhouse. Algae had spread across the glass and the wooden joists were dark with damp. Wild daffodils had colonized it, fighting for space with lime-green nettles and the first exploratory tentacles from a blackberry bush. It was slightly warmer inside that out: the spring sunshine shone wine-green through the glass. I leant Eddie against a sagging wooden bench and undid her trousers. My pebbles spilled on the ground as I parted her with my tongue; she reminded me of a sea urchin split open, salty and fleshy. The muscles in her legs unlocked as if I'd poured oil over a pair of scissors and I stood up and slid inside her. I held her buttocks in my hands, and felt her bones grind into mine. When she came she opened her eyes wide, shocking blue as the blackbird's eggs in the green light of the greenhouse.

I ate at the Greenaun that evening. It was a slow night and Eddie served herself a meal and ate it with me – eating a little at a time in between rushing back downstairs to the kitchen. The food quickly grew cold. She heated it up once and then gave up. Conventionally one would say she ate as little as a bird, but since most songbirds eat twice their own weight a day, this would hardly apply to Eddie. She made me order dessert, but didn't have one herself. It was delicious: frozen yoghurt with a slice of honeycomb, hot ginger wine sauce and thick ginger biscuits to dip in.

'I used to keep bees in my bedroom,' I said, prising apart the waxy comb with a biscuit.

She wrinkled her nose and poured herself some more wine. 'Bees? How can you keep them in your room? Didn't they sting?'

I shook my head. 'They were bumble bees, they live on

76

their own. I drilled holes in the walls and hung little perspex boxes over them. Every night they'd return with their pollen baskets laden – after a while I could tell where they'd been from the colour of the pollen. I used to follow them sometimes when they woke up in the morning and see where they went.'

I hadn't thought about my bees for a long time. I must have had about ten of them. I fell asleep and woke to the sound of their gentle buzzing, each one in its own individual box, shivering to warm themselves up before crawling through the tunnels I'd made them and flying away for the day. In the end one of them got a parasite and it spread to the rest. It was a kind of mite that lives only in the ears of bees, crawling through their teddy-bear-yellow fur to breed and multiply. The bees scratched pitifully and listed when they flew. Finally I killed them all to put them out of their misery.

I glanced up and caught Eddie looking at me. She had that look that women sometimes get when they think you're mad and obsessive but they love you anyway. It only lasted a fleeting moment and then she turned away and called out to one of her friends. We stayed until the restaurant shut and then went to her friend's house. I drank coffee until I'd sobered myself up and then walked through the grey dawn out to my study site. The field between the wall and the pine trees was heavy with dew and I left a dark trail through the grass. As I got to the old stone wall by the short grass at the edge of the beach, the salt-laden wind whipped from the sea brought me an unfamiliar song. I looked over the wall and saw buttermilk light spilling and spreading across the edge of the ocean and a solitary unringed magpie perched on a piece of driftwood washed white by the waves. It was the magpie that was singing,

singing a strange sad song stolen from the tongues of other birds: nightingale, lark, warbler and robin, the notes jumbled and warped as they tumbled from its swollen throat.

*H*atching

One morning at the beginning of April I arrived on the beach to find sand blowing low along the shore like dry ice. Bleached white, it shifted and seethed in ectoplasmic coils, settled between the ribs of a seagull's skeleton, grazed a glass bottle washed up from Mexico, folded between the toes of a jelly-bean-blue plastic sandal. It rustled and hissed round my ankles, and danced in will o' the wisps across the tidemark. How, I wondered, would one calibrate such a thing – the waves on the shore, the sands of the sea? Some days every seventh wave was larger than the rest, thin as a diamond, bright as a gem, its cutting edge splintering into spume. Some days the sea was flat as a sheet of black obsidian; when the sun came out clear pools of aquamarine blossomed like the unfolding of Japanese lilies. What laws of science could determine how water molecules, the pull of the moon, a melting iceberg, flowering algae, and the song of a whale would interact? They say that Chaos Theory can predict these things – collect enough data, use a big enough computer – and from turbulence a pattern will emerge: order from anarchy. I couldn't picture myself as a mariner sampling the seas for the resolution of complexity. Where everything and nothing has an effect, how would one know where to stop? How could one tell whether the slow drift of a sea horse caught in the current, or the sudden snap of an angel shark's jaws, would contribute to change, causing a shift of volcanic sand on the shores of Reykjavik, a bigger bloom of krill in the Antarctic? How could a computer tell you that on an insignificant beach on the north-east of the island of Ireland a tide of moon jellyfish would blow in and leave the imprint of their internal organs stamped into the damp sand as perfectly as the print from a mushroom when the spores fall out in the pattern of gills? I liked my science as precise as the counting of orchid leaves. I liked to know that the animals I was watching were programmed by their genes, their lives unfolding as clearly as if I could decipher the code inscribed in the protein of their cells.

That morning the magpie pair in the pine trees fought. I guess it was inevitable, I suppose you could have seen it coming. The crows mobbed them. The grass below the trees was thick and lush – fine for the crows, but too long for the pies. There wasn't enough food and the female was constantly harassed. At five to nine she left and never returned. I walked in the general direction she took but didn't find her until eleven fifteen. She was with a stranger, an unringed male on a prime territory way down the beach where the grass was shorn by herds of rabbits and there were low-growing thorny trees. She was preening the unknown male, quivering her wings and begging for food with an intensity unrivalled by any courtship displays I'd seen before. The technical term for this is divorce. By remarrying, female magpies move up in status, zeroing in on middle-class territories, pulling themselves up from the lower classes by their bootstraps. I wondered what had happened to the new male's ex-partner, whether she too had moved up in the world or had been injured. Perhaps she was still on the scene and he was embarking on a bigamous relationship.

When I returned to the stand of pine trees the abandoned male was hunched in an elderberry bush. The nest was empty and the ground was littered with bloody fragments of eggshell. That night I had a dream. I dreamt I was eight years old again and I was walking through the dry heat of the desert greenhouse at Kew. The quail were silent and it was dark – the cacti's curved fangs were silhouetted against the milk-white panes of glass. I slid open the door to the Orchid House and entered the moist tropical heat of the jungle. I was surrounded by fleshy leaves. A single spray of moon orchids glittered as pale as moths in the twilight. I walked over to the blackbirds' nest but there was no sound, no tell-tale rustle of wings, or flighty stirrings in the throat of the female. I climbed up onto the wooden bench, pushing pots of orchids to one side. I thought the nest must be empty but as I knelt in front of it and smelt the metal tang from the copper water pipes, I caught sight of the female. She appeared to be wrapped in spider silk as if she had been completely mummified. I reached out and picked her up. She weighed almost nothing. Cushioned in the moss-lined nest three eggs gleamed like sweets, and a tiny fledgling reared its head and opened its mouth to gape silently at me, its stumps of wings raw, its eyes dark as blackberries and sealed with skin. In my hand I felt the still bird's heart beat once, twice and then stop. It was like the tolling of a bell echoing in the curve of my palm.

After that first time with Nadia I returned to the stables again and again, driven by some incomprehensible addiction. I didn't see her for nearly two weeks and I suspected that her job at the riding school was little more than a passing fancy to be entertained when she pleased. When I finally saw her she was curt, and although I was left with tinder-dry fantasies it was little more than I expected. The time after that I was walking along the beach. She came riding towards me, bareback astride her horse, her red cape flickering in the wind. I imagined her wearing nothing but the cloak. At the same time, I wondered at her vanity. I looked up, thinking she might nod to me as she passed, or that at the very least I would catch sight of her face beneath the mane of thick hair, so black it was nearly blue. She slowed the horse to a walk.

'Do you want a ride?'

I looked dumbly up at her, unsure whether she meant I could test drive Gabriel as if he were a new motor, or whether there was some hidden meaning in her question.

'Well do you or don't you? You can get up behind me.'

She wound her cloak tightly around herself and I tried to jump on the horse. I managed on my second attempt, but it was more like a bad scramble than the neat, athletic vault I'd hoped for. The horse steamed gently between my thighs. I put my arms around Nadia's waist, and as we walked towards the wood I unwound the cape, and eased my hands against her hot skin. She flinched at first, my hands were cold, but as I moved them upwards to cradle her breasts she arched her hips and leant back against me, swaying slightly. There was a glimmer of a smile, a glimpse of real feeling when I asked her to put her cloak back on after she had undressed in the stables.

After that, I slept with Nadia occasionally, though the infrequency was not for lack of trying on my part. I was under no illusions. I didn't want a relationship with this woman, and I was certain she felt little for me. She *was* beautiful, but in an impossibly icy yet exotic way. If I'd met her in other circumstances, I doubt I'd have had the courage to speak to her. I think it was her boredom that attracted me; if I created enough opportunities, she might fuck me as the mood took her. I liked to think she found me attractive, but I also knew if I had not presented myself other men would, other men surely had: I was nothing special. When she kept her eyes open during sex, she might as well have had them shut, so cut off was I from what she was feeling, or whom she might be fantasizing she was with, and though this damaged my pride, in a strange and slightly perverse way, it turned me on. There were none of the complicating emotions that are normally implicated in an act that ought to be pure pleasure. I pretended to myself I might get to know her mind if I had sex with her. I was intrigued to find out how she operated, and what might move her; yet I remained completely content to keep our relationship, such as it was, solely physical; knowing deep down that I really didn't care what she thought.

In the meantime things got worse for the magpies. The following day a sparrow hawk attacked the first pair. The domed roof of the nest must have been badly made for the hawk pulled the messy bunch of twigs apart with its hooked claws and seized the female. The male tried to dive-bomb the hawk, but it was too late: the raptor broke her neck and carried her clean away.

For the rest of the day the male flew between the beach and the scrubland, through the wood and across the fields, calling for his mate. I returned at dusk and there was no sign of the male, but I could hear the pitiful cries of the chicks. They were three days old and I didn't think they'd last the night. As an objective scientist, the proper thing to do would be to leave them to their fate; the hawk attack was a natural event, after all. I dithered for a couple of minutes and then pushed my way into the heart of the hawthorn. It took me half an hour just to get a couple of metres off the ground. I had to break some of the branches, and by the time I reached the nest my clothes were torn and my hands and face were scratched. The chicks were cold but still alive. As I put my hand through the opening of the nest, they made a heroic effort to open their mouths and cheep. I took them out one by one and put them in the inside pocket of my jacket. There were five of them and they moved feebly against my chest.

I struggled out of the tree, falling the last few feet, and ripped my coat again. I walked back across the fields in the dark, stumbling into the bitter cold of the stream and bruising my shin on a tree stump. When I got home I put them in a box with a hot-water bottle wrapped in a towel underneath them. I heated up some milk until it was the temperature of blood and added an egg. By hammering the edge of a teaspoon I was able to make it into a narrow scoop with which I attempted to feed the five baby magpies. Most of the milk missed and dribbled over them, but when I was sure I'd managed to get at least a little nourishment into them, I covered them with my pillowcase and left them in a box by the fire.

'Eddie feeding you too many vegetables?' asked Mrs O'Malley as I paid for five cans of dog food. William watched me from a dark corner of the shop, only his hands, pressed together in his lap, illuminated by a still pool of light. The corner store smelled of dried peas and rotten apples.

As soon as I got back home, the babies started to crane out of the box, their tiny overweighted heads lolling on their thin necks like flowers that haven't been given enough water. I mixed up the dog food with more egg and a few oats, and ground in some of Eddie's vitamin tablets. She had innumerable different varieties – she was always complaining that her skin was too dry or something. I told her that if she actually ate anything her skin would be fine – not that I could see anything wrong with her complexion anyway. This time I managed to get a bit more food into them, but even right after I'd fed them, they opened their mouths and begged for more. I was still up when Eddie came home. It was only then that I realized what an intensive and time-consuming job it was for the parents – the babies needed to be fed every fifteen minutes. The noise level increased dramatically every time I went near the box, and, for such small, vulnerable creatures, they were certainly vocal.

Eddie stood in the middle of the floor with her hand on her hip, a cigarette dangling from the other, whilst I tried to explain what I was doing.

'Didn't think you'd be up for my benefit,' was all she said, finally remembering to take a drag.

She went into the kitchen and reappeared a few minutes later with some leftover food from the restaurant. She put the plate on the floor. There were pink onions roasted in sherry and stuffed with almonds and wine-coloured sage leaves, a hot avocado pie that tasted of chicken, red cabbage cooked with cranberries and apple, and chargrilled purple sprouting broccoli. She ticked the items off on her fingers as she enumerated them to me.

'And I recommend a white Zinfandel from California – which is pink,' she added when she perceived I hadn't quite grasped the colour scheme.

I said it all looked rather pretty, but I was too tired to eat much. Eddie sat down on the sagging sofa and got out her knives. She started to sharpen them as fluidly as if she were filing her fingernails and I tried not to look.

★　　★　　★

The next couple of weeks were a complete nightmare. The magpie chicks ate voraciously and it soon became apparent that there was no way I could go out to the field with them at this loud, hungry and needy stage. I tried to enter some of my data into the laptop, but my attention wandered as soon as they started cheeping again. By the time I'd downloaded the same data three times and lost a day's work, I gave up and concentrated on sleeping and watching daytime TV. The only time I ever used my brain was when I did a back-of-the-envelope calculation which I thought would amuse Eddie: an angel, if one really existed, would have to have a wing span of six metres to carry the average male body – plus an extra four stone of chest muscle to power them. And to support this extra weight, he'd need a breastbone like a turkey's but half a metre long. No wonder angels were always saying 'Do not be afraid' every time they cruised in at 60mph heading smack bang for virgins and unsuspecting shepherds.

I realized what a pattern Eddie and I had fallen into. Eddie wouldn't get in until about two in the morning. Twice a week she stayed up until four, sometimes with a friend, sometimes in my house, drinking wine and coffee and smoking dope, before leaving for the vegetable market in Belfast. The rest of the time she would climb into bed and wake me up. I'd doze fitfully and get up at five, whilst she would sleep in until eleven, take a long bath, and dash frantically to work to supervise lunch and prepare the following week's menu. I used to find it exciting being woken by her insistent tongue and hands and making love in a half-dream; now I just felt tired and annoyed. It wasn't that I didn't like giving her pleasure, but I was a little bored of lying beneath her, holding back until she was ready.

For someone who had a very natural look, a large number of bottles containing lotions, creams, unguents and powders had appeared. I'd no idea what they were for, but their smells and contents leaked, spilt, dusted and pervaded the bathroom and bedroom. The kitchen was always scrupulously clean and meticulously laid out, the taps so shiny you could see your reflection in them, the spices and tins in regimental rows in the cupboards, pots of leftovers neatly labelled and sealed with cling film in the fridge – but the rest of the house was a mess. The place reeked of incense, and the bedroom had become a grotto full of wax stalagmites and stalactites. The angels had multiplied too. The wallpaper was all but covered with divine posters and there were gold cherub candles in the bathroom. Eddie liked to bathe in style. I've never been a particularly tidy person myself, but I don't mind my mess. Sometimes she even put flowers in the sitting room. Flowers are for green-houses.

I moved the magpies into the boxroom and put my files and computer downstairs in the living room.

'Are you planning on working down here?' Eddie asked suspiciously.

'Well, I can't work upstairs with the magpies, can I? Their bloody cheeping would do my head in.'

'It does *your* head in? You're the one that brought them home. It's so cramped – I've got nowhere to sit, or put any of my stuff. The whole house is full of magpies and magpie bloody papers.'

'And the bedroom is full of fucking angels. What do you mean you've got nowhere to put anything? Your stuff is lying around everywhere. Anyway, you must be used to being cramped, you're a fucking Catholic for God's sake.'

I immediately regretted what I'd said.

'Why d'you think I moved here?' Eddie yelled in frustration. 'To get some peace and bloody quiet.'

Even I, no great reader of female behaviour, realized she was on the verge of tears as she ran out of the house and slammed the door. I ran after her and caught her by the palm tree.

'I'm sorry, I shouldn't have said that. Look, you wouldn't have wanted them to die, would you?' I asked.

She shook her head slightly.

'And it's only for a little while. As soon as they're big enough, they'll fly off and we'll get the sitting room back to normal. I'll put all my things in the boxroom and you can have all the space and peace and quiet you want.'

I led her back into the house and kissed her. As I slid my hands beneath her T-shirt, she said in a small voice, 'I'm late for work, so I am.'

'Eddie,' I said, 'you're always late for work. Today you're just going to be a little later.'

I peeled her T-shirt off and made love to her very slowly and gently. Soundlessly. I thought I could make things better without words.

One day Eddie decided to sort out her life and went to Belfast. She came home with four almost identical outfits. She was going to be organized, she explained. Two were for when it was cold, two for when it was warm; the difference between them was the thickness of the material and the colour. She hung her complete outfits up, each one on a separate hanger. They were for when she fell out of bed at midday and sleepwalked into the bathroom. She wouldn't have to think about what to wear, she said. Within a week they were lying in mixed-up piles on the bedroom floor, and now that I was home I was privy to her loud and panic-stricken demands to locate a certain T-shirt – the one with the black star on green, not the green star on black – her desperate attempts to find something clean, and her constant queries about what I thought she ought to wear. She would snarl at my attempts to locate items of clothing – how could I possibly think that that shirt would go with those trousers? She would smear stuff on her face, rub gel in her hair, toss my clothes round the room, and emerge looking fresh and perfect save for the slightly agonized expression over how late she was.

Since I was cooped up at home with my magpies, I didn't get the chance to wander along the beach towards the Ismails' wood under the pretext of research, and so I was unable to see Nadia. I missed her exotic perfume, her air of crisp detachment, the way her eyes would suddenly glow with life in the dark of the stables. I missed her striking, almost glacial beauty, so cold I could barely look at her. I missed being able to take her, wide awake and forcefully, holding my hand over her mouth to stop her crying out loud, feeling her teeth sink into the palm of my hand like a horse at the bit, the way she slid and moved beneath me with no jagged edges or stone-sharp bones.

I called David.

'Hey,' I said.

'All right, mate. How's it going?'

'OK. You?'

'Fine. Did another E1 this weekend. I'll have to mail you a spare set of keys.'

'Good?'

'Yeah, great. The wrens are laying. One male had five nests on his territory.'

'Yeah?'

'Should have seen them, they were so perfectly formed.

89

He used bright green moss. I think there's a correlation, you know, number of nests and territory quality.'

'Yeah?'

'Bound to be. We'll have to run some experimental trials next year. You'd better be there to give me a hand.'

'Whatever you say, boss.'

'You bet. All right, you old bastard, see you around.'

I didn't feel any better. I stood in the phone booth and rested my head against the glass for a minute. It was cold. Outside a gale was blowing.

I phoned my mother and immediately felt guilty at the pleasure in her voice.

'Niall! I'm so glad you called. We were worried about you. Is everything all right?'

'Yeah, yeah, fine. How's Dad?'

'Same as ever, Niall. I hardly see him. He's always in a greenhouse, whether it's the one at home or at Kew.' She tried to laugh. 'He's well. He's going to a conference soon, in Germany I believe. On orchids, but I don't know exactly what it's all about. And he's given several talks in London recently. I think one was at the RGS. How's your work? Have you heard from David?'

'He's busy counting wren nests.'

'What about you?'

'Well, things have kind of ground to a halt here. I'm looking after some baby magpies, not getting much done.'

'I'm sure you'll catch up. Whose magpies are they?'

I told her a little bit about the fledglings and then surprised myself by telling her about Eddie. Christ, I thought, I must be in a bad way, talking to my mother like this.

'What's she like?'

I thought for a minute. 'Well, she's like me, but she's not.

Like me that is. She's a chef, she doesn't eat meat, she likes clothes . . .'

I ran out of things to say. How can you sum a person up, I wondered. When I thought of Eddie the images I held in my mind were physical – not sex necessarily, but the way she moved, how she held herself, wielded a knife, walked round the house, strode across the restaurant, bent over laughing, lit a cigarette. Those were the things, I thought, that would remain, long after I'd forgotten what I'd said to her, what she might or might not have said to me, where we'd gone and whom we'd seen.

My mother was still talking. 'I always remember it being cold and damp, but the sea was incredible, the light, always changing.'

'Sorry?' I said. 'Where was the light incredible?'

'Ireland,' she said patiently.

'Oh. I hadn't realized you'd been.'

There was a long pause.

'No, no, I guess not,' she said at the same time as I said, 'Look, I've got to go. The magpies, you know.'

'Thanks for calling, love. Don't leave it so long next time, will you?'

I went back and fed the magpies, then wrapped them up in the pillowcase and headed for the Pink Geranium. Cyril was playing *Breakfast at Tiffany's*. I remember smirking in sympathy at the scene where Holly Golightly is trying to get Paul, her new next-door neighbour, to find her black alligator shoes; he discovers one under the bed, she eventually spots the other in the fruit basket. The last thing I can recollect is Audrey Hepburn declaring she is 'top banana in the shock department.' I woke up with an erection, and a cloud of beer breath in my face. Cyril was shaking me violently.

'They're complaining so they are.'

'I guess they're hungry,' I said, yawning, looking down at the fledglings squirming beneath the pillowcase.

'Not them, you great lump, *them*,' he hissed and indicated the audience with a flamboyant sweep of his arm.

The theatre was filled with old women all of whom were muttering and shaking their heads at me.

'Church outing, so it is,' said Cyril. 'Cakes served in the café afterwards followed by flower arranging.'

I groaned. 'All right, all right, I get the message.'

'You've not missed much anyway,' said Cyril sarcastically, 'I've only had to rewind to the beginning twice.'

I picked up my box and made my way slowly along the aisle, tripping over several artfully placed umbrellas. I took the magpies back home to feed them, then carried them with me to the pub.

'What in God's name are those?' asked George, bending his head over his stick to look in the box. The magpies craned their scrawny necks back at him and gaped so widely I thought they might choke. Their feathers were just starting to poke through their wrinkled pink old-man skin. 'They're queer and ugly.'

I couldn't help but agree.

'The devil's spawn,' he added, somewhat unnecessarily I felt. He prodded one with a gnarled finger, the nail thick and yellow. 'And do you know how the magpie came by his black and white colours?'

I shook my head. I had a feeling I was going to be told whether I liked it or not.

''Twas at the time of the crucifixion. The magpie was the only bird that refused to go into mourning, and so he wore black and white to offend our dear Lord. And the

92

Lord made the magpie wear his two-tone cloth for ever after. Malicious little blighter.'

He took a sip from his beer. Just in case I got the idea he might have been referring to the good Lord, he continued, 'The only animal, the only one that refused to go into the ark was the magpie. The pair o' them, the male and the female, perched on the rafters of the boat and jabbered at the drowning world. Didn't stop them hitching a ride but. Och, they're evil wee beasties indeed.'

He looked sharply at me, his blue eyes as keen as ice picks. 'An' I'm tellin' you, son, you should have left these where they were. No good will come of it, not at all, at all.'

'George,' I said, 'if you don't stop being so bloody melo-dramatic I'll have to go and join the women's flower arranging.'

'It's no laughing matter, sonny Jim.'

'Definitely not. There's a limit to the amount of things you can do with daffodils.'

The magpies liked to be bathed every day. I used the washing-up basin, to Eddie's utter disgust. She shouted at me for a full minute and I thought I was simultaneously going to be ditched for John and end up with a face full of pecan pie. They were at a stage where they would struggle, splash and gape as if they couldn't make up their minds whether to love it or loathe it, and their brains were still in feed-me overdrive. The way I saw it was that they were full of conflicting subroutines for eating, sleeping and playing; they didn't have an overall programme that would act as a long-term guide to co-ordinate their behaviour and allow these subroutines to run concurrently.

At five weeks old they were still incredibly ugly: they looked as if some avian voodoo spirit had stuck them full of quills, and they were as prickly as baby hedgehogs. But at least I could now leave them for longer periods of time. I decided to go back to my study site to see how things had been shaping up in my absence. I gave them a larger feed than normal, laced it with brandy and turned the gas fire in their room up a little higher than usual. That, I figured, should send them into a sleepy stupor for a good couple of hours.

The sky was white, clouds massing on the horizon in heavy brooding grey, the sea a sulky black, savage and sand-laden where the waves hit the shore. Small flocks of dunlin zig-zagged along the water's margins; the odd rain-drop fell across my face and my lips were raw with salt. There was something on the beach that looked like a large white worm. As I got nearer I saw that it was trussed up with wool and strands of weed. Poking from one end were four small hooves, and from the other a muzzle, the lips pulled back to reveal a set of tiny teeth. It was a lamb bound tight as a cocoon. It must have drowned; this was the sea's strange way of presenting gift-wrapped offerings. It reminded me of the bagworm, a kind of moth whose larvae hatch live inside the female and eat their mother from the inside out before attaching silken ropes to her remains and casting away on the wind.

I had to lean into the wind as I walked. It caught a handful of magpies in its grip; they shattered against the sky, wings and tail feathers outstretched, and were swept into the wood. To my surprise I discovered that the male whose mate had been killed by a hawk had not taken another partner but was still hanging round the scrubland. Every so often he would fly aimlessly over the fields calling before returning to his perch. Against the odds, the male who had been abandoned by his unfaithful partner had managed to mate again with a new female who was much younger than him. They were now rearing a second brood of chicks. The third pair and the adulterous female who had married up the social hierarchy also had chicks and were attempting to feed them. All of them were thinner.

I was timing the male of my third pair to see how frequently he returned with food when I noticed something white on the trunk of the tree. I focused my binoculars on it. It was a cross crudely scratched into the bark directly below the nest. I went back to the other nests, even the one desecrated by the crows. They were all marked with a cross.

I figured I had another half an hour or so before I needed to be back home so I cut across the beach and into Nadia Ismail's wood. I wanted to see if the flock of adolescent birds were still around. As I suspected, the stables were empty save for Toby, the white Shetland pony. I followed the path away from the house deeper into the woods. There were wild primroses, and crocuses growing along the verges, and further into the wood lime-green stands of sorrel, the finely veined flowers just beginning to unfold. The wind sliced through the trees and the branches creaked and groaned. The path itself was probably only ever used by Nadia: it was pockmarked with hoof prints and I imagined her riding towards me, her sheet of black hair and her red cloak sweeping around her. I hadn't seen a single solitary magpie and I was thinking of turning back when I saw the gleam of water ahead. I quickened my pace. It was in the wrong direction and far too still to be the sea.

The trees fell back and there in front of me was a small lake complete with several different kinds of ducks. A couple of moorhens stepped gingerly towards the far bank. There were a few water lily leaves in the centre, rolled into tight scrolls by the wind, and a small wooden boat. The path continued on past the lake and crossed a shallow ford laced with the deep butter-yellow of marshcups. I walked round the edge of the lake, sending the ducks and moorhens into squawking flurries and the variegated ducklings scrambling for cover amongst the bulrushes. The sky was nearly pitch black by now and from out at sea an ominous peal of thunder rolled in. I could hardly hear the ducks above the howling of the wind, but one thing I did hear with great clarity was a sharp click and a locking sound as I entered the wood again. I was about to swing round to see what it was, when an arm tightened round my throat and I was hauled backwards. I had a dizzying impression of vast oak trees arching above my head and then I was pushed to the ground.

I looked up at my assailant. He was well over six feet tall, broad-shouldered and stout-thighed. He had a thick head of ginger hair and a beard. Clenched in his left fist was a shotgun with the safety catch off.

'You're trespassing, son. You're lucky I didn't shoot you as soon as see you.'

I stood up. He still towered over me. 'I was just looking for magpies. I study them, you know.'

'Aye, I know all right, you daft bugger.' He spat and turned back to me. 'The only good magpie's a dead 'un. You can get out that way. Don't let me catch you here again.'

I hastily clambered back to the path, tripping over a tree root, and headed away from the lake. I could feel his eyes boring into my back as I stumbled over small stones, but when I finally plucked up enough courage to look behind me, he had gone. The path curved round at the edge of the wood, winding back up to meet the potholed drive and the huge rusty iron gates with their forbidding battlements on either side. They were padlocked together and I had to climb over the wall, half falling into the field below. Just as I reached the road to the village, the sky seemed to crack, there was another roll of thunder and rain poured down in icy torrents. Sheets of water swept in from the sea, obliterating the horizon and turning the road into a shallow river.

The thunder frightened the magpies. They cowered in their box and hardly cheeped when I entered the room. I peeled my wet things off as soon as I got in and fed the magpies wearing only my boxer shorts. I'd almost finished when there was a frantic pounding on the front door. I ran downstairs and opened the door a fraction. I was nearly flattened against the wall by the force with which the door was flung open. Nadia Ismail pushed her way into the hall and stood in front of me dripping with water. Her hair was slick against her skull and drops of rain hung on her thick eyelashes above those impossibly blue eyes.

'You have to feed me,' she said, tearing off her cloak. She tossed the sodden thing over the banisters and strode into the kitchen, flicking her hair over her shoulder. A streak of water hit me across the chest. She left a trail of wet footprints and the longed-for mixture of sandalwood perfume and the sweet smell of hay and horse behind her.

'Come on, Niall, what is there to eat?'

She didn't wait for me to reply but opened the fridge and started emptying it of silver-foil-wrapped dishes. I watched in amazement as she squeezed whole slices of aubergines baked in pesto into her mouth. A dribble of green oil ran over her chin. Nadia bit into a courgette fritter and wiped her glassy lips across the back of her hand.

'It's Ramadan,' she said. 'I'm not supposed to eat between sunrise and sunset. I can't even buy food from Spar without me da finding out. And it's such a long time over here, so many hours of daylight.'

She tore the foil from another bowl and scooped out red wine and mushroom pâté with her fingers. Eddie, I thought, would be amazed that for once I'd managed to eat all the leftovers she brought back. I'd have to tell her I went for a run, or something. Nadia finished the pâté, washed her hands and pushed her hair back from her face.

'Now what have you that's sweet? I need sugar. C'mon Niall, I feel so faint.'

Nadia didn't look as if she were going to faint to me; she was positively glowing beneath the thin sheen of water that coated her skin. I cut her a piece of rum and chocolate cake and steered her in the direction of the sitting room.

'Well don't just watch me,' she said through a mouthful of chocolate, 'put the fire on. It's bloody freezing so it is.'

I went back into the kitchen and started to hunt through the freezer for something I thought she would like. Riffling through bags of ice, I remembered the first time Eddie had come round to the house with enough food and equipment to feed a small army, and I felt myself break out in a cold sweat. What if she came home? She might feel ill, or have forgotten something vital for tonight's dinner. It was highly unlikely, I told myself. I allowed my mind to cloud with images of Nadia glowing like hellebore when the first frosts melt. I went back into the sitting room. Nadia had licked the plate clean and looked as smug as a cat that's just drunk a quart of cream. There was a faint rim of chocolate icing round her mouth.

'Ice cream,' I said, holding out the tub. 'It's home-made.'

For one second she almost smiled. She was about to take it from me, but I kept it out of reach.

'I've a better idea,' I said as I peeled the lid off.

I took a spoonful of ice cream and held it out to her. I watched as she took the spoon between her lips and sipped the ice cream from it. For one heart-stopping moment she looked up at me. I took another spoonful and put it in my mouth. I leant forward and kissed her and the ice cream burnt and thawed on our tongues. Scooping some up in my fingers, I trailed it across her lips before kissing her. I took her clothes off and smeared ice cream across her soft, brown skin, licking it away as it melted while outside the rain hammered on the windows and the sea tore at the shore.

Towards the end of the month I received a parcel from my mother. It was Eddie's day off, and for once she was out of bed before eleven.

'What's in it?' she asked sleepily. She was curled up on the sofa, bleary-eyed and yawning.

'Don't go to sleep on me. We're going out, remember?' She nodded and yawned again.

There was a card, which my father had signed. I wondered if he'd even read it, but that was probably a little unfair of me, and a photo.

'Actually,' I said in surprise, 'it's for you.'

I handed her the parcel which was wrapped in gold and blue paper. She tore it open at once. It was full of clothes. They looked as if they were from my mother's charity shop and had been in vogue about twenty years ago – old Adidas tops and parkas, a stripy jumper and a snake belt, the kind I remember wearing to hold my grey flannel shorts up at first school, and a pair of Farrah trousers. I groaned inwardly.

'You can stick them in the bin, I won't be offended,' I said, not sure whether to be annoyed or amused.

'Oh no, they're great, so they are. Your mother has brilliant taste.' She pulled off her T-shirt and immediately started trying the clothes on. 'They're just so cool. How come you didn't inherit her clothes sense?'

'Must've been on the other X chromosome.'

'I'm going to write her a thank you letter. Give me a bit of that paper.'

'Do it when we get back, she's not going anywhere. Are you going to get dressed at all, or is this the start of your new career as a fashion victim?'

She screwed the wrapping paper into a ball and threw it at me. While she was getting dressed, I looked at the photo. It was black and white, slightly creased and was of my mother and father, looking younger and happier. My father's beard was thicker and glossier than I remembered it, and my mother's face was rounder, firmer. My father had his arm around my mother, and also another woman. She was slight and very young – she couldn't have been more than twenty. It looked as if she were trying to smile, but was finding it harder than she'd expected. There was something familiar about her. I couldn't work out quite what it was at first. The twist of her mouth? She had my father's eyes. Perhaps she was a relative? There was a church in the background. I turned the photo over, but the only thing written on it was the date: 1972.

I put the photo in my coat pocket and shouted up at Eddie.

'Hold your horses, I'm coming, so I am.'

She clattered down the stairs, grabbed her car keys, kissed me and raced out of the house. I followed and locked up. We had planned to drive to Tollymore Forest Park.

The park was on the slopes of the Mourne Mountains, the highest mountain range in Northern Ireland, which sweeps directly down to the sea. For once the visibility was good and we could see the tips of the mountains, shiny as shale with snow trapped in pockets. Driving towards them I had an eerie sensation. I felt a tingling at the back of my neck and a tenseness across my shoulder blades. I could imagine what the mountains were like in winter covered with snow and stunted trees, the last haws wizened on their branches, tiny lanterns of red hope for starving birds; in summer in the full flush of heather, the purple slopes, unfolded into the sea like a falling cloak. Most days the mountains would announce themselves by their absence, a brooding presence shrouded by mist and fog. They must, I thought, control the weather. From somewhere I remembered a saying, 'If you can see the Mourne Mountains, it's about to rain; if you can't see them, it's already raining.'

We parked the car and walked through the ornamental gardens to get to the start of the forest trail. The sensation grew stronger. I started to feel slightly sick right at the point where we walked along a path bordered by camellia bushes, their glossy leaves so dark they seemed to swallow the light. The waxy buds were still wrapped in membranes like the inner eyelid of some kind of reptile. I pulled Eddie towards me and put my arms around her.

'What are you being so soppy for, you great eejit?' she said, pushing me away.

She was wearing one of my jackets – her wardrobe contained a conspicuous lack of anything warm to wear out walking and it had been a struggle to persuade her to take it instead of her fluffy bathmat and a tiny T-shirt that exposed her midriff. I figured our walk was going to be fairly short.

The forest stretched above us streaked with the new leaves of larches.

'You know,' I said, 'I feel as if I've been here before. Just round the bend there's going to be a bridge.'

There was.

'I thought you said you'd never been to Ireland.'

'I haven't.'

'Well there's bridges all the way along this path. We'd have seen one sooner or later.'

'Yes, but I knew it was going to be like this – a rustic sort of feel, and a hiding place carved into the rock next to it.'

'Och, well, you can't expect me to believe you now.'

'Sure I can. It's that déjà vu feeling all over again.'

I hung over the bridge and stared into the water. It was a deep green sinking into darkness. The other side above a waterfall was shallower, stones poked through the surface crowned with moss and grass; below the level of the water they appeared armour-plated, covered with beaten pewter moulded to fit their form. Forests of weeds trailed sinuously across molten-copper-coloured pebbles. I had an image of myself playing with the stones, tripping and falling into the water, so icy cold I stopped breathing, felt the current catch me in its grip, felt the weed slide across my palms as perilous as mermaids' hair. I heard people shouting as I picked up speed and hurtled towards the waterfall, pebbles trickling from my fingers. Someone pulled me out choking and gasping, puking water, and there were adult voices, angry with love. I shook my head. Nothing like that had ever happened to me. I must have seen it in a film or something.

Eddie had used my musing as an opportunity to have a rest. She was inside the cave which was above the river, the entrance screened by a wooden blind. I couldn't see her, but a thin stream of smoke wafted through the opening. I joined her. She was sitting on a bench, hunched up awkwardly.

'I'm cold,' she said.

I sat down next to her and put my arms round her. She felt frail and bony. I wondered what we would look like in the semi-darkness with our twin white faces, black hair and blue eyes. You were supposed to be attracted to people who looked like you. There'd been studies on it: you picked people who were neither more nor less good-looking. The people that you pick match you – not just looks but height, weight, build, even down the ratio of the length of your middle finger compared to the rest of your body, or the size of your ear lobes. Eddie's were small and shaped like teardrops; they melded with the skin of her jaw. She had an outie tummy button and I had an innie; she had a birthmark like a misshapen daisy in the hollow of her thigh just below her hip bone. I had one on my right shoulder blade. My twin, my other half who looked so similar and was so different. And Nadia? Was it an attraction of opposites between me and her? Nadia was small, she barely came up to the middle of my chest; her hair and skin were practically black and the soft curve of her stomach, her full hips and warm flesh were quintessentially feminine. But her eyes were as blue as my own.

'Come on,' I said, taking one of Eddie's scarred hands in mine. 'Let's keep walking.'

We headed back along the other side of the river and Eddie said, 'I came here once with me mammy. It was years ago and we climbed really high, it felt like we were walking for hours. We went right up into the mountains, so we did. She said she had to show me something and she'd brought along lots of sweets to keep me going. I thought it was so strange, just me and her – she left my brothers at home, and the babies weren't born then. It was exciting at first, but then I got bored. I sat down and cried because I was cold and I didn't want to keep walking but she didn't get angry with me like she normally did. She looked worried and sad so I got up. And then we got to this grassy place with no heather. It was almost level, the mountain dropped away steeply below us, and above us it was starting to get rocky. She stood there at the edge of this place and I couldn't understand why – it was just grass and a few stones in the middle of bloody nowhere.

'I said, "Mammy, why've you stopped?" but she just ignored me, and then I got frightened and started to cry, and she took me in her arms and she said, "This is a cillín – these are the graves of the unbaptized babies and you must never forget they are here." The Catholic church wouldn't allow bastard children, or babies who died before they were baptized, to be buried in consecrated ground so they brought them up to this place on one of the mountains and buried them in shallow graves, no names or nothing, just a stone. And if no-one told you, you could walk right across the graves of those babies and you wouldn't be any the wiser.'

She didn't say another word for the rest of the walk and seemed very quiet and withdrawn. I didn't want to intrude upon her thoughts so I said nothing until we got back to the car.

'Shall we go and get something to eat in the café?' I asked.

She nodded and we went in. I was going to take advantage of her unusual quietness and get a bacon and sausage sandwich, but she snapped out of her mood, and ordered us both veggie burgers and salad, with French dressing, no mayonnaise, no onions, and extra ketchup, and mineral water with ice and lemon, but not the kind from Ballywalter. I smiled. She was back to form, and I sat back and waited for the onslaught for the café was a design nightmare – red plastic seats that were stapled to the floor, tacky prints of forest scenes, fake flowers, and everything from sugar to mustard in plastic sachets. The food was the standard junk you get in most restaurants round Northern Ireland – chips, eggs, sausages, and sticky buns. Eddie looked round in distaste, shrugged off my jacket and started rolling a cigarette. She snorted in disbelief at the dressing the chef had attempted to concoct, but didn't launch into a diatribe against the place as I had expected.

Instead she simply said, 'I can't wait to get to London,' and I got that edgy feeling, as if I didn't want to be there, or perhaps more accurately, I didn't want her to be there. 'When are you going back?'

I shrugged. 'Dunno. I don't have any plans to go for a while.' I looked out of the window, suddenly becoming intensely interested in the ornamental gardens below us.

'What d'you mean, you don't know? Aren't you going to see your mammy and daddy?'

'Got to finish my work here. I'm not supposed to be taking a break from data collection. If it wasn't for those damn magpies I'd wouldn't have had to stop at all.'

'I'd love to go.'

'I know,' I said, and I could hear the tension in my voice. And then Eddie surprised me as she usually did by ploughing ahead without me and I didn't know whether to be pleased because there were no strings attached to our relationship as far as she was concerned, or whether to be annoyed that she didn't want to depend on me.

'I'm going over there later this year. I'll stay with a friend of John's to begin with. Just you wait, I'll have a restaurant of my own in London town, so I will.'

'I'll be your first customer.'

'Here,' she said, 'I don't want it.'

She put half of her burger on my plate. Eddie, I thought, was so self-absorbed, though not in a narcissistic kind of way – she'd give you the shirt off her back if you said you were cold.

We drove back along the inland road where the mountains turned into rolling hills and the walls were made of loose granite covered with plates of yellow lichen.

'Just stop here a second,' I asked Eddie.

'What d'you want to look at that for?'

'I just do.'

'I've seen enough churches in my time,' she said, and stayed in the car.

It was small with a circular nave. There was a statue of Mary in a blue and white cape by the roadside. It was dark inside save for white light filtering through the half-open door and a dull glow from the thickened glass in the stained glass windows. A single candle flickered by the altar. The place smelt of cold stone and rotting daffodils.

I found what I was looking for by the font – leather-bound and gold-embossed books of all the births and deaths in the parish – and I took out the one for the year I was born. I didn't know why, or what I was looking for, but about halfway through a name leapt off the page: Jacob Charles Eamonn Edwards, born 2 February 1967 to Sarah Ann Edwards. A coincidence, that was all, that we shared the same surname and were born a few days apart. And the names of my father and my grandfather? The human mind isn't very good at probabilities, I thought as I slid the book back onto the shelf. We search for patterns and meaning, hunt for answers, believe false prophets and cling to old faiths. The probability of being killed by a shark is one in 300 million, yet you only have to spend six hours in a car to have a one in a million chance of dying in a crash, and which do we fear the most? Biologically speaking, that's fair enough: sharks have been on the planet for 38 million years, cars are a new thing on this earth. Maybe in a few more million years we'll evolve car phobia – if we last that long, that is.

On a whim I took out the old black and white picture my mother had sent me. I looked back at the church just as I got to the car. It was almost identical to the one in the photograph. Another of those coincidences the human mind is always being fooled by. I tucked it back in my coat.

That trip to Tollymore was the first time I'd left the magpie chicks alone for any length of time. The problem I now faced was what to feed them. They were old enough to eat solid food but I wasn't about to start collecting grubs and insects twenty-four hours a day. The phone boxes here were still quaint enough to have copies of the Yellow Pages in them, and I looked up 'chicken farmers'. There was an intensive farm not far from the Greenaun, so one afternoon I cycled over.

It took me a while to find it. The farm itself was at the end of a long lane bordered by a dense hawthorn hedge that was just beginning to bloom. The last of the dog violets were withering at its feet, and wild carrots opened their carousels of flowers like floral lobster pots trawling for insects. The road was potholed and stony and I was convinced I would get a puncture. As I reached the crest of the hill, a black mongrel dog came flying towards me, barking with rage. I skidded to a halt, and half fell off my bike. The dog leapt and choked on its collar, spinning on the end of a chain. Its bark became high-pitched and winded, saliva flecked its cheeks, and from my position of relative safety, I noticed that one of its eyes was brown, the other clouded and blue. A whole chorus of dogs joined in, their wounded barks sawing the air. I walked gingerly up to the dog until I was sure of the reach of its chain and then freewheeled my bike past it and into a rutted courtyard made of levelled concrete awash with fetid pools of slurry and cow-pats. Two whippet-thin ginger and white dogs whined and growled from a kennel next to the black dog, which now turned in frenzied circles howling at me, its kennel inching along the concrete as it desperately attempted to seize a piece of my calf. The stench of chicken shit was overpowering.

'Is it lost you are?'

An elderly man hobbled towards me, his legs bowed, his trousers held up by a length of twine. His nose was hooked, his lips were lined as a drawstring and his ears sprouted grizzled tufts of black and white hair.

'No, I think this is where I want to be. Calder's Farm?'

'Aye, that's right. And what will you be wanting?'

'Chicks,' I said. 'Day-old chicks.'

'You'd best be coming in. Speak to me son, Jim.'

I followed him into the farmhouse, a dark, granite brick building, and leant my bike against the wall.

'Sit here, I'll be looking for Jim.' He gestured with a swollen red and crooked finger to a heavy bench attached to a long wooden table. The kitchen was cold, the fire out, and the pots on the range were black with use and caked in congealed fat. I waited, feeling the cold from the stone flags seep into the soles of my feet.

'I hear you want some chicks.'

I looked up at what I presumed was Jim, a man in his late forties, early fifties, broad-shouldered and stocky, his face ruddy, his hair black. In contrast to his weather-worn complexion his lips were thin and white. He was wearing a waxed jacket and his boots were covered in chicken droppings.

'Yeah. My name is Niall,' I said, standing up and holding out my hand to shake his.

His grip slid from mine as if the touch of another hand repulsed him. I explained why I wanted day-old chicks.

'We're not in the business of selling frozen chicks. We use them for bone meal, you see, grind them up. Would that do you?'

'Not really. They need to be solid, something for the magpies to chew on.'

I didn't know which was more ridiculous, the idea of my fledglings with beaks full of teeth, snapping for food like pterodactyls, or of Jim tipping balls of yellow fluff into a concrete mixer.

'Well now, it'd be no trouble to freeze you some specially. How many would you be wanting?'

'I dunno. A couple of bags to be going on with. This sort of size.' I gestured with my hands.

'Martha,' Jim shouted suddenly. 'Do you take Calder's eggs?'

'I'm not sure,' I said apologetically. 'I don't take much notice of the labels on the boxes.'

'Well you shall have some,' said Jim as if there were to be no more discussion on the subject. 'Martha,' he shouted again.

A woman a little younger than him appeared at the door. She was wearing a nylon wraparound pinny; the waxed jacket she wore over the top didn't disguise the rolls of fat around her midriff or her large, pendulous breasts.

'Fry him an egg,' said Jim, nodding at me.

'Oh no, I'm not hungry. Really, please don't go to any trouble.'

The pair acted as if I hadn't spoken. Martha kept her jacket on as she lit the stove and clattered one of the greasy frying pans on top of the flame. Jim sat down heavily opposite me. The table creaked with his weight. He slapped an order book down, carefully placed a piece of carbon paper between two sheets in the book, and laboriously wrote down 'Frozen day-old chicks' and the price, in blue biro. He dated the invoice and tore it out.

'So now, see me da tomorrow morning and he'll give you what you need.' He got up and left without saying goodbye.

Martha cracked two eggs and dropped them into the spitting pan. She ladled oil over them as they cooked.

'Have you been running this farm for long?' I asked, desperate to break the silence.

She didn't answer and I retreated in embarrassment, unable to discern whether she hadn't heard me or was ignoring me. A few moments later she slapped a plate down in front of me with a couple of buttered slices of Mother's Pride and the two fried eggs. She left the kitchen without a word.

I found some knives and forks in the third drawer I opened. The other two were full of cables and syringes, string and linseed oil. I sliced my first egg in half, right down the middle, and as the yolk burst it was marbled with blood. I watched as the two fluids melded and flowed over the bread and trickled viscously onto the plate. I checked that no-one was about to come into the kitchen before tipping the whole lot into the bin.

Old Mr Calder watched me leave, nodding his head slowly at me as I cycled past the three psychotic dogs, and on the way down the hill, freewheeling over the bumps and stones, I breathed in deeply, trying to fill my lungs full of fresh air and the scent of hawthorn blossom. But try as I might, I couldn't rid myself of the smell of Calder's Farm, nor of the image of a plastic bag full of peeping day-old, day-glo chicks, gradually winding down like wind-up toys, the inside of the bag growing opaque with condensation from their tiny breaths, their fluffy feathers wilting and clinging to flesh that changed from pink to blue-grey as their soft and pliable bodies became hard and solid to the touch. I wondered if there was a word to describe this kind of death, this kind of meat; I thought of my magpies and how I was forcing them to cannibalize their own feathered kind.

I'd already been back to the farm and was chopping up the chicks when Eddie came downstairs the following morning. When she saw what I was doing she left for work without a word and didn't come home that night. She went straight to work from wherever she stayed but the next night she came home and made love to me with a passion she hadn't had for a while. Neither of us mentioned it, and the chicks stayed in a bin bag in the freezer. I did wrap the ones I had to defrost in tinfoil, though, so she wouldn't have to look at them.

It didn't stop me borrowing Eddie's kitchen scales. I took them and Ruth's stepladder to my study site – I was going to weigh all the wild magpie chicks. I started with the most difficult ones – the male and his new young partner who had a nest in the pine trees. The stepladder only went a third of the way up the tree. I put the scales in my rucksack and climbed the rest of the way. The crows fell like leaves from the trees cawing hoarsely and the magpies uttered rattling alarm calls. One of the branches I grabbed hold of was short and tinder dry. It snapped off in my hand and I nearly fell. The tree swayed slightly from side to side in the wind and I could feel the dull throb of a splinter in the ball of my thumb. Nearer the crown the branches grew thick and sturdy, but I didn't want to trust the ones lower down any more. I gripped the trunk between my feet and knees, wrapped my arms round as far as they would go and inched up the tree. By the time I managed to grab one of the larger branches at the top I was out of breath. I hauled myself up and sat with my legs dangling into space on either side to get my wind back. From up here I could see the sea, the roof of Nadia Ismail's house, the disused lighthouse on top of the cliffs at the other end of the beach and, behind me, the lough to the far side of the fields. The tree creaked and groaned and the crows' cries filled the air. They were lined up in rows on the other pine trees. The two magpies had given up and flown away. I took my rucksack off carefully so I didn't overbalance and hung it from the branch. I wedged the scales in between the dense, resinous foliage and mat of finer twigs and reached into the nest to remove the chicks. They were much smaller than the others since they'd been born later, and a good deal thinner than my fat blighters had been at their age.

As I held their struggling, scrawny, flesh-pink bodies, I remembered something John had told me. I'd gone round to watch the FA Cup at his house and we'd drunk more than was good for us and eaten wheaten bread with rhubarb and ginger jam and toasted potato cakes in front of the fire because he said Eddie would never give me traditional Irish fare in a month of Sundays. Towards the end of the afternoon I'd asked him about the crosses on the trees.

He said it was an old folk custom to get magpies to abandon their nests. I wondered whether Brendan had scraped away the bark on those trees with his penknife, and if so, was it to frighten me or the magpies? I told John about getting the day-old chicks and he told me the strange case of the chicken child. A few years back a boy was found in one of the nearby villages. He was the bastard child of one of the young daughters in the family and they'd put the infant in the chicken coop. He wasn't discovered until he was seven years old. The boy was malnourished – he'd lived on chicken feed his whole life – and he was seriously deformed: most of the time he'd perched on a shelf, arms wrapped round his knees. He couldn't speak a word: he clucked like a hen and looked at his food with one eye, his head to one side. I suppose any living creature will take on some of the characteristics of those with whom it is raised and I was determined to make sure my magpies knew what they were.

I climbed back down the tree slowly and it was only when I reached the ground that I realized I was shaking. I walked along the beach towards the scrubland. A thick fog was rolling in and seagulls flew out of it as if they were spirits made flesh. I couldn't rid myself of the image of the child, crouched in the dark and filth of the chicken coop, his head tilted, soft clucks swelling from his throat. What must it be like to be locked inside the cage of your own mind for seven long years, unable to speak or communicate? How would you view the world when you couldn't name it? How would you feel when you were released into the blinding light of day where nothing smelt of the familiar musty air of poultry and all about you spoke in an alien tongue?

The other two pairs of magpies had made their nests in

low-growing hawthorns which weren't too difficult to get at now that I had a ladder and didn't have to climb through the middle of the thorns. I still tore my hands, though, but the parents didn't dive-bomb me. To my surprise they sat quietly in a nearby bush and watched. I put my hand into the nest but I could only feel one chick. I thought for a minute I'd got the wrong nest completely. The chick, when I pulled it out, was huge. It overflowed the scales and gaped at me with its enormous beak. Perhaps the others had died for some reason, and this chick had got to eat all the food that should have been shared between its siblings. The other odd thing about it was that it already had most of its feathers. Maybe its accelerated growth had made it sprout feathers prematurely. But as I put the chick back into its nest, I realized that its feathers were grey. I climbed back down the tree and peered on the ground around the roots. The grass was littered with splinters of thin white bones. I folded up the stepladder and tucked it under my arm, then stopped dead. The monstrous chick wasn't the magpies', it was a cuckoo and it must have pushed the other fledglings out of the nest. But I still couldn't understand: magpies were almost never parasitized by cuckoos in this country. Songbirds like reed warblers and meadow pipits were duped into caring for cuckoo chicks because the cuckoos' eggs so closely mimicked their own − but not the magpies: they were too smart to be conned by pale imitations of their own eggs.

I had the answer sooner than I thought. When I reached my final pair of magpies, they were both perched on top of their nest, jabbing fiercely through the roof. I crouched down behind a bush and got out my binoculars. The magpies were tearing their nest apart, and as I watched, the male seized a chick in his beak. He could barely lift it, it was so large. I was too far away to tell whether it was another cuckoo chick, but if the size was anything to go by it couldn't possibly be a magpie fledgling. But before the male managed to pull the imposter clear of the nest, out of the fog came five grey birds which began to dive-bomb the magpies. The male dropped the chick and turned to ward off the attack. The grey birds circled round the pair, darting in and raking at them with outstretched feet and slashing at them with their beaks. The magpies cawed and rattled in response, and shortly their attackers flew away – but not far. They alighted in a neighbouring hawthorn and sat in a row on one of the branches. It was only then that I was able to get a good look at them. To my amazement, they appeared to be large cuckoos. The five regarded the magpie pair with dull yellow eyes, and eventually the male started to forage half-heartedly around the base of the hawthorns, and the female began to repair the nest.

The cuckoos remained watching the magpies until the pair resumed feeding the fledgling before flying off together. I was astonished. Was this some new breed of parasitic bird, a kind of cuckoo mafia that terrorized the magpies into raising their young? If so, they no longer concentrated on subtle tactics – camouflaged eggs and baby birds born to look like their hosts – but used sheer brute force and bully boy tactics to frighten the magpies into submission. I walked home thinking about all this, and worrying about the implications for my own research now that my little population of magpies was sadly diminished.

'I need to go to the library,' I said. 'I wondered whether you fancied a trip into Belfast.'

'So I can drive you in, you mean?'

'Something like that. But we could go out while we're there, go to the cinema. I hear they have colour films.'

'OK,' said Eddie. 'Sounds good.'

'I don't know what you want to do while I'm in the library. Go shopping?'

Eddie looked at me with disdain. 'I'll be in the library too, so I will.'

'What, helping me look up papers on cuckoos?'

'I've more interesting things to do,' she said haughtily.

She didn't stay cross with me for long but I thought I shouldn't be so condescending to her, even as a joke. Eddie chatted about the customers in the Greenaun on the way into town. The ones she liked the best were her obstreperous clients, dragged in by their friends, who demanded to know where the meat was, and whom she tamed, less through charm than through fine cooking; the ones who left feeling full and content even though they'd come in demanding to go to McDonald's on the way home.

When we got to Queen's University library, I searched for papers on the arms race between cuckoos and their hosts, a war of attrition which the cuckoo generally won. Libraries have a soporific effect on me, and as usual I found myself daydreaming – this time about all the papers I would write on the cuckoo mafia I'd witnessed. David would be my co-author, of course, and I imagined he'd want to see the cuckoos in action for himself. I tried to picture David over here and, with a mixture of pride and dismay, I thought that he'd probably fit in well – he and John would get on, and David could charm the pants off everyone I knew, even George and Eddie.

I looked at Eddie. She was hunched over a book, furiously reading and taking notes. Suddenly she got up and strode down the aisle alongside the rows of reading desks and marched past the book stands before disappearing between the stacks. A minute or two later she emerged, a book in one hand, and swung back into her seat. I was at the far end of the library and was aware of the way she attracted people's gaze. Students in libraries always look up at the slightest distraction, but they stared for longer than normal, and I grinned like an idiot, knowing that this woman was with me, smiled at the furrow in her brow, the look of sheer concentration on her face, her complete ob-liviousness of the attention she was receiving, and because I knew that in another five to ten minutes she'd be bored, and would want to leave.

A quarter of an hour later she photocopied a few pages from one of the books, tapping her foot in impatience at the queue, and the Jurassic slowness of the machine.

'I'm ready to go,' she announced, a little too loudly.

'Meet you outside,' I mouthed back.

She was hunched on the front step smoking one of her roll-ups and clutching a plastic cup of coffee to her chest when I came out. The air was dense with the red scent of mulberry flowers.

'Beginning of May and it's still fockin' cold,' she muttered.

'Well, if you insist on wearing . . .'

'Oh, give over, you sound like me mother. She's allus saying my clothes are so thin you could spit through them. Anyway, this is from your mother.'

'Is it?' I said in surprise. 'It looks like all your other things.'

She rolled her eyes at me, then interlaced her fingers in mine.

'So will we go to the greenhouse then?'

I gave her a puzzled look and she added, 'You know,

117

the Palm House. I thought you might want to go.' She tailed off as if she'd had a good idea and was suddenly no longer sure about it.

'Oh, that one. It was built by the same architect who designed the Palm House at Kew,' I said excitedly. 'Yeah, that'd be great. Is it near?'

She smiled triumphantly at me. 'Sure it's just across the road.'

I squeezed her hand, touched that she'd thought of it, and pleased she wanted to go with me. I didn't for a moment think that visiting a greenhouse in the city centre was the way Eddie would normally consider spending her day off.

The Palm House was a smaller version of the one at Kew, with the same characteristic dome built from more small panes of glass than the output of your average Venetian glass-blowing factory. The reflection of ornamental cherries and small shoals of clouds fragmented like a Cubist Monet over its curvilinear surface.

'Designed by iron-founder Richard Turner, his inspiration was iron "deck beams" used in ship-building,' Eddie read from a brochure. 'It's supposed to look like the hull of a boat, so it is. Originally all the glass was green to shade the plants,' she added. 'Sure what they did was practise on us first and then build a proper one at Kew. Isn't that typical of the English?'

Inside it was dank and humid with none of the soaring space between banana trees and strangler figs that was characteristic of the Palm House at Kew. The smell of dense foliage and dank soil reminded me of plants I'd seen in the jungles of Venezuela: Swiss cheese plants with leaves like torn boats snarling twenty metres into the forest canopy, flowers whose plastic petals were shaped like lips and which

118

hung in mid-air as if to ensnare the unwary traveller, the sickly sweet smell of perfume and decay that rose moth-like at night and, of course, the orchids. My father always preferred the tiny ones, their flowers so minute that no-one but he might stop to see, whereas my taste had always run to the big and brash: monstrous orchids as Wilde once said.

'What are you thinking about?' asked Eddie, tugging my hand.

'Orchids,' I said, and realized that was the wrong answer. She gave one of her half-sneers that was supposed to be condescending to me and my one-track mind, but in reality was little more than the twist of a broken smile.

We visited the other greenhouse which had a subterranean basement full of frangipani and cotton trees, and on the ground-floor level red brick ponds bright green with duckweed and giant water lilies.

'How many angels could dance on a lily leaf?' I asked, pulling Eddie towards me and kissing her on the nose.

'Look what I found out today,' she said, pulling out the sheaf of photocopied papers from her back pocket and waving them excitedly in front of me. 'I found another angel of war – Camael. According to some sources he was one of the seven angels of the Lord, along with Michael, Gabriel and Raphael. He had the skin of a leopard, he ruled Mars, and he was in charge of a legion of twelve thousand angels of destruction.'

'Right up your street.'

'I was also reading about the nature of evil,' she said importantly. 'Apparently evil is all part of God's design. When St Paul was alive he visited the third heaven, and he said,' she riffled through her notes, 'it was full of "angels of evil, terrible and without pity, carrying savage weapons". In the Psalms it said that heaven and hell were only a hand-breadth apart. It was only later that they became separate places. What happened,' she continued as we left the greenhouse, 'was that when angels were born they had free will and they were allowed to choose one thing – good or evil. Once they'd chosen whose side they were on, they had to relinquish their free will and stick with that choice for ever.'

'What about us?'

'Oh, we've got free will all right. That's why the angels do the "final reckoning" to balance how much good we've done against how much evil before deciding whether we should be in heaven or hell.'

That we were creatures of good and evil I had no doubt: it was part of our genetic make-up. Free will was a whole other issue, but I didn't want to get into an argument about it with Eddie.

'Let's go and eat, and then go to the cinema,' she said, abruptly changing the subject.

We went to a small African restaurant tucked behind one of the university buildings which had Nigerian prints on the walls and played music from Senegal. We never made it to the cinema and I spent most of the meal on my own, gradually getting drunk on the complimentary bottle of wine that had no label, only a sticker of a zebra pasted on the front. Eddie, after a couple of mouthfuls of the peanut stew and fried plaintain she'd ordered, disappeared into the kitchen to chat to the chef and didn't emerge for some time. When she did, she was brimming with ideas for incorporating peanut butter, okra and cassava into some of the dishes she served at the Greenaun.

As we were driving home, Eddie suddenly pulled a piece of paper out of her jacket pocket and handed it to me.

'Could you just explain to me what this is?'

I recognized it as my handwriting. 'Oh, just doodling, you know.'

'Doodling?' She snatched it back and, balancing it on top of the steering wheel, started reading aloud. 'Flesh, carrion, fowl, sausage, salami, beef, kangaroo, ostrich,' she swerved back onto the left side of the road, 'wurst, jerky, pepperoni, crocodile, brawn, lobster, breast . . . breast?'

'The art of driving is keeping your eyes on the road,' I said dryly, trying not to let any of my terror show.

She tossed the piece of paper back at me. 'What on earth is it, Niall?'

'It's a list of meat. I was trying to come up with all the words we use to describe meat and see if I could separate them from the words we use for animals we eat.'

'Crocodile?'

'Some people eat crocodiles.'

'Well some people will eat almost anything. You don't have locusts or caterpillars.'

'Good point.'

She gave an exasperated sigh. 'But why, Niall?'

'Just doodling, like I said,' I answered irritably, then added, 'I was thinking of meat, eating it, I suppose, since we never do, I mean I don't because I'm with you, and that got me thinking about words and how they define us. There was that myth that Inuit people used twenty-eight different words for snow, and now it turns out it's not such a myth, they do use lots of words for snow and ice. But then, so do we, everything from flurry, to sleet, slush, powder snow . . .' I started running out of examples. 'Anyway, the point is I started wondering about words for meat – I mean, most societies eat meat, it's an integral part of human culture, so it ought to figure highly in our thoughts and that should be reflected in the language we use. The more words there are for meat, the more important it should be for that particular culture — that was my hypothesis, anyway. Language, you see, defines how we think.

'But I haven't quite worked it out. I mean, I don't know anything about the words other languages use for meat, and in English, well, beef only applies to cow, but we don't say let's eat some cow, whereas we would ask for kangaroo meat by name. Then there's words like steak which normally means beef if you don't specify which animal it came from, although you would say kangaroo and ostrich steak, but not chicken steak. I just didn't know how to categorize anything on the list, that's why it's such a jumble.'

'What was the point?'

'I don't suppose there was one,' I said lamely, 'it was just something I did and I've been thinking about.'

'The point is you don't like being vegetarian, so you don't — you don't like having to eat the same food as me when we go out. You'd much rather be eating lobster and steak.'

'No, that's not true,' I said a little too loudly.

She was holding the steering wheel so tightly the scars across the back of her hands were a livid white.

'The point is,' she started again, then stopped herself. 'Niall, did anyone ever tell you you were a queer soul?' She ruffled my hair. 'What about toad-in-the-hole and haggis? Where do they fit into your grand scheme of things?'

The next day I saw something even stranger than the cuckoo mafia. As I was looking for my birds, a movement on the short grass of the beach attracted my attention. It was a white bird, leaping. At first I thought it was a gull but when I looked at it through my binoculars I realized

I was mistaken. I had to put the binoculars down and stare at the wall of mist billowing in before I could look back at the bird and believe what I was seeing.

It was an albino magpie and it appeared to be having an epileptic fit. It was hopping and jumping in a circle, first one way and then another, its wings partly outstretched. Occasionally I saw its thick pink tongue flash from its beak as it uttered a single harsh cry. Then it gave one final leap and struck at the ground with its beak. It had caught a mouse and as I watched, it tore it to pieces bit by bit and ate it, and as it did so, drops of blood beaded its pure white feathers.

Fledging

Once I brought home an old nest. It was a swallow's, made of baked hard mud and bits of twigs, that had been under the eaves of a neighbour's house. I borrowed a stepladder and prised it away from the brickwork, then put it in my bedroom. It was going to take pride of place in my museum collection, which held spore prints from ferns and the gills of toadstools, a rabbit's skull, a badger's tooth, three periwinkles and a top hat shell, a dying lichen on a rock, pressed vetch, and one of my father's orchids in a terracotta pot. The following day, whilst I was sketching swallows to pin on the wall round the nest, I found I was covered in large red lumps. Each was the size of my hand and itched horribly. I thought little of it, but when I woke the next morning I saw a black trail running from the nest, across my desk, and over the end of the bed, before disappearing underneath my duvet. They were fleas and my mother nearly had hysterics. Everything in my room was fumigated. My pet rats were rubbed with flea powder and their bedding was burnt in a ritualistic bonfire in the back garden. I wondered what on earth all the fuss was about. After all, it was me they were eating.

I was reminded of this when my skin started to swell in

lumps across my forearms. I'd de-fleaed the fledglings so I'd probably been bitten when I was weighing the wild cuckoo chicks. I deloused the magpies again – just in case – and myself. Since the nestlings had survived long enough to have grown most of their feathers and no longer looked like road kills I decided to name them: Rinky, Rannee, Rena, Riordan and Ron. It was a fresh breezy day at the end of the first week in May when I took them outside for the first time. They crouched down on a patch of concrete in front of the back door and blinked their eyes in surprise as the wind ruffled their stiff, spiked feathers. I wanted to teach them what it was like to be a magpie. I'd found an old trowel in a cupboard under the stairs which I used to lever out a few clumps of grass and a dandelion from the nearest flower bed. The thick tap root snapped in half and bitter, milky sap oozed from the wound. I persevered and managed to dig out a few earthworms. Rinky, Rannee, Rena, Riordan and Ron huddled together for warmth and squawked pitifully, only becoming animated when I dangled a worm in front of them. They all tried to eat the same one, but Rinky, being the biggest, managed to swallow most of it whole like an outsize string of spaghetti, and Rena snipped off the tail end before it disappeared down her sister's throat. They were probably a little too young to appreciate my labours.

They were old enough to be left on their own for short periods though – as long as they had some food. The room was starting to smell bad although I couldn't understand why because I changed the newspaper that was on the floor every day. Then I started finding parts of the dead baby chicks hidden behind cracks in the skirting board. Their hoarding behaviour was starting early.

*   *   *

The day of the war of the crows the sea was a deep green flecked with wild white horses and gulls peeled off the cliffs and fell about the jagged temples of Skull Island. Where the thin stream from the scrubland met the sea, the water turned brown and froth rose and crumbled in sand-blown faery pancakes across the beach. I climbed over the old stone wall and dropped into air heady with bluebells and sharp with the scent of crushed sorrel. Four magpies flew across the pale sky and settled in a sycamore, their long tails hanging straight as spears.

I recognized two of them; they were one of the pairs that lived in the scrub. The group flew down to the dense grass sweet with mauve flowers below the pine trees. It was hard work for the magpies – the grass was too long for them to be able to forage efficiently – but the pressure of feeding the chicks must have forced them away from the narrow strip of shorn grass by the beach. As if they thought there was safety in numbers, they were joined by the male from the pair in the pine tree, and the second pair from the scrubland. Like a lull before a storm, ranks of crows massed silently in the pines. The trees creaked in the breeze and from far away came voices borne on the wind and the bleat of sheep. Without warning the crows plunged from the branches, wings narrowed, claws outstretched, and descended on the magpies. The field below the pines was theirs long before magpies invaded the island of Ireland. They started to caw and the magpies chattered back, a hoarse death rattle as if their throats were raw with tuberculosis. The crows filled the air like particles of soot falling before my eyes, and those amongst the grass tangled and sparred with the magpies.

I stood rooted to the spot and spoke quietly into my

Dictaphone as any good scientist should whilst three crows killed the male whose nest was in the pine trees, whilst the crows pecked the eyes from one of the females and snapped the leg of her mate. They dragged the fledglings from the nests of their casualties, speared them with their beaks and ripped them wing from wing. The rest of the magpies flew silently across the fields away from the sea. I heard the blind female crying. Eventually she overcame her fear of sightless flight and took to the air. She collided with the branch of a tree and plummeted to the ground, blood running in red tears from her empty eye sockets. Just before she hit the earth she beat her wings and took off again in an erratic course. Two crows followed her languorously, almost lazily, hooded henchmen who were only slow because of the certainty of the crime. The grass beneath the pines was flattened in places and scattered with black and white feathers. One feather had got stuck standing upright and it shone peacock blue in the weak spring light. As I was about to leave, I caught a glimpse of the white magpie perched in a crippled elder, his feathers two-tone shades of parchment and lace, watching through his albino eyes.

I took my usual short cut through the Ismails' wood (which invariably just happened to include a small detour past the stables) and that was a mistake too because one moment I was walking through the pale green and silent light thinking about a battle that had escalated into a full-scale war and in the next breath the wood shattered with an explosion of sound and I was thrown to the ground. I was starting to get up when a violent blow to my stomach knocked me down again and I retched for air and tasted blood on my tongue. I spat out dried leaves and groaned and heaved breath into my lungs.

'I told you afore. This is private property.'

127

I squinted up at Brendan. He was clutching a gun. The barrel smelt of the dead air left behind by fireworks.

'Holy mother of God, you soft get.' He stretched out his ham-sized fist and hauled me to my feet.

I staggered and wiped the blood from my lips, unable to believe that I was not mortally wounded. Brendan spat disparagingly and turned on his heel. For a large man he was uncommonly nimble, and for someone with a flaming red head of hair, he could blend into the damp wood surprisingly easily.

'I did warn you,' said Nadia, when I found her tacking up Gabriel. But she then invited me for supper and I immediately thought not of her family, or the dinner to which I had been asked, nor of being in the great house the colour of a magpie's egg, but of sex with Nadia Ismail without the accompanying heavy breathing of her horse, and of clean sheets without hay, the smell of sandalwood unadulterated by the scent of straw. I thought then that that was worth a cut lip.

'Eat, please eat,' said Mrs Ismail, proffering a plate of pakoras with a dollop of tomato ketchup on the side. 'Growing boy like you, needs to eat.'

The fact that I was a man approaching thirty and hadn't grown upwards for the past decade seemed to have escaped her notice. I took the plate from her although she had already refilled it twice. I was perched nervously on the edge of a green velvet sofa surrounded by the Ismails. All thought of a cosy chat with her parents before whisking their daughter off to the sublime heights of ecstasy had vanished. It hadn't even crossed my mind that Nadia might have siblings, yet here they were surrounding me in droves. She had four older brothers called Rashid, Nazim, Al Karim and Ali, and even more disconcertingly, a twin called Nazir who had the same jet-black hair and piercing blue eyes clouded in the centre with a ring of grey, but where hers were bored and somnambulant, his had a sharp, crafty cast. The four older brothers appeared to run the two hotels the Ismails owned in Belfast city centre. What Nazir did, if anything, was unclear, but he seemed to be surgically attached to a Hitachi camcorder.

The house itself was strange. The long driveway was bordered by lush grass and flanked by stone idols about a foot high with weatherbeaten faces. Their abdomens were flecked with liver spots of lemon-yellow lichen and carved with eroding spirals. A broken fountain, green with age, stood in front of the porch which was flanked by white Grecian-style columns. Inside, the decor was a sublime marriage between Western and Eastern kitsch. The sitting room was wallpapered in green velvet flock, the carpet was a violent mixture of mustard and yellow, and hung between garish Indian miniatures were sombre oil paint-ings of Parnell, a dead pheasant, and a rural landscape in great gilt frames. Lace doilies covered the mahogany cof-fee tables, which were crowned with dried flowers and silk bamboo in porcelain vases; there was a statue of the Great Mosque at Makkah, framed teachings from the Qur'an and several incense-burners made out of what looked like silver putty inlaid with bits of mirror and glass beads.

'You like some rum and coke?' asked Mr Ismail.

'Well, um, but I thought, well, I didn't think you drank.'

Mr Ismail, a small man with slicked-down hair and a too-tight shirt, flapped his hand at me. 'Not in public. In my own home I can do what I like.' He waved expans-ively. 'Come on, man, have a rum.'

'Och, Da, sure he'd rather have a Guinness,' said Rashid in an accent that would have put Ian Paisley to shame.

I cleared my throat. 'Er, if it's no trouble, that would be very nice.' I cringed at how English I sounded.

'Sure 'twould be no bother. Ma.' Rashid nodded at his mother who immediately got up and left the room.

'Me, I'm a whiskey drinker. Johnnie Walker's the best, top brass.'

'Top hole, Da. Niall's not a bit interested in your old whisky anyway.'

'So tell me, son, my daughter says you are studying these goddam birds that are all over the place, what are they called? These black and white fellows?'

'Magpies.'

'Those are pesky blighters, they're eating all my ducklings and game birds. They should be shot.'

'They are shot, Da,' said Nazim. 'That's what we employ Brendan for.'

'Now don't be giving me any of your lip, son. Why can't you be studying something sensible?'

'Like sociology, or metallurgy?' asked Nazim.

'No, no, like medicine. There's a top brass job. All my lazy good for nothing sons are too damn stupid to be doctors, but a bright fellow like you, you could be making good money.'

'It's your lazy good fer nothin' sons that keep your hotels making a tidy wee profit,' said Nazim.

Rashid added, 'And in case you hadn't noticed, there is a national health service in this part of the world and it pays its doctors bugger all.'

'Wash your mouth out, son.'

'Niall is a doctor already,' said Nadia, looking disinterestedly at her fingernails.

130

'Sure that's only a bit of paper,' said Ali. 'Da means a proper doctor.'

'Aye, a GP who doesn't know his arse from his armpit but makes a queer an' good job of writing penicillin a hundred times a day,' said Nazim.

'Stop your damn fool swearing,' said Mr Ismail, swirling his Johnnie Walker on the rocks so violently the Scotch spattered on his trousers.

Mrs Ismail sailed back into the room like an ocean liner decorated in an icing-sugar-pink *shalwar kameze* with lime-green edging. She was carrying a Guinness in a brandy glass and had poured the rest of the can into a glass jug which she placed on the coffee table next to me. Rashid started to snigger.

'Have some more pakoras.'

'Oh, they're very nice, but I really don't think I could.'

'Have a heart, Ma. You've already stuffed the poor boy to the gills and we haven't even had tea.'

Mrs Ismail threw a disapproving look at Rashid but put my plate down without refilling it. 'So I think we eat now.'

We all followed her, me clutching my jug and glass of Guinness, the others carrying cans apart from Mr Ismail who topped up his tumbler with more Scotch and burped loudly. Nadia rolled her eyes at Nazir who gave her a side-long stare and linked his arm with hers. The dining room had dark red velvet wallpaper, the chairs were upholstered to match and set around an enormously long dining table that gleamed dully in the light of an overhead candelabra which instead of candles held bulbs shaped like miniature flames. Mr Ismail made me sit at one end of the table, and he sat at the far end. A black velvet scroll hung above him painted with the prophet Muhammad on the Mount of

Light receiving revelations from the angel Gabriel. To my right was an oil of some dead mackerel and lemons lying on a wooden slab; the other wall was almost entirely taken up with a large mirror in an ornate frame.

Mrs Ismail started to serve us with a variety of curries from silver plates. She passed round a tray piled high with chapattis.

'So, Niall, what are you thinking of Ireland?'

'Well fer sure isn't that a loaded question,' interrupted Rashid. 'D'you mean what does he think of the English in Ireland, or the Irish in Ireland, or whether we should be referred to as the island of Ireland, or does he not think we're grand as we are, all under the bonny banner we so lovingly call the Union Jack?'

'My damn fool sons, I'm telling them, don't be getting mixed up in this politics business.'

'If it wasn't fer politics you wouldn't be where you are today, and that's a fact,' retorted Rashid.

'I've never been involved in all this tomfoolery, never have and never will be.'

'Aren't you allus telling us how we were the first Asian family to arrive in Northern Ireland because everyone back home was too scared to come fer all the talk o' bombs, an' how we were the first people to open a shop in the heart of Belfast when all around us was nothin' but rubble, and how we bought the Dalriada for a song because it had been gutted seventeen times before and no-one who wasn't soft in the head would touch it with a ten-foot pole? If that's not profiteering from politics, what is?'

'Your mother and I didn't raise you to be so damn ungrateful.'

'Och, I'm not ungrateful, so I'm not,' said Rashid. 'I'd

drink a toast to the British any bloody day.' He raised his can at me and took a swig.

'Eighteen times,' said Ali. 'It was bombed eighteen times, and Da found the last one and . . .'

'. . . he picked it up with his two bare hands and carried it out into the street and put it in the middle of the road and he shouted "Bomb!"' chorused Rashid, Al Karim, Nazim, Nadia and Nazir, 'and everyone ran for cover and it blew up and not a soul was hurt but you could hear the echo from here to Tipperary.'

At this point I blew into my napkin loudly. Nazir sniggered.

'Ma, you haven't made it mild enough for the white boy.'

'Hush, son. Have some more chapatti,' she said, turning to me. 'And take more of the korma. Go on, take, take.'

She was right. The lamb brought tears to my eyes, the lime pickle made me weep, and the mushroom curry, although mild, was unexpectedly full of sticks of cinnamon and cardamoms which I kept biting into by accident, but the korma was pleasantly sweet with coconut, almonds, cream and apricots. None of them tasted remotely similar to the usual assortment of baltis, bhoonas and vindaloos I'd indulged in during my Cambridge days.

'You know I hate curry. I want an omelette,' said Nadia.

Mrs Ismail, who hadn't touched her own food, she'd been so busy serving the rest of the family, left the table and re-appeared ten minutes later with an omelette and more Guinness.

Mr Ismail tried again, 'So. Niall, tell me, what kind of car are you having?'

Nazir and Nadia smirked at each other.

'Sure he has the two-wheeled variety,' said Nazim.

'Two wheels? Are you telling me you're having a motor bike?'

'No, Da, he has a wee bike, you know, a push bike.'

'No car?'

I shook my head almost shamefacedly.

'And why not? Why not? I have just bought a Cappuccino.'

I stared at him in amazement as I wondered what on earth coffee had to do with cars.

'Sure an' don't you look a sight, driving round Belfast in your wee tin can, embarrassing me an' all me friends,' burst out Nadia.

'It's a very good car, sports car you know, but low on petrol, four wheel drive, made by Suzuki, limited edition – they're only bringing one thousand five hundred into the country.'

I nodded as if I did know.

'And by the country we mean, of course, England,' said Rashid.

'And wasn't that a palaver, we had to drive the old man over the water to pick up his car, and himself insists on driving the tin can back to Belfast via Holyhead, and your man here doesn't know London from Liverpool, plus the car's so wee, he could hardly see over the wheel to follow the Range Rover,' added Nazim.

I nodded again. It seemed the best response.

'Kulfi?' asked Mrs Ismail.

'I beg your pardon?'

'It's Indian ice cream,' said Nadia with a sigh.

I felt about an inch tall.

'He'll have some, Ma, and bring me some yoghurt,' she added, and then shouted after her mother's retreating back, 'with diet sugar, don't you be putting any of the real stuff on it, I can tell.'

Mrs Ismail served the kulfi in tall cocktail glasses with paper umbrellas and maraschino cherries on the top, but the ice cream itself was gorgeous; it was smooth and creamy with chunks of frozen pineapple and tasted of almonds and cardamoms. After we'd drunk coffee, Rashid winked at me and said, 'Nadia would probably like to talk to her friend.'

Mr Ismail swilled his Scotch at me. 'Yes, yes, off you go.' He turned to Nazir. 'Go with them.'

The twins linked arms once more and I followed them a little sheepishly as they ascended a great sweep of stairs. It seemed to take for ever to get to Nadia's room. She had a four-poster bed draped with heavy red velvet. Indian muslin prints hung from the ceiling, and surrounding the door was a multicoloured cotton frieze studded with mirrors. Nadia lit incense sticks and candles and then sat on the edge of her bed with her arms wrapped round her brother. I perched on a sofa opposite them and wondered what was going to happen. I was quite prepared for them to chat cosily amongst themselves, and then suggest I leave.

Eventually Nazir tousled his sister's hair, stood up and winked at me.

'So long, sailor,' he said, and then, very oddly, said to Nadia, 'Just give me a minute.'

She nodded and yawned and fixed her blank gaze on me. She patted the bed next to her. I walked over in a daze with that slightly sick feeling you get at school parties when the girls are watching. I noticed there was a large painting of an angel hanging above Nadia's bed. What was it with women and angels? I stopped and looked more closely.

'Azrael,' said Nadia, 'angel of death. Michael, Gabriel

135

and Israfel were supposed to collect seven handfuls of earth to make Adam, but they failed. Azrael succeeded, and because of that he was officially allowed to separate men's souls from their bodies.' She yawned again. 'We have to be quick in case me da comes up to check Nazir is still acting as chaperon.'

'He's got a lot of wings.'

'Four thousand, and he has seventy thousand feet, and as many eyes and tongues as there are men in the world. It's not a bad painting,' she added. 'Me da bought it — unusually good taste fer him.'

She took her shoes and socks off. As she lay back on the bed, I stopped looking at the painting and became mesmerized by the soles of her feet: they were so perfect and unblemished. I cupped them in my hands and ran my tongue along their length. I traced a line across her thigh and watched her eyes close, the lashes long and dark against her cheeks. I held her in my lap and rocked her, her nipples hardening against my chest, her hair falling over my face. Her skin, the colour of tea without milk, tasted of salt and fresh wood, apricots and incense. Keeping one hand underneath her back, I pushed her down on the bed and she wound her legs round my waist, her heels digging like spurs into the base of my spine. I wrapped her mane of hair round one of my hands, holding it tight enough to be taut until she opened her ice-blue eyes and I felt as if I were being sucked in by the widening blackness of her pupils. Nadia, between sheets, and without a strand of hay, was everything I'd hoped she'd be.

Rinky, Rannee, Rena, Riordan and Ron were having a field day. There was silver foil strewn all over the kitchen floor, Ron was skittering about in the sink pecking at his reflection in the taps, and Rinky and Riordan were standing in the open cutlery drawer arguing over a spoon. Rannee and Rena, in between shredding up the foil, were going through their whole repertoire. They barked like next door's dog, whistled like the milkman, sang like the blackbirds that had nested in the garden, and honked like the lorries that hooted as they eased round the sharp bend in front of the house. They also made a noise which sounded like 'T-shirt' and must have come from Eddie running round shouting for her clothes. On the other hand, it could have been 'oh shit'. Rena hopped onto my shoulder and started preening my hair. She cocked her head on one side and closed her inner eyelid. She was flirting with me. I ruffled her feathers. The magpies were now nearly fully grown. Their plumage was still crumpled, and their flight jerky and erratic, but it wouldn't be long before I could let them go.

I was chopping up bits of fresh liver, a special treat for them. Rinky and Riordan seemed to have sorted out their differences and were now systematically hiding every piece of cutlery beneath the oven and under the mat. I fed a small piece of liver to Rena. Ron remained obsessed with his own image, and Rannee was rolling a foil ball between my feet. Rena begged for another piece, opening her beak wide, crouching down and splaying her wings so her feathers poked uncomfortably into my neck. I handed her a sliver. I carried on giving her small scraps as I sliced up the quivering mass of spongy meat. After several minutes I felt something wet touch my ear. I shook my head, but it made no difference; the object, whatever it was, was being forced into my ear. I let out a shout and Rena fell in a tangle of feathers to the ground; all the others, apart from Ron who was still in the sink, ran into a corner of the kitchen and huddled together. Rena had stuffed the last bit of liver in my ear: presumably the dark cavity looked like the perfect place to hoard her food.

I carried on cutting up the meat, and as I did so I unconsciously licked my fingers. The taste took me aback. That bitter iron tang. I licked them again. I had eaten almost no meat for months – Eddie refused to have any in the house and if we ever ate anywhere apart from the Greenaun she always made a fuss if I wanted to order meat. I tried a tiny bit of the raw liver, and then nibbled another corner of a chunk I had cut for the fledglings, and then another, and before I realized, I had eaten the whole piece. I felt a little disgusted at myself, and guilty. With a start I remembered that I was using Eddie's chopping board for the liver and she would be furious. I tipped the meat into a dog bowl on the floor, and the four female fledglings dived at it, squabbling and clattering their bills furiously. Ron was doing a magpie version of ice-skating in the sink. His wings caught a mug and sent it crashing to the floor. I picked him up and dumped him unceremoniously in the middle of his siblings before attempting to scrub the bloodstains out of the board.

As I did so, I became gripped with an overwhelming desire for meat; it wasn't hunger exactly, but a gnawing sensation that made my hands tremble. I left the water running across the chopping board and started frantically riffling through the cupboards. There were tins of shiitake mushrooms, asparagus spears, artichoke hearts, flageolet beans, several cans of baked beans, and twenty tins of dog food, but all my sardines had been thrown out. The fridge was full of the usual leftovers, half a passion fruit cheesecake, a spinach and wild mushroom lasagne, creamed celeriac and buckwheat crêpe. I discovered some ancient cheese triangles with an old garlic clove, and, welded into the freezer, half a loaf of Mother's Pride and some day-old chicks. I considered the possibility of eating the chicks, but dismissed the idea quickly. I could actually go and buy meat, I suddenly thought, but then realized that Mrs O'Malley would be sure to tell Eddie when she next saw her, and I couldn't make the excuse that I was buying yet more scraps for the magpies . . . at least, not until tomorrow.

The answer was to cook something, and quickly. The shiitake mushrooms were the most likely to resemble meat, I thought. I got out a frying pan and added a dollop of margarine. As it was melting, I hurriedly opened the can and poured out the water. I tipped the mushrooms on top of the half-melted fat and shook the pan. They were large and flat with gelatinous, glistening caps. I felt slightly revolted. I touched one experimentally and a thin trail of slime clung to my finger. Perhaps a bit of garlic would help. I prised out a segment from the clove and started to chop it up. A ladybird wandered across the kitchen shelf and climbed laboriously onto the board. There was an absolute plague of them this year; I had never seen so many in all my life. Every morning when I came downstairs, the tiny red and black bugs would be swarming out of the cracks in the wooden window frames. Drifts of them, like fragile fragments of enamel, washed up on the doorstep, and the dead roses in the back garden were clothed in a seething, vibrant skin. I liked the way they split open their carapaces and hoicked their wings up into flight position like some kind of James Bond bugcopter – but I was less enamoured of them when they were bumbling around the bathroom. The ladybird on my chopping board had got stuck in a drop of water. I gave it a tap with the tip of my knife to release it. I didn't know why there were so many; maybe it was because the winter had been harsh and spring was exceptionally mild.

I scraped the garlic into the pan and gave it another shake. As I put the board down I realized the ladybird wasn't there. It wasn't on the floor either, although it could have been amongst the innumerable ones crawling about the work surface. The magpies pecked half-heartedly at them, almost out of habit, but they didn't like the taste. I had a horrible feeling. I looked in the pan and saw the ladybird on its back, its wing-cases roast-pepper red, its legs crisped. I suddenly felt sick. What was I thinking of? What kind of half-baked idea was this – slimy mushrooms, garlic wedges and a fried ladybird? I threw the whole lot out, but I couldn't rid my mind of the image – biting into a mushroom with all the culinary charisma of a shellfish and feeling the crisp body of the insect between my teeth. No good would come of this, I felt sure.

I could go to John's. That way I'd have an excuse to visit the butcher's shop and I wouldn't get found out: it wasn't as if Eddie would be likely to pop in there for half a side of tofu. I fetched my coat and bike and whistled to the magpies. They hopped after me. I opened the front door and a draught of cold air swept into the hall and they blinked in surprise. I wheeled my bike out and whistled to them again. They came and crouched on the front doorstep in a row, examining the racing clouds and the flailing palm. I shut the door behind them and started to cycle away. For a moment they continued to sit on the step looking dazed, fluffing their feathers out, then they erupted into rattling alarm calls, jumped across the pavement and broke into ungainly flight. I cycled through the village with a cloud of magpies flying around my head. I figured that if they got tired, they could always cling on to my shoulders – I wasn't pedalling fast. I was enormously proud of them. Several of the villagers stopped to stare. Even William, Mrs O'Malley's son, who was sitting outside Spar in the weak afternoon sunshine, slowly raised his eyes from his hands. And just as slowly he made the sign of the cross as I passed him by.

'Well holy mother of God,' said John when he opened the door. He had a roll-up stuck to his lower lip.

'Can you keep an eye on them? I have to get something.' I said, pushing my bike into his sitting room.

One of John's cats hissed and spat and retreated behind a sagging armchair. I ushered all the fledglings inside and shut the door, then, checking John wasn't looking out of the window, I darted into the butcher's shop. It took a moment for my eyes to become accustomed to the gloom. There was sawdust on the floor and a whole pig with glazed black eyes and its ribs exposed. A brace of pheasants hung by the door in a flurry of bronze and gold. The smell of the place caught me by the back of the throat.

'So what can I do fer you?' The butcher wiped his hands on his white bloodstained apron.

It had to be something I could cook quickly and easily. It also had to be something I could palm off on the magpies if Eddie found it. My hands started sweating. Why was I doing this? John would probably fry me a sausage if I asked him to. I had a sudden vision of myself tearing into a thick slab of meat, pulling the sinews apart with my teeth. I wiped my forehead. The counter was divided up into fields of crushed ice hemmed in by plastic hedges. I inspected the chicken breasts, slick, shiny and dull purple, and the sausage meat, pink with fat and minced into worms.

'Take your time, take your time,' said the butcher, turning to serve another customer.

I watched as he split apart a huge slab of pork with his cleaver and wrapped it up in greaseproof paper.

'Missus not around today, and you haven't a clue what t'buy?'

I nodded and asked for some stewing steak.

'It's the safe option now. But could I not interest you in some pork chops? Put meat on your bones so they will, and they're easy to cook.'

I coughed and said a little hoarsely that I'd stick with the steak.

'Right you are,' he said cheerfully and started to whistle.

I walked out of the shop with a small plastic bag in my hand, the meat cold and malleable. I put it in my coat pocket and could feel its dead weight pressed against my thigh. I felt, for some strange reason, guilty as hell.

'All done?' asked John, when I pushed open the front door and went in.

I nodded and wondered whether he was looking at me in an odd way. He went back to stroking the magpies who were huddled together in one of the armchairs by the fire. There was a half-empty bowl of bread and milk on the floor.

'They're shagged, so they are, the poor wee critters,' he said, running a finger down a wing feather that glinted metallic blue in the light of the flames. 'So what'll it be? Are you taking tea or will we have a drink?'

'A drink,' I said, my hand still tight round the meat. The cat stalked back in and came and sat on my knee, throbbing as it purred. I wondered whether it could smell the faint aroma of raw steak as I stroked it.

'Have you heard about the crucifixion?' asked John, handing me a can.

'Yeah, it was nearly two thousand years ago in a place called Golgotha.'

'Very funny. No, the one that happened the other day.'

'Is this going to be a tasteless joke?'

'I'm not kidding you, a man was crucified.'

I stared at him in disbelief. 'Here?'

'Aye, a couple of miles from the lough.'

John described how a farmer had discovered the man early one morning. He'd been walking through one of his freshly ploughed fields and he thought he saw something white fluttering in the middle but it was misty and he couldn't see properly. It was only when he got to the other side of the field and looked back that he thought he saw a body. He went a little closer but the mist closed in again. He'd walked right up to the man before he realized what he was looking at. It was a young man stretched out on the ground, naked save for a white loincloth, blue with the cold. His chest had been shaved and there were long razor marks across his skin. He'd been nailed into the frozen field with great iron spikes, one through each wrist and one through his crossed ankles.

'The IRA?' I asked.

'Or the UDA or the UVF. No one's owned up yet, but who cares? He raped an eighty-six-year-old woman.'

'Is he dead?'

'Aye. They severed an artery. Bled to death.' Into the silence John said, 'Course, they might not have *meant* to kill him.'

He turned on the TV. It was the local news headlining with the crucifixion story. The newsreader was talking

atonally over panning shots of muddy fields and trees, their
newly minted leaves opening. I turned over and flicked
through all the channels before turning it off.

'John, let's go to the pub and watch Sky sport and for
once, could you try not to tell me anything grisly?'

John grinned at me and said, 'I'll shut the cat in the
kitchen then – unless you want a pile of black and white
feathers as a wee souvenir. You can always take them wit'
you,' he added, picking the cat up off my knee, 'but I don't
suppose they'd like the spitting.'

'What are you on about?'

'Have you not been spat at yet?' he shouted from the
kitchen. 'It'll happen, believe you me. If they don't make
the sign of the cross, they'll be spitting. Still, as long as you
make sure they don't fly over the roof of someone's house,
you'll be all right.'

'Why?'

'Means there'll be a death in the family.' He shrugged
his coat on and said, 'I've got another one fer you: one's
sorrow, two's mirth, three's a wedding, four's a birth . . .'

'This is the same as the last one.'

'Shut up and listen. Five's a christening, six a death,
seven's heaven, eight is hell, and nine's the devil's own self.'

'I liked the old one better – seven for a bitch, eight for a
whore – gave me hope.'

'Aye, and nine for a burying. Come on, it's your turn to
buy the drinks, you tight bastard.'

I got back late, much later than I intended, and Eddie was
already in bed. John had lent me an old canvas bag to put
the magpies in on my way home and they stirred sleepily
and cooed softly as I lifted them out and put them in their
nesting box in the spare room. I felt the meat squash against

my leg. I checked on Eddie. She was fast asleep. I went back downstairs and got out a frying pan and some fat. What, I wondered, would happen if Eddie heard me and came downstairs? How would I explain myself? I couldn't exactly say I was making a fry-up for five magpies who were fast asleep.

I unwrapped the meat and stared at the chunks of sinew moulded together in the shape of my pocket. I peeled one of the chunks off and ate it raw. It felt tough and tender at the same time, heavy with the taste of blood. I ate another cube. As I stood in the kitchen that night, my heart trembled in time with the rhythmic pulse of the sea and the moonlight glinted off the polished carapaces of dozens of ladybirds clustered along the window sill.

A couple of days later as I was cycling down the main road in the village, a small, shiny bubble of a sports car careered towards me. As it jerked to a halt on the wrong side of the road and Mr Ismail stuck his head out of the window, I had a sudden image of Toad of Toad Hall.

'Ah, Niall, I see you have your two-wheeled car. It's not in very good condition, if I may be saying so,' said Mr Ismail, looking at my bike. 'How much was it costing you?'

'About thirty quid.'

'Well no wonder, no wonder. You should be getting yourself a nice bicycle at least.'

'It gets me around and I won't be taking it with me – I've already got a mountain bike back home.'

'So now, I want to make sure you're coming on Saturday. It's our annual charity do, we're raising money for cancer this year. Mrs O'Malley has the tickets. Go on and get them from her, it's all in a good cause, go on now, we don't want you to be forgetting.'

He waved me on and revved up the engine. I half wheeled my bike towards Spar intending to cycle on as soon as Mr Ismail had gone, but I changed my mind and thought I might as well get a ticket while I was there. It didn't commit me to going.

'So what's going on?' I asked Mrs O'Malley.

'Sure we have one of these dos every year. It's in the village hall – a bring-and-buy sale in the afternoon with wee cakes and cream teas, and it turns into a disco in the evening.' As if she could read my mind, she added, 'It's good fun, so it is. Everyone goes.'

What the hell, I thought, I might as well go and buy a couple of cakes, keep the old folks happy. I wondered whether Nadia and her entourage of brothers would be there. Their names and faces were all mixed up in my mind, apart from Nazir, her double image with his cunning smile and chill blue eyes.

That night Eddie woke me up as she climbed into bed. She laid the length of her body along mine.

She whispered in my ear, 'I've got us both tickets for the charity ball this Saturday.'

'Ball? Isn't that a bit grand?'

'For a poky wee place like this?'

I yawned. 'No, I meant for a bring-and-buy sale and disco.'

'So you know about it then?'

I thought if I admitted I'd only bought one ticket, I'd lay myself open to all the usual accusations about being selfish, not doing anything together, never saying 'we'. 'Mr Ismail told me about it today,' I said reluctantly, and then added, 'I didn't think you'd be able to go.'

'I'll go along in the afternoon for a wee while and then come back in the evening – I'll leave the restaurant early.'

I wondered if Eddie would ask how I knew Mr Ismail. It would be easy to explain since everyone in the village had heard of him, he was the Asian equivalent of landed aristocracy after all. But Eddie had a singular mind.

'What kind of cake do you think I should make?' she asked.

'Is it a kind of entrance badge? No villagers allowed in without cake.'

She pinched me. 'A chocolate one might be nice, but then everyone does them, and sponge cakes with butter icing. They're so boring, so they are. I want to do something different. What do you think, Niall?'

I sighed. 'Eddie, it's two thirty in the morning and you're asking me about cake. I wouldn't know a jam tart from a chocolate log unless it said so on the wrapper. Will you go to sleep? Ask someone at the Greenaun. There's bound to be a budding cake expert lurking in the kitchen.'

'I am a cake expert,' she said indignantly, ' I just don't get the chance to exercise my skills. People want dull cakes – passion fruit and carrot and blackcurrant cheesecake. I want to make something a wee bit special.'

'I'm sure you'll think of something,' I said, turning over. I yawned and added, 'Make an angel or something.'

There was silence, and then she said suddenly and loudly right in my ear, 'That's not such a bad idea, Niall Edwards.'

A moment later I heard the bed creak as she got up. A cold draught swept into the room as the bedroom door slammed shut and she rattled down the stairs.

Jesus, I thought, the villagers could eat cake for all I cared, but did she really have to start designing angel-shaped cakes for them in the small hours of the morning?

About eleven the next day she pushed open the sitting room door and collapsed into the armchair, pulling her dressing gown tightly around her. I was perched on the sofa, hunched over my laptop, surrounded by crescent-shaped pieces of card and curls of paper.

'So what do you think?' she said.

'About what? My sitting room as the headquarters of the latest paper-recycling project?'

She scrunched up some paper and threw it at me. 'You don't always have to be so smart. Look.'

She took a few pieces of card and laid them out on the floor. 'My angel. I'm going to cut these pieces out and then stick them together with butter icing. I don't know whether to do it traditional, you know, vanilla sponge, a long white gown and yellow wings. It would be a queer shock for them if I made it a chocolate cake. Or iced his wings green.'

'Green?'

'Yeah, Michael had green wings like a bird's. Bird of paradise or something, that's how I imagine it. And he could have been black.'

'Really? Well, that would look fantastic.'

'But would it sell?' she brooded. 'And they might just think I'd made a mistake, you know, run out of yellow food colour. They don't know anything about angels.'

'Eleven fifteen,' I said, looking at the clock on my computer.

'Fuck.' She ran out of the room. Pieces of paper drifted and swirled in her wake.

In the silence after Eddie had left, I was struck by a terrible thought. Both Eddie and Nadia would be at this event on Saturday. Did Nadia know about Eddie? Probably – it was impossible for anything to remain a secret here. Did she care? Presumably not, but then I really had no idea what Nadia thought. But she might behave towards me in such a way that Eddie would think there was something going on. And what about her father and her brothers? What if Nazir told anyone, or made some sneaky comment? I would either be married to her by the end of the night if they found out what I'd been doing to their little sister, or – and this was more likely – strung limb from limb across the front of the village hall, if not by them, then by Eddie.

I tried to picture Eddie and Nadia talking to each other (had they already met?). I failed dismally, but this didn't stop me feeling tense at the thought of it. The solution was not to go. After all, I was an outsider and they all thought me a bit weird anyway. I could always make the excuse of work, or just not say anything to anyone – slip out to my study site or even get the bus into Belfast. I was perfectly aware this was the coward's way out, but the more I thought about it, the more I could see the pitfalls in that too. I might bump into someone – Ruth, for instance, walking her dog along the beach. She'd be bound to demand why I wasn't with Eddie at the disco. And what would I do in the evening? More to the point, what might happen in my absence? At least if I was there I could make sure no-one said anything suspicious to Eddie.

That was on Wednesday. By Friday night I was beginning to wish I'd never heard of Mr Ismail and his cancer fête. I'd made up my mind to go, if only to chaperon Eddie and make sure no-one said something to her they shouldn't, but the situation was made worse by Eddie's constant queries about her cake, usually at two a.m. Her first cake didn't rise properly, then she couldn't cut the wings out so they were even and by the time they were symmetrical they ended up being smaller than she'd wanted them to be. Her icing bag broke and I had to get the bus into Newtownards to buy her a new one, she didn't know whether pale or vibrant yellow was better for the wings, and how in God's name did I think she should ice the features on his face?

On Saturday morning she left for work before I got up to try to finish the cake and do a whole afternoon's work in the morning so she could come home early. She left me a note saying I had to wait until she got back so we could go together. That was fine by me.

At three thirty the doorbell rang. Eddie pushed past me balancing a silver board.

'I'm sorry I'm so late. I stayed until the end of the lunches and then helped Daniel set himself up for the evening. He's going to stay and work tonight so I don't have to go back in,' she said as she rushed into the kitchen and slid the board onto one of the work surfaces. 'I hope he'll be OK.'

'You practically run the place. Give yourself a break. You're not the manager and you almost never take any time off. Anyway, I'm sure he'll be fine, I bet you gave him a list of instructions a mile long.'

'Well, there's so much to remember and it's a tricky menu this week. But I've pre-prepared most of the dishes. Do you want to see this cake or not?'

'Of course.'

She'd covered the cake with a tea towel which she now folded back to reveal the angel. It was made from vanilla sponge (with a hint of orange) and his face and hands had been left the natural golden brown of the cake mixture. She'd used what looked like felt tips – but she assured me they were edible – to shade his face and draw the eyes and mouth. His gown was long and white with a Celtic pattern along the hem and the edge of his sleeves in a green so pale it was nearly white. He clasped a tinfoil sword with both hands, and his heart was made of red fondant icing surrounded by leaping flames. Eddie had decorated his wings by cutting out pale yellow lozenges from fondant icing and overlapping them to create a feathered effect. The whole cake was surrounded by ivy, and in his hair he wore a black crown of ivy berries.

'I'm stunned,' I said, putting my arm round her shoulders. 'It's more than a wee bit special, it's bloody amazing. It looks far too good to sell. Couldn't we just keep it?'

She smiled up at me. She was too tall for me to rest my arm comfortably round her shoulders and as I slid my arms round her waist, I realized how tense she was. It struck me for the first time that she was nervous. I suppose I should have noticed before, but I thought she was just being her usual impatient self about the angel cake.

'Want me to go and run a bath for you? We've got loads of time, especially if you don't have to go back to work.'

'We don't want to miss the bring-and-buy bit.'

'I'm sure we won't, but your cake should be sold on its own. It should have a bring-and-buy sale just for it, and if the disco's already started, well, too bad, we'll have to put a stop to it until everyone's admired your angel.'

I poured a quarter of a bottle of bubble bath into the bath, and went into the bedroom thinking Eddie would want to ask me what she should wear and then ignore my suggestions as she usually did. It was a ritual I thought she might take comfort in. But instead of flinging her clothes in piles round the room she was sitting on the bed with a forlorn expression, a flush creeping beneath her translucent skin.

'What's up?'

'You forgot to take the clothes to the laundry.'

'Oh fuck. So I did.' Eddie normally did it but she'd asked me to do it yesterday. I cleared my throat a little nervously.

'Um, was there something in particular you wanted to wear?' I asked, knowing the answer to that one.

She nodded.

'Oh.' I sat down next to her. 'What can I say? I'm really sorry. Look, what did you want to wear?' I started riffling through the bag of dirty clothes. I held up a couple of T-shirts. She didn't respond. Finally she pointed at a cropped fleece with a zip.

'It's not that dirty. You could just shake it out. Put a bit of deodorant on it. Hey, we could iron it. I used to do it with my shirts at Cambridge. You can wear things for an extra couple of days if you iron them after you've worn them for a bit.'

'You can't iron a fleece.'

'Couldn't you shout at me or something? I'd feel better. This isn't like you at all.' I had a slightly sick feeling she was going to cry and this coupled with my increasingly guilty feelings about Nadia was more than I thought I could handle. 'All right, so ironing is out. Ironing is not a good idea. You've got lots more clean clothes. Come on, there must be something else you can wear? Shit, the bath.'

I ran into the bathroom only to find that not only was the water pouring down the overflow outlet but the room had turned into a spare film set for Willy Wonka's chocolate factory: there were bubbles everywhere. I waded through a mass of peach and jasmine scented foam to turn the taps off. I tried dumping armfuls of the bubbles in the sink and toilet. I tried mopping them up with one of Eddie's towels. She walked in as I was standing there, soaking wet, her towel dripping, the toilet, sink and bath overflowing with sparkling soap suds, and started laughing and crying at the same time. I was at a loss to know how to respond.

Still crying and hiccuping, she took the towel from me and wrung it out.

'Go and get changed and leave me be,' she said, giving me a little push. 'Put your blue T-shirt on,' she yelled after my retreating back.

Two hours later we were ready to go.

Outside an eerie light lay along the length of the sea; a slick of burnt copper floated on the water where the sun had gone down. A thin wind peeled back the feathers of the gulls lining the harbour wall. I carried the angel cake through the darkening village before uncovering it and handing it back to Eddie at the entrance to the hall. Mrs Ismail in a yellow and purple *shalwar kameze* collected our tickets.

'What a beautiful cake you are baking,' she exclaimed in delight when she saw Eddie. 'So kind. Take it to Mr Ismail, he'll sort it out for you. Come in, come in, Niall – we want you to spend lots of money and have a good time.'

The place was quite full – there was not much bring-and-buying going on, but a lot of cake-and-tea eating. At the back of the hall Rashid, Ali, Al Karim and Nazim were hanging up lights, presumably for the disco, and a couple of youths I recognized from the Sandpiper were rolling barrels of beer over towards the tea stand. Cyril waved at me from one corner of the room and smiled, his gummy mouth full of mashed cake. I found Mr Ismail and steered him towards Eddie who was still standing by the door looking like a wilting Cleopatra, brandishing the angel cake around her clavicle.

'Maybe we could auction it, sell it to the highest bidder. It's too good just to go on a stall,' I said.

'Top hole idea, top hole,' said Mr Ismail. 'Now we will be wanting maximum publicity on it.'

As if on cue Nazir minced over and filmed the cake, panning across its length and tilting very slowly up Eddie's chest to her face.

'Not that kind of publicity, you useless good for nothing. Put your camera down and take the cake around. Go on, show, show everyone. You must go with him, you are the prize cake-maker. Interest must be drummed up.'

The odd couple, Nazir with his camera dangling round his back bearing the angel cake, and Eddie trailing reluctantly behind him, slouched round the room to show the villagers her latest creation.

I grabbed a milky cup of tea and a plate of something called 'Death by Chocolate' before sliding into a wooden seat next to George.

'Bit of a hit with the women, George,' I said, biting into the sickly sweet goo. He was sitting bolt upright, both hands on his cane, his white hair freshly brushed and swept back, surrounded by five old ladies from the flower arranging class, all of whom were trying to make him eat their buns.

'It's a simple thing, so it is,' he confided. 'You just have to say no several times, and then when they're looking desperation in the face, you say, so I'll take a tiny bit, and they're happier than if you'd eaten the whole damn lot in the first place.'

I'd missed seeing Nadia in my first feverish sweep of the room. Now I was doing my best to avoid looking halfway down the hall on the left where she was standing by a table with the sticky remnants of what must have been a mountain of Indian sweets, wearing a scarlet *shalwar kameze* that fitted her breasts perfectly before flaring out at the waist. In the course of not looking at her, I saw her sweep a red gauze scarf back over her shoulders and arrange a fold of it carefully over that thick, dark hair. As she moved, heavy gold earrings swung against her cheeks.

I was not destined to die of chocolate poisoning.

'Niall, I have a small favour to ask. Please come over here.'

I followed Mr Ismail to a slightly quieter spot where the temporary tearoom bled into the embryonic disco.

'So talented, such a good girl. She will be a great chef,' said Mr Ismail. He abruptly came to the point. 'It's Nadia.'

I choked on my cake and looked wildly around to see how far I was from the door. My heart started beating faster.

'She's not a very good girl.'

I put my cake and tea down on the nearest trestle table.

'This horse riding business, it's a hobby really, that's all it is. She hardly ever goes to the riding stables and she's never there when she's needed. She's not, how shall I put it, reliable. And Gabriel, some days she's with that damn fool horse every minute of the day, next moment she couldn't care less about him. Now of course I want her to get married, but first she needs a good education, or at least a good job. It's not as if she helps in the house either. Totally lazy. Niall, I want you to talk to her. You're a good, hard-working young man, you must tell her, it is in her own best interests to go to school or do something useful with her life.'

'Me?'

'Yes you. You might have some influence over her. So skittish. Never sticks to one thing. She has no, no, what do you call it, spunk.'

I swallowed. I begged to differ. 'Now?' I croaked.

'No time like the present. Make hay while it's good weather and all that.' He flapped his hand at me.

I looked around. Eddie was sitting down talking to two old men and Nazir was standing in front of them looking bored. I looked across at Nadia. She was staring right at me and her father with an 'I don't give a fuck about you' expression on her face, chewing gum and looking even more bored than usual.

'Right,' I said. 'I'll go now.' I didn't move.

'Yes, go, go, she's not busy now. We've sold so many barfi, so many jellabie.'

I walked over.

'What did he want?'

'Wants me to tell you to do something useful with your life like go to university or get a job.'

'I've got a job already, in case you hadn't noticed, doctor, so stop sticking your nose into other people's business.'

I held up my hands. 'Nothing to do with me. I don't mind what you do. Your father said the riding school was a hobby and you should do something else more constructive. I'm merely reporting what he told me to tell you.'

'Like a good little boy,' she sneered.

'Well, neither of us is exactly what I'd call good,' I said. I was standing close enough to be able to smell her sandalwood perfume.

She smirked and raised one eyebrow. 'And I'm merely filling in time until I get married. Personally,' she added, 'I think I've managed to be exceptionally constructive, so I have.'

'You think potential husbands will be queuing up for you, do you?'

'But of course. Me da will whittle the numbers down, though. You know, maybe it's not such a bad idea. I could go abroad, go to art school in Italy. There'll be more opportunities.'

'Opportunities for what? I didn't think you were interested in art, and I know you can't speak Italian.'

'You know nothing,' she said in a fake Italian accent overlaid with her Irish brogue. 'Anyway, do you seriously think I'll need to be talking in Italian to those Latino men?'

'If I were you,' I said, trying to conquer a stupidly irrational and raging jealousy, 'I'd go to Norway or Sweden. Amongst those cold, white-blond Icelandic types, you'll get a little more attention.'

'Maybe I will learn Italian then. It'll add to the glamour.'

I couldn't help myself. I asked, 'Are we going to meet up? I wouldn't want you to use your time less than constructively before you leave for the Continent.'

'You know something?' said Nadia sweetly, leaning towards me and arranging her chiffon scarf over her hair.

'What?' I asked, bending my head a little towards her.

'I think your girlfriend is planning to kill me.'

I stood up abruptly and stepped back. Eddie looked away as I turned round.

'I'll talk to you later,' I said.

Nadia smirked at me again and in spite of everything, in spite of thinking that she was shallow and vain and quite possibly malicious, and in spite of the fact that I was making a fool of myself in front of her and Eddie, I was filled with an illogical desire for her, and I knew she knew how I felt. I strode back over to Eddie, half wondering how I'd managed to become so sleazy and half knowing exactly how it had happened. Ten years of practice, that was what it was. I'd almost reached her when Mr Ismail banged a spoon against a beer bottle and coughed loudly.

'Ladies and gentlemen. May I have your attention please? First of all, I'd like to thank you all for coming and donating so grandly to our charity. I hope by now you will have seen this magnificent cake made by the finest chef this side of the Mourne Mountains. We are making an auction for this angel. I want you all to reach deeply into your pockets and be as generous as possible. It was a positive work of love. I myself will put down the first bid – five pounds. Does anyone want to raise me to eight pounds? Eight pounds for the angel.'

The bidding was amicable and Michael was eventually sold to Ruth who gestured quickly, almost with a sleight of hand. She must have arrived whilst I was talking to Nadia as I hadn't seen her before. She was wearing a pale grey wool suit and an olive shawl so finely crocheted it could have been made of heavy spider silk.

Ruth came over and kissed Eddie briefly on the cheek and asked her to cut the cake. Eddie, taller than Ruth, bent over the cake, scowling in concentration but expertly cutting smooth even pieces, the knuckles of her right hand white where she gripped the knife, and as she breathed deeply I could see the rise and fall and the faint outline of her ribcage. Ruth, in contrast, with her easy smile that hid, I couldn't help feeling, some deep-seated sadness, was altogether more rounded, like a pebble worn smooth by the sea and laced with a skein of coral weed. Ruth handed out pieces of the white cake to the villagers until every man, woman and child from Ballynanane had eaten part of Michael, angel of war and chaos, and I wondered idly who had received his heart.

Later on the disco got going: a heart-pounding mixture of warm beer, oily gin, undiluted lights and Eighties chart hits. John's timing was impeccable. He breezed in and was handed the last piece of cake and the first pint; he was given the leftovers from the Indian sweet stall and had the first dance with the last old lady to leave. I was about to join him on the dance floor when a hand clamped down on my shoulder and Rashid spun me round.

'A word to the wise,' he yelled at me.

'What?' I shouted back.

'I'll keep it brief and to the point, so I will. Stay away from our sister.'

'What?' I yelled. 'I was only talking to her because your father asked me to.'

'I'm not talking about today,' he said, still holding on to my T-shirt round the neck. 'I just don't want you to be getting any ideas, that's all.'

I relaxed slightly. At least he thought I was still at the ideas stage.

'Right,' I said. 'Got the message.'

'Good.' He patted me on the back and went to dance to 'Eye of the Tiger'.

I got myself another beer and a gin for good measure. Ruth, I noticed, was talking to George.

'Listen, Niall, I've a wee something I want to tell you.' I looked up. It was Nazim. I braced myself.

'It's about Nadia,' he shouted.

This could get boring, I thought. I hadn't realized she had a team of German shepherd dogs as siblings.

'I saw her coming on to you tonight,' said Nazim. 'She's a bit of a one is our Nadia. You just got to watch yourself, man. She knows how to treat men real badly, so she does. Believe me, I've seen it before. You want to take care of yourself, 'cos you don't want to be getting caught, if you know what I mean. The old man wouldn't like it. Och, he's a nice enough guy, but he's a bit soft in the head when it comes to Nadia.'

I nodded. 'Yeah, thanks for the warning, Nazim, but it's all right, honestly. You know I'm with Eddie.'

'Aye, I know. But I know how these things go.'

Yeah, I thought, don't we all. I looked up to see Nazir filming me. A little later I felt a tentative hand on my arm. It was Al Karim.

'Look,' I said belligerently, 'for fuck's sake, just fucking believe me when I say I'm not into your sister, all right?'

He looked at me in surprise and said, 'I was just going to ask you how you got your job. I'd really like to be a zoologist.'

Oh, I thought, that was clever, Niall. And I remembered, as Al Karim started to back off, that the poor guy was so shy he hadn't said a word to me or anyone else when I was at the Ismails' house. I grabbed his shoulder and said, 'Let's go over there and talk. Bit less noisy.' He nodded and followed me.

Eddie was too gauche to dance, but at midnight and half plastered, she dragged me onto the dance floor. I was thankful for small mercies. Nazir might have metres of videotape, but David would never see me dance to Adam and the Ants and the Bangles. Didn't they do Ecstasy over here, I wondered.

'Do you think I'm a real pain?' Eddie asked suddenly.

'No,' I said automatically, and then more warily, 'Why?' And why, I wondered, did women insist on asking questions they didn't want to know the answer to, and hammer on about always telling them the truth? Before you did.

'Oh, you know, all the fuss about the cake, and my clothes.'

'No,' I said staunchly. 'And it was my fault about the

clothes. I should have remembered to wash them.'

We could have stopped talking right there and everything would have been satisfactory all round, but Eddie persisted. 'Yes, but it's not the first time. I know I'm always bothering you with things like that.'

'It's OK,' I said, 'honestly. I don't mind. I don't know anything about cooking or clothes, but lack of knowledge has never stopped me giving you an opinion on anything before now, has it? Besides, it's not as if I'm the easiest person in the world to live with, is it?'

She smiled wanly. 'Shall we go now?'

'If you like.'

'I've got something I want to tell you.'

I felt I'd had enough people tell me enough things all night, but I just nodded. I couldn't work out whether Eddie was only drunk, only miserable, or both; if one had brought on the other, and if so, which had led to what.

'Are youse leaving?' asked John.

'Yeah,' I said.

He leant forward and kissed Eddie on the cheek. 'Eddie love, can you wait here one moment? I want a word with Niall.'

She nodded dumbly.

'Niall, boyo,' he said, putting his arm round my shoulders and leading me away. 'I'm only going to say this to you once, so don't be taking it the wrong way. Eddie's a grand lass and you were making her a wee bit unhappy tonight.'

'She's all right. She's just been drinking, that's all.'

'Niall, catch yourself on. Every time you looked up, your eyes got snagged on Nadia Ismail's tits. OK, so she's got a great pair, and the wee red dress does stand out a bit, but honestly, man, have you no self-control?'

Easy answer. I looked at my feet sheepishly.

'Go on now, get on with you. Make a happy woman of her.'

I caught up with Eddie and followed her outside. I had a sinking feeling in the pit of my stomach.

'I wanted to tell you how I got the scars on my hands.'

I looked at her sharply. She had such a capacity to floor me by saying things when I least expected them.

I thought hard for a minute and then said, 'But I know how you got the scars. You told me before.'

She shook her head. 'I made that up. I didn't want you to know how it really happened. I went to a Protestant school. I think there was only three Catholics in the whole place. They always used to say, "Three Fenians too many."'

She was weaving slightly as she walked and making a real effort to try to speak clearly.

'There was one young boy there, he was always picking on me. I'm sure he bullied everyone else too but for different reasons. With me it was because of being a Tag, but he knew I wanted to be a chef and he was allus making fun of me because of that too. Said I'd never get anywhere, I'd be washing dishes in Newtownards if I was lucky.

'We had a home economics lesson, and I'd made a vegetable quiche and a soufflé and our teacher, Mrs Jarvis, said to all the class how good my work was – and it was, too: my soufflé had risen and the quiche was really pretty, so it was, all covered with slices of peppers and mushrooms round the edge and a sprig of parsley in the middle. Not very adventurous, but I was only twelve. On the way home this boy, his name was Darren, got hold of me, and he and his friends held me down. He was leaning right over me and saying, "So you think you're going to be chef, do you? You're not fit to wash me feet, never mind dishes. You'll end up some wee Tag's whore, cooking bangers and mash, and that's the closest you'll ever get to any fancy bloody cuisine." And he made the others hold my hands flat on the ground and he took a kitchen knife and he cut my hands all over and then he poured salt into every cut.' She stopped and took a deep breath. 'After that he and his wee friends would catch me in the playground and pull the skin on my hands apart so the scars took a long time to heal. He stole sachets of salt from the canteen at dinner time and kept them in his pockets. He said he wanted me to be branded for life.'

I stopped walking. I didn't know what to say. I felt sick. I turned and hugged her tightly to me.

'Niall?'

'Hush,' I whispered, 'it's OK.'

'Niall,' she said more urgently, pushing me away, 'I'm going to be . . .'

And she was.

On Monday I went back to work. I was still carrying on with my usual observations, but David was excited about the cuckoo mafia. He said so long as my head hadn't been turned by too much Guinness, it was an astonishing finding and I should look into it in more detail. At first I took the fledglings with me to my field site, but that caused too many problems. The resident birds attacked them and they didn't know how to respond. It upset the fledglings, upset my data collection, and ultimately I would have to go and rescue them. The result was that I ended up being treated like an honorary magpie as the territorial pair rattled and screeched at me to get off their patch of land. In the end I left the youngsters at home, but tried to take them out for a short time every day by cycling through the village with my little flock following me. John was right. It wasn't just William O'Malley, the residents did either spit or cross themselves when they saw me with five magpies swooping round my bike. It tended to bring traffic to a standstill.

I decided that taking them to the pub was also likely to be more trouble than it was worth, but it didn't stop George saying sourly, 'If it's not our magpie man,' when he saw me. He was on his own, leaning on his stick and staring balefully at the youths playing pool. I bought him a pint and joined him.

'Where's Cyril then?' I asked.

'Sure I get sick o' the sight of him. You must too, you spend a queer amount o' time in the Geranium.'

'I don't have to look at him, he sits at the back and falls asleep.'

'Aye, and you sit at the front and nod off.'

'Hey,' I protested, 'I managed to stay awake for the whole first half of *The African Queen*.'

He snorted and we sat in silence for a while. He suddenly said, 'You know, you should look after that wee girl of yours.'

I looked at him warily. I hadn't seen Nadia since the cancer fête.

'A good woman is hard to find,' he said, turning to look at me. His eyes were watering.

I took a sip of my drink. I was drinking cider that night – I wanted something thin and sweet to remind me of home.

'I was married once. Aye, an' I had a grand wee daughter. You don't appreciate these things while you have them. I'm telling you this now, afore it's too late.'

'Too late for what?'

'Too late fer you. My daughter was eighteen, so she was. A bonny girl, full of life. She was learning to drive – we had a car – an there weren't many o' those to the pound in Ballynanane at that time, I'm telling you. It was about a week before her driving test. She wanted to go to a dance up Lough Erne way. She had a young man. I said, "Why can your young man not pick you up?" and she said, "Och, Daddy, don't be so old-fashioned." "Old-fashioned" she said and that was forty-one years ago. She said there was no point in him coming all the way over to get her when he lived near the dance hall. And he didn't have a car so she wanted me to drive her. I was in here. It's allus been called the Sandpiper, you know. I'd been drinking an' I didn't want to leave. Fair near broke her heart. She kept saying, "Oh go on, Daddy, let me go, just this once." So I said she could take the car. She was a sensible girl, good at driving.

'She looked so pretty that day. She had on a white dress with a frill round the hem. She'd made it herself – allus was good wit' her hands. Her mother had given her a touch of make-up and her cheeks were glowing. Worst decision of my life it was, sending that wee girl off on her own.

'Some people came over from the next village later that night – came to the Sandpiper. Did anyone know anything about a blue Ford. I was still in the pub. "Aye," I says, "I've a blue Ford."

'"Well, you'll not be driving it much more," this man says to me. The car was at the bottom of the sea. She'd driven off the edge of the cliff. To this day I don't know what happened – whether something went wrong with the car, or a rabbit ran across her path, or whether someone frightened her. All I know is my wee girl was gone, and I should never have let her try to drive to the dance on her own.'

He put his pint glass down, the inner surface webbed with froth, his hands shaking slightly.

'My missus died of grief. The year after she faded to a thin stick and then passed away one night. 'Twas of a broken heart. The doctor said she had cancer, her body was riddled with the tumours, but these things will never attack a person who is healthy and happy. I lived for a long time with this great emptiness inside me. All I had loved I had lost, an' I never realized how much I loved until it was gone.'

We sat in silence for a while and I felt as if I were absorbing the old man's pain.

'An' another thing, Niall,' he suddenly said with his usual fierceness. 'I'm telling you this fer your own good too. Those men over there, you're to stay away from them.'

'They're harmless,' I said, thinking he was talking about the pool players.

'They're not harmless. Will you look where I'm telling you?'

I followed the toss of his head and his sharp blue eyes and saw Brendan with his flaming hair and thick beard at the far end of the pub. He was surrounded by three other thickset men. They were all wearing boots and gaiters and their guns were propped up against the bar.

'You've rubbed people up the wrong way, wit' your damn magpies an' all. It's Brendan's livelihood, and he's not the one to let anyone stand between him an' a silver shilling. So now I'll be going. I'm tired of your company too, so I am.'

He stood up slowly, his hand grasping his stick tightly, his eyes clouded. I resisted the impulse to give him a hand.

I tried not to watch as he shuffled towards the door, attempting to straighten his back bit by bit.

At low tide you could sometimes see the bones of a ship that had shattered on Skull Island. I stared out to sea, looking for some sign of the skeletal boat. In a line along the horizon the sky darkened from pearl to black. Faint lines of light strobed by the waves as they raced to the shore. I sipped my gin slowly: it was sharp with lime juice and the ice in my glass cracked and spluttered.

'OK, you can come and eat now.'

I sat down at the table. The first course was laid out beautifully: a small white goat's cheese rolled in crushed red and black peppercorns resting on a bed of nasturtium leaves, decorated with one brilliant orange flower, its throat a deep yellow.

I smiled. 'It looks amazing.'

'The cheese is made from my goats' milk,' said Ruth, 'and the nasturtiums grow in the garden – they're pretty hot and peppery, so be warned.'

Ruth had lit candles throughout her long, white room. They gave off the faint scent of vanilla. Pale green candles and yellow nasturtium flowers floated in a crudely carved marble bowl, and the old ship's light dripped internally as the waterfall of wax that had encrusted it slowly melted.

For the main course Ruth had baked polenta marinated in a pesto sauce; there were roast artichoke hearts, char-grilled aubergines and a white haricot bean salad with lettuce and chives. Eddie would have approved, I thought, and felt a twinge of guilt. When Ruth had invited me to dinner, I hadn't even asked whether Eddie could come; I'd made no attempt to choose a date when she wouldn't be working, and had, in fact, not even told her.

'This is delicious,' I said to Ruth.

As we ate I told her about Rinky, Rannee, Rena, Riordan and Ron; how they scared the life out of the postman by hiding underneath the letter box; when he put the mail through, they burst into a chorus of dog barks. I thought Riordan could count up to five because if I showed her five pieces of meat and then hid four of them in their room, Riordan would pick out the four and then look around as if wondering what I'd done with the fifth. Either that or she was constantly hungry and couldn't believe I wouldn't have left more food. Until I looked after the fledglings, I'd thought that the idea that magpies hid shiny objects was a myth, but I was proved wrong. Anything that glinted was unsafe. I watched one day as Rannee tried to tuck one of Eddie's necklaces underneath a rug. It was a silver spiral fixed to what looked like a shoelace. I took it off the magpie and put it back on the coffee table. Rannee paced up and down. I must have looked out of the window at one point because when I turned back, the necklace was gone. I could just see the shoelace sticking out from underneath one of the armchairs. I continued trying to work, but glanced up in time to see Rannee surreptitiously trying to put the necklace back under the mat. When she saw me looking she stopped what she was doing immediately and flew onto the coffee table. It was only when she thought I was staring at my computer again that she returned to her task of storing the silver spiral.

Ruth brought out a yoghurt mousse in a Grand Marnier and raspberry sauce and a dessert wine the colour of honey which tasted of champagne.

'You're really spoiling me.'

'I don't often get the chance to entertain, and I love to cook. I guess we have that in common.'

I looked across at her in surprise and she added, 'With Eddie, of course. I don't suppose you're a dab hand with anything more than tinned sardines.'

'Oh, there's an infinite variety of things one can do with canned sardines – you can eat them right out of the tin, or put them on toast, or have them with baked beans. They're nearly as versatile as Spam.'

Ruth made a face. She bowed her head, and then looked directly at me. 'I phoned the Greenaun but they said Eddie was working tonight.'

'You didn't speak to Eddie, then?'

She shook her head. 'Come and sit down.'

We took our drinks and the clouded glass bottle of wine to the window. I felt as if I were a lighthouse, the candles guttering around me, outside complete darkness and the hiss and lash of the sea. From far away came the distant sound of a foghorn.

'Sometimes there are lights at sea, almost like a mirage, or a will o' the wisp, but they come closer and closer until I can see fragments of small ships where the light from the lamps bleeds and catches the rigging or the edge of the hull. They pass to one side of the house and moor over there. Then they extinguish the lights.'

'That's where the Ismails' wood is.'

She nodded and I thought of the small concrete harbour near the stables, the underground tunnels dripping with rancid water, the poisonous ragwort and the bay of pink stones.

'Why?' I asked.

'Why should small boats arrive at night? I've no idea, and I've never seen any during the day. The Ismails have a yacht, and sometimes I see one of the young men out on a sailboard. Maybe they're smugglers.'

She smiled up at me and the candlelight caught the soft down on the curve of her cheek. Her eyes seemed to have darkened with the wine and the night; I imagined they would turn from soft green to sharp emerald in the sea. I thought of her beaded in salt water, and as she moved and turned towards me, I caught traces of her perfume, light and fresh like the scent of snowdrops. Scientists say that women choose perfumes that amplify their own natural scent. We were sitting at either end of a small sofa that faced out to sea. I had my arm along the back and if I'd stretched out my fingers, I could have touched her hair. I wondered if she wanted me to, whether she had really wanted Eddie to come too, or if she had merely phoned the Greenaun for the sake of appearances. Her grey silk dress flowed and pooled in the space between us.

'What brought you over here all those years ago?'

'To Ireland? Or to this particular village?'

'Both.'

'Oh, it's a long story.'

'I've got time.'

'There was a man. There always is, isn't there? I met him in Russia. I spent nearly a year there during my third year at university – I studied Russian and French. I was on the lookout for Russian men who would sweet-talk me into marriage just to get out of the country but I had no defences against charming Irishmen.

'He was a ship's captain and he used to bring me back gifts from the places he visited – a bottle of rosewater from Turkey, a carved stool inlaid with brass from Morocco, an embroidered wall hanging from Pakistan. I suppose it sounds terribly innocent and naive, but I didn't realize that I had fallen in love with him until he asked me to marry him.

170

'I had another year of my degree course to do back in England, but I left and we got married. He insisted we live in Ireland, and I was happy to. I spent most of my time at sea. I had a choice – either I could live here and see him for short stretches of time, then let him go for four, six, sometimes even eight months. Or I could travel with him.

'The places I went to – I've seen most of the ports in most of the world. I've spent my life in the company of men. Those times at sea could be long, and monotonous, but I finished my degree through a correspondence course. I took up painting and I learnt to sew and knit. I practised my Russian and French, and picked up a little Urdu, Spanish and Arabic. I could say "Hello, how are you?" and "How much is that?" in ten different languages.'

Ruth took a sip of her drink and sighed. 'After several years we decided to have a child. I was reluctant at first because it would have meant staying behind in Ireland while he continued to travel, but he said that he would spend less time at sea. I was in my late twenties and I suppose I thought my biological clock was starting to tick. We had a few false starts, nothing too serious. And then I finally became pregnant and carried the child for longer than two months – that was a real breakthrough. I felt fantastic. Alan, my husband, wanted me to go home, thought it would be better for me and the baby, but I didn't want to. I wanted to be with him. In any case, it would have been difficult – we were halfway into a six-month journey. I thought arriving back home five months pregnant was ample time.

Anyway, to cut a long story short, after four months I started to feel a sharp pain in my stomach. I didn't say anything about it – what could anyone have done? One

night the pain became extreme. I was in my berth, grip-
ping on to the side of the bed. I could hardly move. I
managed to make it to the door and shouted. Someone
came, I can't remember who, and I screamed at them to
go and fetch Alan. When he arrived I was drenched in
blood, I felt as if my insides were being torn out. Alan put
his hand between my legs and caught the child. It was tiny,
bloody, it fitted in the palm of his hand. Not yet fully
formed, but almost perfect.'

She stopped speaking and in the silence I heard the waves
whispering against the shore. She swallowed uncomfortably
and continued.

'It damaged something inside me. The doctors told me I
would never be able to have children again. I went home,
rested and started to recover – physically, at least. Alan
never returned.'

'What happened to him?'

'Oh, he's not dead, if that's what you mean. He just
didn't come back. I don't know where he is, or who he's
with. I don't know why. I think he blamed me – I should
have gone home when I was in the early stages of preg-
nancy. And he wanted children so much and after I told
him I'd never be able to have any . . . well, I didn't hear
from him again. I waited and waited. In the end I sold our
house and moved down the coast to Ballynanane. I chose
this house by the sea.'

What she didn't say, and she knew I now knew, was that
she was still waiting, watching the shore in case she ever
saw him and his ship again.

She reached over and taking my hand gently said, 'So
there you are, that's why I'm still here. It's ten years to the
day since I came back from that ship without my child.'

I didn't know what to say. I marvelled at the woman

– at women. Here she was, still grieving for her child and her lost husband, and I had no words of comfort to offer her, yet she perceived my distress and held out her hand to me.

When I left I took her in my arms and kissed her on the cheek. She held her body rigidly and then relaxed into me. She tilted her face up to mine and kissed me back fleetingly. On the lips. She half turned away from me, but as I walked away she watched me from the open doorway and my heart turned within me. It had started to rain. The village was silent save for the crash and suck of the sea and the faint moan of the wind. I thought of George's daughter, her white dress spread around her, sinking to the bottom of the ocean; George watching his wife dying, her life ebbing away; of Ruth and Alan locked together in a small berth in the bowels of a ship, crouched over the bloody body of a tiny child, Ruth, walking the length of the beach every day with her white dog, staring at the rainwet sky. I didn't think I could stand the pain. My worst suspicions had been confirmed: if this was what intimate relationships were all about, I wanted none of it. There was a three-quarter moon, bitter yellow and shrouded in cloud. I climbed the stairs in my house slowly and quietly. Eddie was in bed, naked and only half covered by blankets. She had her back to me and in the dark the ribs of her spine and her shoulder blades glowed bright bone-white.

I thought she was asleep, but she said, 'Where have you been?'

When I didn't answer, she turned to face me and the corners of her eyes trapped the light.

'I had a meal with Ruth,' I said heavily. 'I'll tell you about it in the morning.'

'Can't you tell me now?'

'No,' I said.

'Why? Did you . . .?'

'Did I what?' I asked shortly.

'Sleep with her?'

'Don't be ridiculous.'

I started to get undressed. So quietly I barely heard her, she said, 'I love you, Niall.'

I got into bed and lay next to her staring at the ceiling where the moonlight broke in waves of light and trembled against the walls and I couldn't find the words within me that needed to be said.

And to my shame, the next day when I saw Nadia Ismail gallop by carving a trail of hoofprints across the pristine tideswept bay, I dropped my binoculars and my Dictaphone in the scrubland and ran through the torn sand in her wake, fancying I could smell traces of her horse, and her dusky perfume. I caught up with her by the stables as she slid panting from Gabriel's back. When she saw me she dropped the reins and grabbed hold of my belt buckle, pulling me towards her. I bent my head to hers and kissed her forcefully before dragging her into the stables. I wondered whether this was a set-up and all the Ismail brothers were lined up outside ready to tear me apart, but that thought vanished as quickly as it had come as I slid the folds of Nadia's riding habit apart and pushed myself inside her harder than was strictly necessary, pounding expression into Nadia Ismail's face, fighting pain with pain. And afterwards I wiped away the one tear that had burnt my hand, and was gentle with her; she unfurled beneath my hands like a flower in the heat.

As I left she called, 'Ciao, bellissimo,' and I couldn't turn to look at her but saw her in my mind naked save for her cloak being unwrapped like a Christmas gift by men with skin as white as wax and hair as white as snow and eyes as hard and white as diamonds who fell upon her body with words as harsh and alien as bird calls and I felt the beginnings of a nameless guilt with sharp feet and hooked claws crawl across my stomach.

About a week later I woke and didn't know what had woken me. I heard a noise, a sharp rattling sound. It came again and I realized dimly that someone was throwing handfuls of gravel at the window. Eddie must have forgotten her key. I shoved open the window.

'Fer God's sake, you sleep like the dead. Come and help me.'

'It's two in the morning.' I leant out of the window and looked blearily down at John.

'Get some clothes on and come down here.'

I hastily pulled on some jeans and a jumper, scrawled a quick note to Eddie, grabbed my jacket and ran downstairs. We drove out of the village, but instead of taking the road to the lough, John followed the coast.

'Where are we going?'

'Newcastle.'

'*Newcastle?* What for?'

'There's some old railway sleepers buried in the sand. I need you to help me dig them out. I don't know if it's exactly *illegal*, but I don't want to risk doing it by day.'

On the empty roads at the dead of night it didn't take long to drive to Newcastle, the seaside town cradled in the lap of the Mourne Mountains. We parked by the beach and John took two spades, a torch and a flask of coffee out of the boot of the car. We leapt from the concrete promenade into the darkness and hit the sand with a spine-jerking thud. John turned the torch on.

'Look at them, they're beauties.'

The line of sleepers poked out of the sand at drunken angles. John ran his hand over the fissured, salt-worn wood.

'They were put here as an erosion barrier over a hundred years ago. But sure they won't miss one or two. What are you waiting for? The spade's there.'

John made a mound of sand and propped the torch up on it and we started digging. It was heavy going. The first layer of sand was fine and dry, and kept rustling back into the hole. The next layer was waterlogged and it was back-breaking work lifting heavy spadefuls of the stuff. The sleeper was much longer than I'd thought and we could barely see what we were doing.

'What are you going to do with it?' I stopped for a breather. Sweat trickled down my face and back and immediately turned cold.

'I'm going to carve them, but try to retain the shape of the log. I dunno what yet, but I'm sure I'll be inspired when I get them home. Come on, keep going. It'll be getting light soon, and we've still got another one to dig out.'

The top part of the sleepers was sharp with tiny barnacles and draped in skeins of dried seaweed; the bit below the ground was dark, damp and malodorous. We hauled the first one out and started on the second a little further down the beach. It was just getting light as we extracted the sleeper from its sand pit which quickly filled with water. I turned towards the dark body of the sea and saw that the beach was full of pebbles. The white sand had disappeared and the stones stretched as far as the eye could see, slick with clotted blood in the light of the rising sun. I closed my eyes and stood still for a moment. When I opened them the beach was back to normal, a vast spread of sand that swept round the bay, the incoming tide a thin varnish of pale opal.

'Hey, do you not want any coffee?'

'No thanks. I'm just going to walk for a bit.'

I knew as surely as I knew anything that once that beach had been full of stones. For decades there was sand, one morning there were stones and sometime later they were all washed back out to sea and the sand remained. Some freak of nature, some chain of ozone destruction that melted part of an iceberg that had last been flowing water five million years ago, an addition to a current, a change in the tidal ebb. For some it was an omen, for others a symbol. And I felt delight at this sudden gift. What was I talking about? I didn't know anything about Newcastle and its beach. A trick of the light, that was all it had been.

I crossed over to the dunes that ran alongside the beach. There was a path full of twists and turns and in the half-light I stumbled and tripped. A smell caught at my throat, instantly familiar and yet unrecognizable. It was a little like toasted coconut combined with the sweet scent of charred wood. I rounded a corner and there was a patch of gorse burnt to the roots. They set fire to it along here – several park wardens stood around with giant beaters in case the fire spread, but it was a fantastic sight all the same, the flames leaping from the sand, poppy red, engulfing bushes of yellow flowers that cracked and spat, and the air, heady with the summer scent of gorse, was masked by acrid woodsmoke.

Further on was a valley between two dunes, the sand

completely level. It was carpeted in a green–gold moss and brilliant turquoise lichen. It was there that we had sat, the day the stones arrived, swapped pebbles, tapered as guillemots' eggs, veined like marble, traded them for bright beads of green glass ground by the sea, a fair-haired boy and me. We'd made little piles of them on the moss and bartered for them, and then he'd shouted 'Follow me' and we'd raced down to the sea and combed through the stones again. I remembered his eyes, large and blue; he felt as close to me as if he were me, or I were him, but I couldn't think of his name. My head was swimming and I felt sick. I ran out of the dunes, aware that I was retracing his footsteps, my pockets heavy with pebbles, and was surprised when I hit the wide expanse of sand instead of a field of stones.

I ran back to John. He looked up at me in surprise, but only offered me the coffee flask. I shook my head.

'Let's get these buggers in your car.'

We had to fold down the back seats and lay them at an angle across the boot. They were heavy, difficult to lift, slimy and coated in sand. I cursed John and his bloody carving, but as soon as we'd levered the second one in the car, he slapped me on the back and grinned.

'Thanks, mate,' he said.

'Any time.'

He unlocked the car and was about to get in when I said, 'Actually, I'm not going to come back with you. I'll, well, I'll stay round here for a bit.'

He scratched his head and left a trail of sand in his hair. 'What for?'

'Just,' I shrugged, 'go for a walk or something.' I scuffed at a stone with my shoe.

'How will you get back from here? It's bloody miles to Ballynanane.'

'Hitch a lift, or something. It's not so far.'

He nodded. 'Right you are. Thanks for the help.'

I watched him drive away.

It took me a couple of hours to climb the hill out of Newcastle up the winding road along the slopes of Slieve Donard to the old church I'd visited with Eddie, the one that had the same domed chapel as the church in the photograph my mother sent me and the parish record books with the entry for the child, Jacob Edwards, who shared my name. It was light now, but the sky was the colour of iron, and it was drizzling. The church was set in its own grounds, the lawn manicured, the flower beds full of navy pansies and mulberry-red primulas. I wandered round looking at the gravestones. Down below me the town was shrouded in mist. I could feel the rain seeping through my clothes and I felt cold, wet and thoroughly miserable. I left the church abruptly and was about to head back into Newcastle when I saw another grave-yard. At least, I assumed it was a graveyard, but it was difficult to make out what it was. It was possible that it might have been the original site of the church. All around me the slopes of the mountain stretched away, dull green and barren save for the odd twisted hawthorn. Along a muddy track pockmarked with quartz was a roughly circular enclosure bounded by stone walls. It appeared to be completely overgrown; I could just make out the head of the Virgin Mary over the top of the wilderness. I walked up the path towards the graveyard and pushed open the rotten iron gate. The place was full of calla lilies growing so abundantly that they almost completely obscured the graves. They were in bloom and the giant, waxy flowers were heavy with scent. They called them funeral lilies over here. I pushed the leaves back to see the graves. They were Celtic crosses – the crucifixes had halos; some were carved with ivy, all were weatherworn and shrouded in lichen. In the centre of the graveyard was the Virgin Mary, the white marble blooming with a copper-green mould. My shoes were filling with water; a tiny stream had burst its banks and the ground was sodden. Behind a clump of wild iris, and concealed by the lilies, I found a small headstone. There were no carvings on this one, only the words: Jacob Charles Eamonn Edwards. Born 2 February 1967. Died 1 June 1972.

It was the boy I'd seen in the church records. Poor sod, I thought, only five when he died. I pushed the dripping leaves further back and uncovered another small stone. I could hardly read the words, but it appeared to say Sarah, something Edwards. She died three months after Jacob. Born in 1951. His mother, I remembered, Sarah Ann Edwards. She'd been twenty-one. I released the leaves and a thick rain of pollen dusted the headstones before they were hidden by the lilies and the iris once more.

As I was leaving the graveyard I saw glass glinting in the old stone wall. It was a bottle, jammed between the stones. I held it up to the light and sniffed its contents. It was three-quarters full of neat gin.

I hitched a lift home with a young salesman in a big Vauxhall that smelt of new plastic. I think he was a little disappointed I was only going as far as Ballynanane. For some reason I didn't want him to know where I lived and so I got him to drop me off in the middle of the village. It was approaching midday and I wasn't sure whether Eddie would still be in or not. In my emotionally unstable state, I didn't think I could face seeing her right then: she might start asking me all the questions I knew I ought to answer. Then again, she might say nothing and I didn't know which would be worse. To be on the safe side I made my way down to the harbour instead of going home. It was quiet at this time of day – all the boats that could sail had sailed. A few were moored at the side: *Boy Jonathon*, *Duchess*, *Pebble*. There was a huge pile of lobster pots, new ones made from blue plastic barrels, and much older ones with a dense cobweb of orange twine suspended from metal frames. By the lobster pots an old pumping machine was decaying, its rusted sides thinning; a viscous iron-red liquid oozing from holes in its flanks had congealed in a pool beneath it. The place stank of fish; a few scales turned in the wind like sequins fallen from some terrible glamour dress.

I stared into the water. A light film of oil fragmented across the surface, hazy with rainbows. I could just make out the bleached skeleton of a catfish on the sea bottom. I walked along the harbour wall. Here there was no clarity to the water; it was black and choppy and the dark grey horizon melded with the edge of the sea. There was something floating below me. I looked more closely. It was a boy. He rolled over and started to kick and scream. I stood rooted to the spot. He sank beneath the waves for several seconds before resurfacing, thrashing and shouting. I felt my knees buckle beneath me, my mouth filled with salt water. I was choking. I tried to breathe and water rushed into my throat and lungs. My hands were raw and bloody where I'd scraped them on rocks. Flashes of sky were cut off by the waves, interspersed with the dark depths of the ocean. I glimpsed the boy in front of me, his thin white legs kicking. For one awful moment his pale face and dilated eyes rose up in front of me, before sinking without trace. I thought, if I dived down I could reach him, but my grasping hands only trapped sea water, and the sea tossed me back towards the rocks, its current like a living thing.

I was shaking, trying desperately to breathe, clinging hard to a stone. When I opened my eyes I realized I was crouched down by the harbour, clutching at the wall. I was soaked through from the rain, and water had run into my eyes. I stood up shakily and wiped my face. I looked out to sea. There was nothing as far as the eye could see save the dark water. I turned round slowly but I was alone. I could hear children calling as they played on the swings in the village, and the cry of the seagulls wheeling above my head, and in my mind's eye I saw the image of a boy resurrected from the sea. He was white as the corpse of a fish and there were strands of seaweed wound into his fair hair.

I went to the Sandpiper and bought a couple of pints and carried them over to the Pink Geranium. Cyril welcomed me with a toothy smile and announced that we were going to watch Hitchcock's version of *The Birds*. I staggered out a couple of hours later, still damp, slightly shaky and befuddled from the drink. I stood in the middle of the road in the centre of Ballynanane and tried to pull myself together, rid myself of the wretched images that fogged my mind, and the nameless sorrow that clung to me like a thin skin of rainwater. Out of the leaden sky, a large white bird flew towards me. It was the albino magpie. It alighted on the top of the O'Malleys' roof, cawed, tipped its tail twice and flew on. I remembered that I hadn't fed my magpies for twenty-four hours.

Flying

I woke from a dream of sand as bright and blue as snow, of sand trickling from my pockets, caught in the spirals of snail shells, chalk white and liquorice-whorled. We'd collected the shells from where they had been beached between blades of marram grass, the fair-haired boy and me. I pricked my finger on a sea holly whose veins had turned bone white and opened my eyes to the aftertaste of blood on my tongue.

Although a week had passed since I'd gone to the church in the Mourne Mountains, I was still plagued by nightmarish dreams. I got up and went down to the seafront and wandered up and down the scrubland watching my magpies attempt to feed the cuckoo fledglings whose voracious appetites appeared insatiable. Even though it was early, the sun quickly became as sharp as a razor blade and the seaweed started to stink. Overnight the beach had become choked with plastic and cracked shoes and there was the faint smell of sewage. From a dead bird on the sand poured a thin stream of tiny black ants, connecting the carcass to the colony by a fragile chain. Each ant was blindly following the scent laid down by the ant that had gone before it, a feed-back loop continually being reinforced by the passage of the ants. I followed it back to the anthill. The colony itself was like a super-organism, a fluid intelligence flowing through the wood. The individual ants were little more than miniature robots, blindly obeying their instincts, programmed by their genes. And yet from this simple genetic blueprint, from a collection of insects that could make decisions no more complicated than whether to work or not work, the resulting behaviour could even rival our own. Some ants grew crops, harvesting a fungus they cultivated in the heart of underground caverns. Others kept cattle, milking bugs for sap, herding them from plant to plant like a nomadic tribe in search of sweeter pastures; others fought wars with neighbouring colonies, took captives and reared them to be their slaves. Ant societies evolved two hundred million years ago but although they've grown highly advanced they are completely chemically controlled and genetically governed. With a powerful enough computer, one could map the growth and behaviour of a whole colony. Ants, I thought, reflect more than most animals the total absence of free will in the biological world. I remembered Eddie telling me that angels lacked free will, it was a sacrifice they made in order to become servants of the Lord. It is only people, she said, who can choose. I disagreed. In the end, we were all little more than ants blindly obeying our biology.

As I wandered along the sheep-bitten grass by the edge of the shore I found a bee orchid in bloom. It was early June, the start of their flowering season, and I suppose I had been unconsciously obeying my instincts: my father had said I should keep a lookout for them; it was the last thing he'd said before I left for Ireland. The orchid's two lower petals were wavy and pale pink, but the rest of the flower was shaped, as its name suggests, like a bee, brown and furry with a shiny thorax. I remember the first time we found one, my father and I. It was July and school had finished. We were on a family holiday in Sussex. It was a hot day and we were walking across the chalk downlands. There were banks of sloes in flower and I thought of how they'd look in winter, an impregnable fortress of thorny branches glowing with sloe-black, coal-black fruit, a silver bloom on them like a slice of frost. I'd been reading *Under Milk Wood* and I chanted the opening lines in time to my footsteps as I marched over summer's parched earth.

My father told me that bee orchids' flowers were an example of floral deception. They fooled male bees into thinking the flowers were females; the males would grasp hold of the flower and try to mate with it. We sat and waited until a bee came by.

'Watch,' whispered my father, and I watched the bee's inept fumbling, its wings humming, its legs grasping, abdomen curled in a scorpion sting as it tried to impregnate the flower. As it drew away, I saw its back was clouded with pollen.

'Sperm,' said my father. 'It's the flower's sperm.'

He told me that the next time the bee visited a bee orchid, it would dust the pollen onto the female parts of the flower and fertilize her: the bee believed it was mating with another bee; in reality it was having three-way sex with flowers.

The sun hot on my neck, I felt my face flush. I was eleven years old and I was fascinated by the bees and the flowers; at the same time, I wanted to choke back the giggles that threatened to burst out every time my father mentioned sex and sperm. My tongue was sticky, glued to the roof of my mouth, and there were odd pictures in my head, hot as thermal images: of frustrated bees, and female parts, fleshy lobes and flowers with hairy petals, all jumbled up with

186

feelings that had little to do with science and could not be named.

We walked on over the wide open downs, the sky like a cathedral, and he told me about evolution. He said that when the sperm and the egg met, half the genes from the male and half the genes from the female fused together to make a new being. This creature, their child, would share some of the male's features, and some of the female's, but because the two sets of genes were mixed together it would be a whole new entity in its own right. And I remember, though I may be misremembering the date and the time and the place, looking up at my father, and wondering what manner of creature was I? Eleven years old and I was already level with his shoulders. Two days in the sun, and his skin was heavily freckled and blond highlights glinted in his ginger hair; his grey eyes reminded me of the maps of the moon I pored over at night. What kind of hopeful monster was I with my coal-black, sloe-black hair and brittle blue eyes? He talked about Mendel and peas, about Darwin and earthworms; then as now I couldn't find the words to ask the questions I really wanted to know the answers to.

Later on in the day I went back to the house to feed the fledglings and eat small scraps of meat. I almost felt like a bird myself, uncovering pieces I'd hoarded away – small pieces of stewing steak wrapped in foil and tucked at the back of the fridge inside a jar of sickly sweet jam Eddie would never touch, a tin of Spam hidden behind cans of dog food, mince sealed in cling film inside the bag of day-old chicks in the freezer. I thought about the list of meat I'd made and wondered how my consciousness was now being defined by words for processed animal flesh combined with words for subterfuge, deception, concealment. As always I felt guilty about it: the hiding, the consumption, my hunger for meat, though God knows, if I wanted to eat a sausage or steak and chips there was nothing to stop me save for Eddie's sharp words and reproachful gaze.

I was overcome with a strange kind of lethargy and went and lay down. Too many dreams of a fair-haired boy with pebbles falling from his hands, too many nights where I choked for breath, not dreaming, but drowning. It was hardly peaceful: next door the magpies whistled and sang, squawked and babbled at each other, and my room was gold with angels. The sun's harsh light reflecting from the sharp surfaces hurt my eyes. Another couple of months or so and my field season would come to an end. It was quite likely that some of the magpies would lay more eggs and raise another brood, but after that there was little point in staying on. I might have to return in winter, and it would certainly be interesting to plot the rise of the cuckoo mafia. But if I left in late summer, I wondered whether Eddie would come home with me. Somehow I thought not. Cambridge would be too quiet and quaint for her. She wanted the bright lights of the big city. Maybe we'd travel to London together, perhaps we'd still see each other. Fanciful dreams. I wanted something, I didn't know quite what, to remind me of this time, and of Eddie – I wanted to preserve her, my research on magpies, and my mixed-up emotions about Ireland in layers like a terrine embalmed in aspic: something discreet and neatly packaged that I could examine from every angle, and view in multicoloured slices. There must be something, I thought, of hers that I could keep which would be quintessentially Eddie.

I surveyed the room, the bottles of creams and lotions with sticky rims and missing caps, underwear and T-shirts spilling from the chest of drawers and strewn across the floor, and the angels, one at every corner of the bed, and a roomful of them to guide me. There was no way I was going to take a gold cherub. I spotted a silver spiral she used as a pendant and slipped it in my pocket. But instead of keeping the pendant as some poor romantics might, in a wallet or at the back of a drawer, I wondered whether I should conceal it somewhere, a good-luck talisman to draw me back and keep everything else here the same. Or simply as a mark that I'd been, my stamp upon this corner of the earth.

It seemed appropriate to hide it where I found my fledglings; they, like me, would have to leave but they might return to the same spot. I roused myself and walked out into the burning day. I should have taken the magpies to give them some exercise, but I couldn't face their noisy demands for food and attention, nor the hostility of the villagers. I walked through Ballynanane, across the fields and into the small wood. The hawthorn where the magpies' nest had been was thick with blossom, but when I pushed back the branches, the cross gouged into the wood was still visible. Brendan's handiwork – of that I had no doubt – had been remarkably successful at bringing the magpies bad luck. I cut the cross off the tree, and below the new scar I made an incision in the bark. I slid the pendant into the slit. It would be there waiting for me next year.

And by that token, I needed something of Nadia's too, to remind me of her, to bring me back, perhaps even to keep her in the country wearing her red cloak and galloping with Gabriel across the sands, unchanged by time, or marriage, untouched by other men's hands, be they Italian or Scandinavian.

I walked along the beach in the direction of the Ismails'

wood. Clouds of flies rose from the banks of sun-blackened seaweed and hung about my face. It was mid-afternoon and I figured there would be no-one in Nadia's house, except perhaps her mother, and maybe Nazir, who seemed to drift around aimlessly with his camcorder. Nadia's bedroom was at the back of the house looking out to sea and I thought the quickest and safest route would be from their harbour, but without my usual detour via the stables. Standing on the shore with my back unprotected, the forest rising in front of me, I felt isolated and vulnerable, exposed to any watching eyes. I left the beach as quickly as possible and took a thin and twisting path that ran in the general direction of the house. There were pools of water on either side so that it appeared as if I were walking along a draw-bridge, but one whose moat was full of stagnant water choked with sedges and bulrushes. Tiny gnats swarmed from the dank pools and stung my hands and face. Dark and stricken alders soaked their roots in the torpid water; above them reared privet gone wild and become trees with white, wood stems, and clouds of blossom, ripe with scent. At one point I thought I heard a sound and wheeled round suddenly, but there was no-one there, no-one with a gun and a beard and hands poised to seize my throat. I continued along the path, past waxy-leaved shrubs with brilliant pink flowers; the first swallows of summer wheeled and called through the dead branches of dying Turkey oaks. The whole place felt like a rotting, tropical forest, reminiscent of the fetid corruptness of the jungles in *The Heart of Darkness*.

I heard the noise again and stopped to listen. It was a thin, slightly high-pitched cry which faded as quickly as it had come. I walked on cautiously. I could hear something else too, a kind of shuffling. For once I was not equipped with my usual paraphernalia – binoculars, Psion, Dictaphone – and should someone suddenly appear, I would be at a loss to explain my presence in the middle of a wood on private property. I couldn't even hide in the bushes because that would have meant wading through the deep pools on either side of the path. I stood stock still and tried to calm my breathing and listen for the crack of a twig, the soft sound of a footfall. Nothing, and then the shuffling again. Sweat trickled down the back of my neck. I walked on cautiously, and rounded a bend in the path. Hanging from a tree was the cause of the noise. It was a wire cage about half a metre long suspended at chest height. Inside was a magpie, her feathers slicked down in terror, beak gaping. She was running from one side of the cage to the other, her feet skittering on the metal grid. There was a hunk of meat tied to the inside of the wire and a small dish with a few drops of water. It was a Larson trap designed to catch other magpies. Attracted by the sight of the captive bird, they would fly down to attack. If they landed on the roof, a spring door would open and they would be trapped inside the cage. The gamekeeper could then dispose of them at his leisure: wringing their necks was thought to be the least painful way. The decoy bird had laid a couple of eggs. They'd smashed against the hard floor of her cage, probably as she ran frantically from side to side, and the yolk had oozed out and congealed in a glutinous puddle on the ground beneath. I opened the door of the cage and reached in. The magpie ran to the far side and attempted to spread her wings, but the cage was too small. She rolled her eyes and opened her beak even wider, but there was no sound beyond the faint high-pitched cry I'd heard earlier: she was too dehydrated to give an alarm call. I left the door open and stepped back round the bend in the path. It wasn't long before I heard the beat of wings, and when I looked again, the rocking cage was empty. I released the catch on the spring at the top so that no other birds would be trapped, and continued towards Nadia Ismail's house.

The path ended abruptly in a tangle of rhododendrons, but through the branches I could see the wide sweep of lawn that surrounded the house. Walking straight through the garden might not be the best policy, I felt, so I skirted round the edge by climbing through the rhododendron bushes. It was a slow and tortuous process – I didn't want to shake the trees and the branches were finely interwoven. I scraped my shin and had to grit my teeth to stop myself from crying out.

When I was opposite the side of the house, I peered out cautiously. There was a medieval knot garden between me and the gable end, shielded in places by clematis. I stepped out into the open and made my way through the garden, pausing behind each of the trellises before darting to the next. Set into the wall was a door. I took a deep breath and opened it. It led into a corridor. I stepped gingerly inside and closed the door behind me. It was dark, and I could hear the rattle of pans. The kitchen must be off the corridor to my right. I had banked on the fact that in a house like this there ought to be a back staircase, and indeed, a little further along the corridor, I found some small, winding stairs and started to climb them. The third stair creaked horribly, and I stopped and listened. I could still hear noises coming from the kitchen, so I continued, treading carefully and slowly. Even so, many of the stairs squeaked painfully. Nadia's bedroom was on the second floor I remembered but that didn't help me much. I'd approached it from the front of the house, not the side, and

Flying

faced with a corridor that disappeared into the gloom, and branched off in several directions, I was at a loss. I opened a couple of doors experimentally, but the first room was empty, and the second was full of furniture shrouded in dust sheets. I wandered down one corridor before realizing that it was doubling back to face the front of the house, so I retraced my footsteps. After a couple more false starts, I ended up in the right section of the house. By this stage I'd been indoors for a full twenty minutes. There was at least one person at home, and who knew how many others might be around. The sooner I found Nadia's room, got what I came for and left, the better. I was also uncomfortably hot, for the house was stuffy and airless. Outside the heat was stifling and there was no wind. My clothes were stuck to my body. I opened a door to what appeared to be a boxroom, and hastily shut it. The room next door was Nadia's. I went in and leant against the door inhaling her scent, and the smell of sandalwood and incense. The room was gloomy, she hadn't opened the curtains and the bed was unmade. I walked around wondering what I could take that was small and would remind me of her. Although the dressing table was overflowing with trinket boxes full of jewellery, I never remembered her wearing any when I'd met her at the stables. And as with Eddie, I certainly wasn't interested in her bottles and tubes of make-up. I picked up a couple of gold rings but they didn't appeal. A thin silk scarf draped across the back of a chair smelt of her; I could almost feel the warmth of her neck when I brushed it against my face. I put it in my pocket and was about to go when I saw a large wooden chest at the far end of the room. It was almost covered in scarves that had been carelessly thrown across it. I brushed them aside and lifted the lid. It was full of videos. Someone with round handwriting

193

had numbered and labelled them, not with the names of films, but with the names of men. I scanned the cassettes furiously. My own name, spelt 'Neil', jumped out at me. I picked up the video and tucked it in my coat pocket. Before I left, I moved the rest of the videos a little to cover the gap, closed the chest and threw the bundle of scarves over the top.

I fought the urge to race down the wide staircase, burst through the front door, and run as fast as I could down the drive and away from the Ismails' house. Instead I hurried along the endless corridors as quickly as I could, only attempting to slow down a little when I got to the creaking staircase. As I descended to the ground floor I could hear Radio 1 and someone humming. I heaved a sigh of relief. Whoever was in the kitchen was still busy, and I was almost home and dry. I practically jumped down the last stairs and turned the corner, ready to make a dash for the door, when a dark figure stepped out of a doorway and blocked my exit.

'Well, well, if it isn't the magpie man. And may I ask what the fock you think you're doing snooping round my house?'

He took a couple of paces towards me and I drew back involuntarily. It was Nazir. I felt the video burning a hole in my chest.

'I came to see Nadia,' I stuttered.

'Isn't it usual in normal, polite society to knock at the door and wait to be invited in?'

'No-one heard me,' I said, 'so I thought I'd try and find her myself.'

'Fockin' in the stables not good enough fer you any more?'

I tried to swallow but my throat was dry.

'And sure you know that Nadia works during the day. What were you really after?'

'Nothing. I mean, I thought she came home early sometimes. But anyway, she's not here, that's clear, so if you could just tell her I called, I'll be on my way.'

I made a move to pass him but he stepped to one side to head me off.

'You want to risk going out the way you came? Is that wise, Dr Edwards? Who knows where Brendan is? And if he knows what you get up to in his woods. He's a little possessive is our Brendan, of his woods and of his precious charge. He'd crucify anyone who touched his master's darlin' daughter. D'you know what I'm saying? We wouldn't want you to meet with an accident . . . just yet. You can go out the front. We've had enough of your furtive scurrying about fer the one day.'

I turned round and walked back along the corridor. Nazir was right behind me. He was so close I could feel his breath against the back of my neck and my skin crawled. When we got to the hall, he stopped and watched as I swung open the giant doors. Sunlight flooded in and I blinked and sucked in air as if starved of oxygen. I wondered whether he was going to make a mad dash at me and punch me from behind. Every muscle in my body was rigid with tension. I stepped outside and let the doors swing shut. For a long moment I stood on the porch and surveyed the dense trees around the dead fountain. The strange pot-bellied statues stared back at me with their sightless eyes. I could see no sign of Brendan, but I walked on eggshells down the gravel drive until I was round a bend and out of sight of the house, and then I ran as fast as I could and didn't stop until I'd left Nazir and the wood a long way behind me.

★   ★   ★

I'd been racking my brains on the way home to try to work
out how I could watch the video, but it wasn't until I was
almost home that I remembered Mrs O'Malley had once
said she'd hire me her video recorder if I wanted it. I went
into Spar.

'I'd like to take you up on your offer of the video
recorder.'

'Right you are. I'll just go and get it from the house. Will
you mind the shop fer me now?'

'Of course. Where's William?' I asked, peering towards
the gloomy depths of the shop.

'He's poorly so he is.'

The shop was so dismal with its rows of wilted lettuces
and yellowing cabbages, it was little wonder that Eddie
refused to buy anything from it. I gave Mrs O'Malley a
fiver for the loan of the video, and carried it back home.
There was a note from Eddie stuck to the TV. I peeled it
off and read it. She'd forgotten to tell me, John had called
her at work the day before yesterday – he wanted me to
go round this afternoon. Well John could wait, I thought,
as I slotted the video into the machine. I pressed play and
crouched down in front of the TV. There was an annoying
glare across the front of the screen, so I jumped up and
yanked the curtains closed. When I turned back, the picture
had flickered into life. It was taken with a camcorder, there
was a date and time code on the bottom of the screen. Even
though I had some idea what might be on the tape, I still
felt a sickening lurch when I recognized the man crouching
at the end of the bed sucking Nadia Ismail's toes. It was
with a kind of horrific fascination – a blend of sheer embarrassment, repulsion and narcissism – that I watched the
whole sorry incident. I even found myself becoming aroused

as I glowed with humiliation. Whoever had recorded Nadia and me – and ignorant as I was about film-making, I knew enough to know that this was not taken on the self-timer setting – the amateur cameraman was heavily into crash zooms that smeared from a blurred image to rather more pin-sharp than one would wish. The scene was filmed from the right hand side and slightly above the bed. And then I remembered the boxroom.

I yanked the video out and looked around for somewhere to hide it. I tried not to think how many tapes there'd been in Nadia's trunk. Glancing at my watch, I realized I was an hour late to meet John. I shoved the video under the coffee table and dumped a pile of newspapers and magazines on top of it. I'd figure out where to put it later. I hastily threw some food at the magpies, checked they had enough water, grabbed my bike and cycled furiously over to John's house.

'And what the fock time d'you call this? We're late now. Hey, are you OK?'

I nodded. 'Yeah, fine. Look, I'm sorry, Eddie didn't tell me till today.'

'Eejit girl. She'd forget her head if it wasn't screwed on.'

The word 'screwed' immediately conjured up quite another picture in my mind and I looked at John almost with loathing and imagined him and Eddie together, viewed from the right and slightly above. I wondered if his timing would be as good as mine.

'Come on now, leave your bike here and get in the car.'

'Where're we going?'

'To see a friend of mine. Thought you'd like to come along, but I was just about to go without you.'

The car journey made me feel sick – it was probably all the tiny winding roads which John took at breakneck speed.

There was a smell of gorse, so strong it was suffocating. I had no idea where we were going, we were surrounded by hills, and dry stone walls, the interminable gorse bushes and the glint of water, navy blue under the leaden sky. Mercifully we stopped just before I was about to throw up. We were next to a small farmhouse by a lake. I followed John round the back where there was a whitewashed barn.

I thought I heard a child call my name and whipped round, but there was nothing, only lapwings calling and mewing as they flew low over the lake, and scythed the water with their sickle-shaped wings. They say that they are the souls of sailors drowned at sea, destined never to find rest.

'Used to be a gunrunners' hideout – they kept all their weapons here,' said John, looking at me strangely, 'which is sort of appropriate.'

I felt a pricking sensation at the back of my neck, and my stomach convulsed. 'Why?' I managed to croak.

'You'll see.'

He swung open the heavy sliding doors and ushered me in. I stepped over the lintel, and as my eyes started to adjust to the gloom, I had the impression of movement. A man darted forward and, to my horror, I realized he was clutching a sword. He brought the blade sweeping down in front of me, a deadly curve of flashing light. I cried out and staggered back, tripped over the lintel and collapsed on the floor.

John and the man burst out laughing and clapped each other on the back.

'This is Mike,' said John, a grin splitting his face. 'He makes swords.'

I stood up and dusted myself off. 'You miserable buggers,' I said, trying to make myself smile at them.

'It was worth it fer the look on your face,' said Mike and slapped me across the shoulders. 'No hard feelings, eh? Come on in and have a drink.'

I followed them to the other end of the barn where there was an old sofa leaking stuffing and a couple of armchairs. Mike propped his sword up against a rickety chest of drawers, took some cans of Murphy's out of an icebox and tossed them at us.

'Murphy's, eh? Can tell we're nearly south of the border,' said John.

'Aye, there was a time when you wouldn't have set foot in Cookstown country.'

I looked around. In the middle of the barn were trestle tables, heavy duty work benches, piles of tools and tractor-blue machines for grinding and cutting metal. There were no windows, but some of the roof slates had been replaced with opaque corrugated plastic and the light that filtered in was the colour of honey. It hit the walls and shattered into silver fire. The walls were lined with swords. I got up and walked towards them. They hung, scabbard up, blade down, and they were beautiful. Wrought from cold, pure silver, the blades were razor sharp and the handles were covered with intricate patterns: Celtic knots, haloed crosses, faces from legends, Deirdre of the Sorrows, and silver swans bleeding into the blades. I picked one up and tried it for size. I held it out straight in front of me, swung it into a couple of fencing postures, and added a few thrusts. John and Mike cheered and I grinned and sparred with an imaginary partner. The sword felt heavy and unwieldy in my hand. Mike made armour too, and chain mail; they were draped over shop dummies sprayed lacquer black.

'Is there much call for swords?' I asked.

'You'd be surprised. Museums often want them as replicas

199

of the originals, but most of my commissions come from the English. They play these games, re-enacting battles, and they like to dress up and have all the proper gear.'

Mike was small and wiry; the muscles of his forearms were sharply defined. He had a rather sly, pointed face, accentuated by a goatee beard and dark hair cropped short and close to his skull. It was indeed an irony that long slim boxes containing lethal weapons were packaged and shipped to the English from the Catholic heart of Northern Ireland.

'They're pretty good,' I said, nodding my head at the glittering walls.

Mike inclined his head in acknowledgement. 'Feel free to look around.'

I picked up more of the swords, balanced them on my palms. Although they were beautiful, I found most of them weighty and cumbersome, but there was one that sang in my hand like a dream of a bird. I swung it a few times, carved slices of that rich air, and it seemed a natural extension of my body, transferring thought to action with a fluid economy of motion. There was an angel carved on the handle, one that Eddie would have appreciated: an angel with burning eyes holding a bunch of calla lilies, an angel with long flowing hair whose robe was embossed in Celtic patterns.

We spent the rest of the afternoon at Mike's, drinking and talking. John wanted Mike to inlay some silver into one of his sculptures, but they didn't spend much time discussing it.

'Surely,' Mike had said. 'Bring it over when you're ready.'

It was dark by the time we left. As we were about to go, I picked up the sword one last time, hefted it in my hand, and traced the outline of the angel's wings.

'Take it with you, if you want,' said Mike.

'Oh, I doubt I could afford it.'

'No, no, as a loan,' protested Mike. 'You can bring it back when John brings his sculpture over.'

I was at a loss to know what to say. It seemed too generous a gift, if only a temporary one, but at the same time, I couldn't put the sword down. Such an easy gesture, a few words would be all it would take, but I stood in the middle of the barn, rooted to the spot, clasping the sword in my hand.

'I'll make sure he takes good care of it,' said John. 'You know what these student types are like, live in godawful homes, eat shite food, look after nothing right.' He winked at Mike and punched me gently on the back. Mike put his hand on my other shoulder and they steered me out of the barn. I felt like TK, our golden retriever, being given a few encouraging pats.

When I woke up the next day, I felt like shit. Getting up at four a.m. is not easy, but for the first time since I'd been in Ireland, I'd slept in. Light was streaming in through the thin curtains from a sky patchworked bright blue and steel grey. Occasionally rain dashed against the window pane in phlegmatic gouts. It was eight o'clock. I groaned and tried to sit up. I felt rough as a dog. The first thing I saw was my sword, propped up against the wall, half the blade glittering, the angel's face in shadow. I picked it up and pointed it at John's carving. Fencing a couple of times, I aimed a thrust at the wooden angel's abdomen, parried its flaming torch, and swept the sword in an arc as if I were slicing its head off. Feeling foolishly pleased, I staggered into the bathroom and ran some water into the basin. I leant into the hot water and stared at my reflection in the bathroom cabinet. When I looked down, my hands were covered in blood. I let out a cry and hurled myself backwards. I stared at my shaking hands, but the drops that fell from my fingers were definitely water. I peered back into the basin. Clear water. I thought I'd try washing myself in the kitchen sink.

The magpies, hearing me moving about, started an infernal racket. Over their calls and clatter, I could hear something else coming from downstairs. It suddenly hit me that Eddie was not in bed, and had not come to bed; at least, I couldn't remember her coming home last night. Maybe she'd been on one of her benders, and had stayed over some place. I walked gingerly down the stairs; I ached all over. The sound was louder, and it was coming from the living room. I jumped down the last few stairs and banged open the door. Eddie was crouched on the floor clutching the remote control in one hand. I stood horrified as Nadia Ismail orgasmed and the camera focused in on my heaving buttocks and arching back. Eddie switched the video off, and in the silence, the wind howled. She turned towards me, and I swear I will never forget that look as long as I live. She was even paler than normal, and there were deep shadows under her eyes. There was a look about her of someone who has cried until there are no tears left. I opened my mouth to say something, but I had nothing to say.

The doorbell rang. Upstairs the magpies started barking.

'I'll get it,' said Eddie.

I sat down on the sofa miserably. I wondered how the magpies knew it was the postman.

'It's for you,' she said dully, holding out a long, thin white box.

I groaned. Today of all days. I thought I'd escaped this

year. I took the parcel and propped it on my knees. My name and address were written on the box in copperplate. The writer had used a dark, mulberry ink but the address had been crossed out and rewritten by my mother.

'Aren't you going to open it?'

'No,' I said, and put the box on the floor.

She started to unwrap it. The best course of action would have been to throw it out directly, but that would only have made Eddie suspicious. And at this stage, I didn't have much further to fall. She prised off the lid. Inside were a dozen dead black roses. When she touched one gingerly, the petals crumbled into flakes of dried blood.

'Who are they from?' she asked in a small voice. She didn't look at me.

'My ex-girlfriend.'

'Why?'

'I guess she doesn't like me very much.' There was a pause and I added, 'She sends them every year on the day when it would have been our anniversary.'

'You'll have to tell me more than that.'

'What's to tell? We split up. End of story. Maybe she's jealous. Or wants me back.'

'Bollocks,' said Eddie, but she said it quietly. 'What did you do to her?'

She was using this as an excuse, a way to get at me without either of us having to face the real issue.

'No, let me tell you. You cheated on her, didn't you?'

I nodded. Spectacularly.

Eddie snorted. For one moment I glimpsed the feisty woman she usually was before she lapsed back into a frail sadness. 'Don't ever think I'd waste my money buying you flowers, even if they were dead.'

She got up and a minute later the door slammed. I heard

the rev of the car engine as she drove away. She must have been up all night. I sat for a couple more minutes with my head in my hands and the desiccated roses at my feet, before going into the kitchen to chop up some dead baby chicks. I'd release the magpies in a few days. I tried to think straight. The bodies of the chicks with their pale coating of down swam in and out of vision and I ignored as best I could the crying of a boy calling my name. A boy, a boy in the street, that was all. I was finding it difficult to breathe. Some mornings I woke up and my lungs felt full of water.

Today I would do a magpie census, I thought. It was too late for my usual observations, but I could count the number of magpies I saw in the area, see if I could spot any of the birds I'd ringed. I tried not to think about Eddie. When I ran the tap and the water playing over my hands was stained with blood, I tried to pretend it was dye. My father, I thought with an effort, used to make dyes when I was young. We would collect onion peel, grass cuttings, ivy berries, bright yellow vetch, and boil our findings up with bits of wool and scraps of material. We used zinc oxide or alum powder to fix the dye. My mother once sewed a patchwork cushion out of all our bits of scraps but when she bought the new cooker we had to stop. She said we always splashed the dye everywhere and it stained her saucepans. I forced myself to look back down at my hands. They were slightly pink and my skin was corrugated but the water was now running clear.

There was something cathartic about wandering around the countryside looking for magpies and thinking of nothing. I walked for four miles along the beach and out along the headland. When I reached the disused lighthouse on the tip of the cliff, I turned back inland. By mid-afternoon I was exhausted. I'd been walking for the best part of seven hours and I'd had nothing to eat or drink. I felt light-headed and dizzy, but I was determined to continue. I'd pretty much covered the area directly south of Ballynanane, including most of the land up to the lough, although I'd left out the Ismails' wood. I turned reluctantly back towards the village, trying not to think about returning to the wood. After all, it was unlikely that Nazir or Nadia would be hanging round the stables or walking through their extensive grounds at this time of day.

I reached the wood in the early part of the evening as the June shadows were cast long and blue across the stones and the water boiled along the shore. The tide was coming in. One of the sails from the small boat had got loose and it flapped in a sudden gust of wind, startling both me and a magpie that cawed and alighted in an overhanging tree. I was about to scale the harbour wall and climb into the wood when I heard the soft clink of stone against stone. I turned to see Brendan standing behind me. He must have been hiding in one of the outhouses. In the summer light his hair was haloed with a fiery red, and his eyes were hidden in the dark recesses of his face. There was utter silence. Even the sea seemed still.

Without a word he advanced towards me. I couldn't believe what he was doing. I took a couple of steps backwards but it was all a little too late. Brendan was close enough for me to see the heavy lines burnt into his face from the wind, and smell the yeasty tang of beer on his breath.

'How did you know I'd be here?' I said, to play for time.

Brendan didn't break his stride. He drew back his fist, and I felt it connect with my jaw bone. The force knocked me to the ground and for a moment my vision went black and my head seemed to swell and explode with the pain

205

that ran across the side of my face and seared the back of my neck and spine.

'Sure I knew you'd be here. I was watching you,' said Brendan, looking down at me sprawled at his feet.

I scrambled up, breathing heavily. I could feel and taste blood pooling round one of my teeth. I took a swing at him which he dodged, but as he wove back I caught him on the nose. It wasn't a great punch, nor did it have the same force as Brendan's, but a streak of blood and mucus spattered across his cheek.

'You little shit,' he said, so quietly I could hardly hear him. I didn't want to think about what he'd be like when he got really angry.

He reached out and seized me by the throat. I flailed about trying to punch him, but my weak thrusts were ineffectual. His arms were so long I couldn't reach him properly. He kicked my feet from under me. I managed to take a deep breath before he plunged my head into the sea; the shock of the cold made the muscles round my skull contract, the pain drilling into my brain. Brendan lifted my head out of the water by my hair. He was holding both my hands twisted behind my back and the muscles along the backs of my arms and across my shoulders ached. I took a ragged gasp of air, and heard him say, as if from afar, 'Don't ever be meddling with my magpies again,' before he thrust me back under water. My lungs felt as if they might burst. The sea roared around my ears; I could hear the stones turning with the tide, and a faint sound that might have been crabs waltzing over rocks, a slow tango of claws and hooks and the clinch of carapaces locking together. And as I battled with myself, trying not to suck in a lethal breath of salt water, I half expected to see the image which floated before me. The boy was suspended in the green-grey depths, his skin bleached rotten as coral pickled in vinegar, his face peeling into tissue-paper-thin strands, his slight body bloated. The fish had nibbled away his eyelids and his lips, and he drifted towards me, smiling wide-eyed, wide-mouthed, murmuring 'Jacob is my name' although I knew he had no tongue.

Brendan hauled me out of the water and left me choking and vomiting sea and bile on the pink granite stones, one or two of which were flecked with blood drying into iron stains. I was freezing cold, my jacket and jumper were sodden with water, and the side of my face was starting to throb; my jaw felt puffy and tender. I got to my feet and limped home. When I reached the house I went upstairs to run a bath. My head swam as I climbed the stairs, and I nearly blacked out before I got to the top. I pulled off my jumper, fumbling with my swollen hand, and dropped it on the bathroom floor. I leant over to turn the taps on and drew back sharply. There was a body in the bath. A woman. She was naked and deathly white. The water was dark with blood. One of her arms hung over the side of the bath, and blood dripped down the porcelain from thick gashes along her wrist. I walked quickly out of the bathroom, shut the door and leant against it, took a few deep breaths and went back in again.

There was nothing. No woman. No blood. Only wax congealed over a golden cherub, my wet jumper, and a pile of spent matches on the floor. I ran the bath and stepped into it gingerly. My whole body was sore; there were bruises round my throat and over my ribs. As I slipped beneath the water, I tried to blot out the woman with her eggshell-blue lips and bruised eyelids; the faint echo of a child crying, calling for his mother. Some freak effect due to lack of oxygen to the brain. I felt the knuckles of my hand, the skin so stretched it was shiny. I didn't think I'd broken any bones though I knew I might have a hairline fracture. I'd bandage it up and put ice round it, I thought. Going to casualty for tapping Brendan on the nose was the last thing I needed right then.

I slept fitfully, half expecting Eddie to come home, but she didn't. The following morning I looked at an OS map of the area. There was another wood due west of Ballynanane. It was about the same size as the Ismails'; if I surveyed it for my magpie census, any birds I saw could stand in for those I might have seen in Nadia's wood. I realized later that the flaw in my reasoning was that if my census was going to be scientifically accurate, the wood needed to be the same kind of habitat as the Ismails' and what I hadn't realized was that the new wood was part of a peat bog. It was wet and overcast, the rain had settled into a thin and steady drizzle. If I were honest with myself, I would have recognized that it was futile to count magpies in the rain when they were probably sheltering in the densest parts of trees, or even to count magpies in the Ballynanane wood at all. But I was not being particularly honest with anyone.

I gritted my teeth, trying to will away the pain in my hand, and the ache in my ribs and back. The road stretched straight in front of me before disappearing into the black-ened middle distance, the tarmac dark with rainwater; on either side was bleak moorland. There were trenches dug parallel to the road, the drying peat face cracked as a lizard's skin. Slabs of turf cut into blocks were piled in stacks, or heaped into heavy duty plastic bags; garishly coloured and out of place, they were like giant tutti-fruttis scattered by some monstrous hand. There was no-one about. A muddy track led into the wood to my right. It was a strange wood; the trees were mainly silver birch, but they were half dead and leafless, the branches rotting, dark olive fungal outgrowths sprouting from their trunks. As I walked further the trees closed in around me, the thin twigs knitting ever tighter together, and the path narrowed. The rain dripped incessantly, icy drops trickling down the back of my neck. There was a dangerous yellow cast to the rain-aching sky which promised thunder. The density of the branches made it an ideal nesting place for magpies, but the wood felt lifeless. I was debating whether to turn back when I saw a bird perched a few metres ahead of me on a tree stump. It glowed as white as the silver birches surrounding me. I stopped and the bird regarded me with its head on one side. I started forward and the albino magpie let out a harsh rattling alarm call and took flight.

A little further on the wood opened up into a large clearing bisected by peat trenches. The level of the ground must have been much higher at one stage because in front of me was a wall of peat several metres high. The bleached, fossilized bones of oak trees entombed thousands of years ago had been revealed as if by archaeologists unearthing old graves. Any peat that had been excavated from this side was heaped in ramshackle pyramids, as messy as haystacks. Pine trees grew round the clearing and there was an old tractor, iron-red with rust, mired in one of the bogs. On slightly higher ground heather grew in twisted, dank clumps; the rest of the clearing was waterlogged. I could feel the water seeping into my shoes, and the many puddles of clear, brown water-covered grass appeared as if preserved in aspic. I walked over and looked in one of the trenches. The water was so dark I could only see my reflection as a dense shadow against the glassy sky.

For one brief moment, the clouds lifted and the light

brightened. Something glinted in the pale sun and then the sky darkened again and it started to rain more heavily. I walked through dense cushions of sphagnum moss, and over tiny carnivorous plants, drowned in their own acidic juices. In front of me was another trench, and whatever I'd seen was sticking out of the top. As I approached, I thought I recognized it. I took another couple of steps forward. All thought of trying to stay as dry as possible were gone. It was a sword sticking out of the peat bog, the angel on the handle glowing darkly. I hurried forward, thinking it was another illusion, but when I got to the bog I was able to reach out and touch it. There was no doubt about it – there were the calla lilies and the robe with its intricate Celtic knots woven across it. The blade of my sword disappeared into the peat-black water. I could just about reach the handle, but when I tried to pull it free it wouldn't budge and I was in danger of slipping on the uneven sides and losing my footing. I was determined to get the sword back. I took off my coat, jumper and T-shirt. Wrapping the T-shirt round my hand, I knelt down by the trench, leant over and grasped the blade of the sword low down near where it disappeared into the water. With my other hand I held on to a hank of heather. The rain poured down my naked back and ran into my eyes. I could barely see. My arm ached with the effort of trying to lift the sword. Finally I felt whatever it was stuck into start to rise to the surface. The water eddied and swirled and there was a sucking noise as the peat released its grip on the object. Just as it began to break free of the water, I let go of the heather and reached out to touch it. I intended to push the log, or whatever it was, away as I pulled the sword free, but as I touched the chill water I felt something soft beneath my fingers. It appeared to be material and I grabbed hold of it. It was unbearably heavy and I couldn't hold it up with my left hand. It started to sink back into the water and I slid towards the mouth of the trench. I desperately tried to keep a grip on it. Letting go of the sword with my other hand, I reached down, grasped the material and, holding it with both hands, tried to wrench it free. I leant back and pulled as hard as I could. I slipped against the mud as I struggled to get a purchase and thought for one dreadful minute I was going to slide into the bog. Then the thing erupted through the water, and I stared down in horror at what I had uncovered. I was clinging to a shirt, once white, now stained with peat. It was the body of a man, and the sword was plunged through his heart. With a cry I let go and the body fell back into the water. His face and shirt glimmered deathly white before subsiding deeper into the murky depths.

I turned and ran out of the clearing. The clawing twigs of the birches snapped across my face and scraped at my eyes. I stumbled and my feet slid from beneath me. I landed heavily in the mud, picked myself up and continued to half run, half stagger out of the wood. When I reached the road, there was still no-one around; only a handful of gulls broke the monotonous grey of the sky. I set off at a run back towards the village. I had left my coat and jumper in the wood and the stinging rain felt bitterly cold against my naked skin. My trousers stuck to me and were heavy with water, making it difficult to move. I settled into an uneasy rhythm, my breath laboured and rasping, my lungs aching, a stitch searing my side. I had to tell someone, get help, but I didn't know whom I could trust, whom I could turn to. Still no-one had driven down this way, and the roads were bleak and empty, the wind and the curlews keening in sympathy. Eddie, I thought, would know what to do. When

I reached a fork in the road, I took the right hand one that led out to the lough, instead of continuing towards Ballynanane.

It took me another hour to get to the restaurant. The road that curved round the lough seemed interminable. Eventually I burst into the restaurant and pushed open the door to the kitchens. The two chefs and one of the waitresses turned towards me. I watched their faces fall before the waitress rushed away to get Eddie. I looked down at myself; I was soaked to the bone, half naked and covered in mud. I stood and dripped miserably.

'You look a real eejit, so you do. Look at the state of you,' said Eddie, when she saw me.

'You've got to come with me, Eddie,' I blurted out.

'I'm not going anywhere with you.'

I tried to still my ragged breathing. 'It's important,' I gasped.

'What have you been doing? Rolling in the mud with Nadia Ismail?'

I shook my head dumbly. 'Come on, I'll explain in the car.'

'Niall, I can't go with you, it's coming up to my busiest time.'

I grabbed hold of her arm and tried to drag her out of the restaurant.

'OK, OK, I'll come, just let go of me, will you?' she said quietly.

She snatched a tea towel from a rack by the door. 'Here, dry yourself with this.' Eddie unfastened her chain of knives and picked up her coat and keys. 'Put this on,' she said, handing me her coat, 'before you freeze to death. Cover for me, will you, Daniel?' she shouted over her shoulder.

'So where's it we're going to?' she asked as she put the car in reverse.

'There's a body. In the peat bogs.'

'The ones behind the village?'

I nodded.

'Och, catch yourself on. You're being a total gobshite. What is it you really want?'

'You'll see,' I said, 'you'll see it.' Eddie's coat fitted me across the shoulders, but I couldn't do the zip up. I started to shake with cold. She turned the heat on.

'Whatever it is, it better be quick.'

I wasn't aware of our journey back to the woods, only of huddling in the car and watching the windscreen wipers sweeping hypnotically across my field of vision, the world outside blurred by the rain.

When we reached the bogs, I led her along the path into the woods. It was early evening, but already the sky was dark. Eddie was furious. He trainers, never meant for anything strenuous, were covered in mud, and as she was only wearing a thin, short-sleeved T-shirt she was soon wet through. We pushed through the veil of crabbed branches, and slipped in the mud. The first peal of thunder cracked over to the east, and the atmosphere seemed to draw in.

'What in God's name were you doing here? Why would anyone want to tramp around a fockin' peat bog in the rain?'

'I was looking for magpies.'

'You and your damn magpies. It's all you ever think about. That and Nadia bloody Ismail.'

There was another roll of thunder. I wondered who could have killed the man.

Eddie staggered and nearly fell. 'They make such a racket. And the whole house stinks of rotting meat, it's like a fockin' slaughterhouse. And I can't find anything. They're always hiding my necklaces and rings. Why don't you let them go, Niall? They're big enough to fly. You're just hanging on to them out of some kind of twisted perversion.'

I pushed through the last of the branches to reach the clearing.

'Niall, Niall, are you listening to me?'

The wind was howling through the gnarled pines, and I could hardly see for the rain.

'Niall, have you ever considered you might be losing your mind? You're not very fockin' well.' Her voice was torn away by the wind.

There was someone standing by the trench. I wiped the water from my eyes and walked into the clearing. The man turned towards me. He seemed to glow with an inner light. He had blond hair, and a faint golden down across his naked arms. As I stood transfixed, he held a sword up in front of him, blade pointing uppermost, the silver darkening in the dull light. And then he opened his wings and I saw that they were green, each feather touched with a faint iridescent gold and cobalt-blue sheen like a magpie's tail. I turned to Eddie. She was just entering the clearing. She glanced around and frowned at me. I looked back. The clearing was empty. There was not a soul here save for the two of us. I stood stock still and listened to the rain and the wind. I felt a coldness deep in my bones.

'So where is it then?'

I pointed wordlessly to the peat trench and walked towards it, keeping my eyes fixed on the ground. When I reached it, I looked up. My jacket and jumper were lying in a sodden heap next to the trench, but there was no sword sticking out of the bog. I knelt down in the mud, took a deep breath and plunged my arm in. I felt nothing save the silky iciness of the peat-saturated water. I tried again. I moved a little further up the trench, and leant in as far as I could. On the fourth attempt, I felt material beneath my fingers. I grabbed hold of it and braced myself to heave the body to the surface, but fell backwards almost immediately. It was my T-shirt.

'Well?'

Eddie's lips were nearly blue and the black shadows beneath her eyes had deepened. She hadn't slept for a day and a half. Her hair was plastered to her skull, and she'd wrapped her arms round herself to try to stop shivering. The skin of her arms was raised in goosebumps and her teeth were chattering.

'Someone must have found it. Or whoever put it here must have seen me. They know I know and they've moved it.'

She turned on her heel.

'It was right here! I swear!'

Eddie carried on walking. I wrung the water out of my clothes and picked up the muddied bundle. I got out of the wood just in time to see Eddie get in the car and drive off. I stood in the middle of the road and watched her go. I watched until I couldn't see the car and then I watched some more.

I went back home, turned the TV on and slumped in front of it with a packet of aspirin, a plastic bag full of ice for my hand and as much alcohol as I could find: two cans of lukewarm lager, half a bottle of pudding wine, and a full bottle of brandy. There was some vodka too, but I left it in the cupboard as there was nothing to mix it with. I wondered vaguely if there was anything else I could get to

dull the pain in my hand and my heart but came rapidly
to the conclusion that anything of any worth could not be
obtained from a well-stocked chemist's, let alone over the
counter in Spar. I should, I suppose, have reported the incident to the police, but it seemed a little ridiculous – they
wouldn't believe me any more than Eddie had. Still, I might
let them know, in the morning perhaps.

The pudding wine curdled in my stomach with the lager.
How on earth did Ulster TV get away with so many hours
of shite? Who paid for this crap? I opened the brandy, and
only after the neat spirit burnt a hole through my chest did
I allow myself to think of the apparition in the peat bog
who'd unfurled his wings like a bird and stared into my
soul. I was getting maudlin on the drink. The events of the
last few days had taken a toll and were making me see and
hear strange things. Either that or it was a side effect from
taking too many aspirin. I'd look it up in our medical refer-
ence book when I got back to my parents'. In any case, I
was bound to be OK soon. I wanted Eddie to come back,
I just didn't want to have to speak to her about it. I hoped
she would forgive me, slide nonchalantly through the door
and start talking about clubs in Belfast, the nightlife in
London, the meal she'd made that night as if nothing had
happened.

In the small hours of the morning I crawled upstairs to
bed, holding on to the banisters and the walls to stop the
house sailing away from me, staggered into my bedroom
and sank into the bed which rocked and swayed beneath
me as I fell into a heavy sleep. But in my dreams, a waterlogged body rose from the marsh and fell towards me with
outstretched hands, and in the first light of morning I felt a
small child's hand hold mine. As the sun rose, his fingers
turned cold and stiff. I reached out and touched the place

where Eddie used to be and it was cold and smooth.

I had the hangover from hell, and would have taken anything, from day-old chicks to raw eggs, to relieve it. I got up and threw up. The smell of brandy in my vomit made me sick all over again. The noise from the boxroom, the magpies' cawing, barking and singing, chiselled into my skull as if the sound were peeling my brain like an orange. I chopped up food for them, pausing to throw up in the sink. When I took it in to them they were fighting with each other in a very unbrotherly fashion. One of them had drawn blood; it was flecked across Rannee's white wing feathers. I had to release them soon. If I plotted the results of my survey, I could decide the best place to let them go, a territory that was still free of adult birds.

From the sitting room I surveyed the wreckage of my life: cans and bottles strewn across the floor, black rose petals and wrapping paper, piles of papers and notes, several discs for my Psion, battery chargers and a video more lethal than any battery acid. There were piles of wet clothes everywhere, the bed was unmade, there was vomit on the landing floor, and I'd found my Dictaphone and binoculars in the bathroom. I took a couple of Pro-Plus tablets and three aspirins and drank two cups of extra strong coffee with sugar and a little brandy. Hair of the dog, I told myself, and after the first few gulps I didn't feel quite so queasy whenever I caught a stray whiff of brandy. By this stage my hands were trembling ever so slightly, but I felt able to resume work.

The first thing to do was reorganize my office so that I could begin data-collection again and finish my survey. I gathered together all my papers and started to sort through them. There was some therapeutic value in this: I put them in order of when I'd first acquired them. It took a lot longer and required far more thought than merely arranging them in alphabetical order, or under subject headings, but I was eventually able to chart the course of my own history of discovery, my scientific journey into the how and why of magpie biology as I had come to understand it. The first papers and the final ones were the easiest to remember: the last papers I'd photocopied were on the arms race between cuckoos and their hosts that day in Belfast with Eddie. I remembered how her eyes had lit up in a glasshouse in Belfast when she talked about the leopard-bodied Camael and his twelve thousand angels of destruction. God, that seemed so long ago.

At about six thirty there was a knock at the door. It was unlikely to be Eddie, and she had her own keys, but even so, my heart skipped a beat. I wondered whether to wait a few moments just to make it look as if I were busy and was a fully functioning member of society. But I didn't.

It was Ruth. She didn't say anything for a minute, just stared at me. I realized I must look pretty rough. I'd thrown on whatever had come to hand that morning and I hadn't shaved or washed properly.

'I was wondering whether you'd like to come round and have some dinner at my place tonight,' she said a trace too brightly. 'It won't be anything special.'

I remembered I hadn't eaten all day and I nodded. 'Yeah, I'd like that. I'll just get my coat.'

I grabbed my jacket and keys and followed her through the village, stopping briefly at Mrs O'Malley's to buy wine.

'It's not exactly Oddbins, is it?' said Ruth as we came out, but I merely shrugged.

I was beyond caring what I drank so long as it had alcohol in it. I'd bought two bottles of red so I wouldn't have to wait for Ruth to chill it. When we got to her house

I opened the wine, poured us both a glass and then took mine up to the bathroom. Even I was shocked at how bad I looked. I was as pale as a reformed alcoholic with dark rings under my eyes and a green and yellow bruise down my jaw. I washed and shaved using one of her Bic razors, managing to cut myself only twice, and ended up looking vaguely presentable.

'I can see your face now,' said Ruth, touching my cheek lightly.

I smiled, grimacing slightly at the pain, and poured myself another glass of wine.

After a moment Ruth said, 'I'm sorry about Eddie.'

'I'm not. She'll be back.'

Ruth winced but had the good taste not to say anything. I sighed. Who was I fucking kidding?

'How did you know?'

'Oh, Mrs O'Malley noticed Eddie's car hasn't been parked outside for two days now. They've nothing better to talk about, Niall. Don't get angry.'

'I'm not,' I said, a little too loudly.

'Come and eat.'

Ruth had made a pasta dish with mushrooms and cream, garlic bread and salad. I was still hungry when I'd finished even though I'd had a second helping. I tried to quench a brief fantasy about rare steak and concentrate on what Ruth was telling me. With green peppercorns and fresh parsley, the juice so fresh it was tinged with blood. Ruth was talking about her latest job, translating for an art gallery in Moscow.

'Funny to think of you sitting here in touch with Russia. I can't even e-mail England.'

I opened the second bottle of wine and added, 'You're very kind.'

'Are you OK? Do you want to talk about it?'

I figured she meant how I felt or how Eddie felt; maybe she even wanted to bring in Nadia and John. She didn't mean a dispassionate account of what had happened, a blow by blow description of what I'd done to Nadia and what had been done to me, all lovingly recorded by Nazir and his camcorder. It reminded me of research carried out on dolphins in Shark Bay, Australia. The sea was so clear the researchers could see everything the dolphins did and would cruise along next to them describing their actions into a Dictaphone. What the adolescents did was have sex most of the time and the transcriptions were vivid accounts of who put his penis where and who rubbed against whose dorsal fin. Occasionally I wondered if anyone transcribed the tapes with human names instead of the cutesy Star Warsesque names the humans gave the dolphins. Nazir was like some kind of alien anthropologist documenting his own species. I suppose I should have been thankful for small mercies: there was no running commentary.

'No,' I said. 'Thank you.' An honest description of events might have lain within my capabilities – but only just. An emotional analysis was a whole different ball game.

I wondered whether I should tell her about the body in the bog, or the other thing, with wings. My aspirin dream, I could call it. I wondered if it would glow in the dark.

'You know,' she said quietly, 'we all get hurt from time to time, but that doesn't mean you have to withdraw from intimacy. Pushing people away from you when you're feeling vulnerable doesn't work in the long run. If you don't take risks, you won't be able to have a true loving relationship.'

I wondered who she thought had hurt me. Do unto them before they can do unto you had always seemed to be my motto. Later that night it started to rain, a few drops at first, as if the sky was bleeding, and then the rain came down in torrents. Ruth lit the candles and we sat on her small sofa and stared out to sea, hardly able to hear each other over the sound of the downpour. We could barely distinguish where water ended and the land began, where the horizon started and finished. Dark clouds stained the sky like ink flowing from a fleet of squid, and where stray lights caught the waves the sea shone sharp as jet.

'There was one exhibition that I translated the blurb for – it was called "Sea" and it was a series of photos of the sea, only sea and sky, from one woman's house, the same perspective every day for one week. The brochure said the colours changed both infinitesimally and enormously. I'd have liked to have seen that.'

'My mother liked the colours here too,' I murmured.

I held her hand in my left one, and put my other arm round her. The feel of her warm skin made me keenly aware of what I had lost.

'Niall, you can stay here tonight if you want.'

I nodded. 'Yeah, I'd like that.'

'I'll make you up a bed on the sofa. You'll be soaked if you leave now,' she said as she fetched sheets and a duvet.

I stretched out in the bed she'd made, listening to the wind keening round the house and singing through the metal sculptures and driftwood offerings in the garden. I wondered whether I should go and knock on Ruth's bedroom door. I imagined her soft skin beneath my hands, smelling light and fresh: snowdrops in June. But I thought she might send me away, and I stayed where I was.

The following morning I got up early and washed the dishes and folded my sheets. I left before Ruth was up, and walked along the beach to get home. After the storm that night, the waves were angry-looking and the sea was dark brown, churned through with mud and dirt. There was a dull lead-yellow light in the sky. I picked my way disconsolately through the debris the sea had thrown up: one trainer, one patent shoe. Why was it always the rule that pairs should be separated? Or did people only ever lose one shoe? How can you lose a shoe? For all but students from the Damien Hirst school of beachcombing, today was a bad day: yards of twine, acres of chipped plastic, parts of TV sets, toilet seats, a bit of a fridge, a dead piglet, and a catheter were strewn across the sand. The sea had uncovered the etiolated roots and stems of aged horse hair: the primitive, jointed plants looked like the chitinous tentacles of some alien probing the surface before venturing forth. I felt slightly queasy.

I knew there was something wrong as soon as I was fifty metres away from the house. The front door was open and banging in the wind. I sprinted down the road and ran inside. The house was ominously quiet. I crept along the hall and peered into the sitting room. It was empty. The wretched videotape was still lying in the middle of the floor and scattered across the carpet were the rust-red petals of the dead roses – I hadn't got round to tidying anything else up apart from my papers. I backed out quietly. Whoever had been here might still be here, hiding somewhere, waiting for me. I edged my way towards the kitchen. The door was closed and I leant against the wall, trying to get my breath back. I tensed to throw open the door and surprise them. There was an almighty crack and the door burst open. I let out a shout. I grabbed it before it could close. The back door was also open and hanging loose from its hinges. Whoever had been in the house had used a crowbar to force the locks of both doors. It wasn't a subtle break-in.

I stood in the kitchen, a tunnel of wind blowing through the house, the three open doors slapping and cracking in their frames. There was something in the back garden, a row of pinkish hooked things that twitched. I couldn't work out what they were at first and stood like a dumb thing looking at them before it suddenly dawned on me. I ran out of the kitchen, and leapt up the steps to the garden. Someone had planted two stakes in the middle of the lawn and strung a length of rope between them. Hanging from the rope by string wrapped in a noose round their necks were my five magpies. Three of them were clearly dead: their eyes were glazed and their wings hung slackly by their sides. Rannee and Riordan were still alive, just. They kicked spasmodically and gaped soundlessly for air. I ran back into the kitchen, grabbed a thin knife and cut them down. I slid the knife carefully between Rannee's neck and the string and severed the noose, then I did the same thing for Riordan. I massaged Rannee's neck and throat gently. Her eyes rolled back in her skull and she closed her white eyelids. Her wings opened slightly and quivered. A dense green bile flecked with blood oozed from her beak. She convulsed twice and lay still. I held her breast in my palm, but I could not feel a heartbeat. I picked up Riordan and carried her inside. I held out little hope for her. When I stroked her throat feathers she too vomited up bloodstained bile. I wrapped her in a tea towel and put her inside my shirt while I boiled the kettle for a hot-water bottle. I heated a pan of milk and laced it with a little brandy and loaded it with sugar just as I had done for the magpies when they were fledglings. Riordan struggled feebly against my chest. I found the old spoon I used and attempted to force her to drink some of the milk. I squeezed the base of her bill to get her to open her beak, tipped a teaspoon of milk down her throat and massaged her neck and stomach. It was slow process, and much of the milk dribbled over me and seeped into her feathers. I soaked a few bits of bread in the milk and gave those to her too, but I didn't want to give her too much in case they got stuck in her gullet. Finally I made up the hot-water bottle, wrapped it in a towel and put it in a box. Riordan croaked pathetically when I put her down, and struggled against the tea towel she was wrapped in. After a moment, she lay still. Immediately I thought the worst and bent to touch her. She opened one eye and closed it again. I defrosted some vegan sausage mix in the microwave, added an egg and some brandy, and ground a couple of vitamin tablets into it. Riordan took barely a couple of teaspoons before sinking into a kind of stupor. She refused to open her beak, and I thought I would hurt her if I forced her. I put the mixture in a small dish in the box, and put the box in the airing cupboard. It was then that I had a sudden thought, one of those nagging feelings that had been at the back of my mind over the last couple of days. I looked in the bedroom. The sword was missing. I was sure it had disappeared the day I'd seen the body in the bog. It had to be the same sword. Here was the proof I needed. I wasn't mad — I hadn't imagined the body.

Outside, the bodies of the other three magpies were rocking in the wind, their heads lolling at an awkward angle. I cut them down and brought them into the kitchen. Their feathers were damp and spotted with blood. I suspected they had been poisoned first and thought I ought to do a post-mortem.

★　★　★

It was mid-morning when Eddie walked in.

'The front door was open,' she called from the hall and I heard her slam the door shut. 'I've just come back to get my things, Niall, I'm not staying . . .' She opened the kitchen door and froze in horror. 'Niall,' she whispered, 'what in God's name are you doing?'

Originally I'd started doing a post-mortem on Ron. I'd found some partially digested meat in his stomach, and since I'd fed them chopped-up chicks that morning, someone else must have given it to him and the other magpies. Having established that they were probably poisoned, I couldn't take my analysis much further – I couldn't tell what kind of poison it was. Then I started thinking about the magpies and their short lives; how I'd miss them, and how funny they had been, and I wondered was there something I could keep that would remind me of them? I thought of my father, and his voracious appetite for taxidermy in the days of his Peruvian expeditions. He'd tried to teach me when I was younger using dead rats, though I only produced animals that looked like over-stuffed sausages with vestigial limbs. But in my museum I'd kept collections of small skulls and bits of bones I found and that's when I got the idea of preserving the magpies' skeletons. I could wire them back up the way they did with dinosaurs at the Natural History Museum. There wasn't time to put the bodies on an anthill and allow the ants to pick the bones clean. I had to use another method. I'd already stripped the flesh from Ron's bones and put them in hot water with the closest equivalent to neat alcohol I could find – Eddie's nail varnish remover and some vodka – in a saucepan on the cooker. The whole mess was boiling away, and I'd written 'Ron' on the side of the pan in black marker pen. I was going to put each of the magpies into a different pan so their bones didn't get mixed up. I was cutting up Rinky – it was a fiddly task as bird bones are so tiny and fragile, and, as the magpies hadn't been dead for long, somewhat messy. All the surfaces in the kitchen were covered with a thin film of blood, bits of flesh, organs, and feathers.

Eddie put her hand over her mouth and retched. I guess the smell was terrible; I'd kind of got used to it. It was only when she ran from the room that I realized what she'd said. What *was* I doing? It was only a matter of time before I would become a wanted man. Whoever had killed the man in the bog had used my sword. It had my fingerprints all over the handle, microscopic filaments from my T-shirt across the blade. I wondered whether I'd even get out of the country. They might have alerted the harbour police. On the other hand, it depended who'd found the body. If whoever had killed him had moved him, then I had a little more time. But if it was the police, or anyone who had told the police, it wouldn't be long before the sword could be traced to Mike, and then to me. How much time did I have? Days? Probably less. I needed to prepare – pack some clothes and get some food together, just in case. Whoever had killed the magpies had been watching the house. He'd seen me leave the night before, although maybe he hadn't bargained on me returning so soon – presumably he thought I'd go straight out to the field until my usual time. And here I was creating mementos to nostalgia out of my dead magpies' bodies as if I had all the time in the world. I washed my hands and ran upstairs. Eddie was sitting on the bed crying. She wiped her eyes when she saw me.

'I've got to go,' I said. 'They're after me.'

'What are you talking about?' she asked, sniffing.

'The body, you know,' I hissed.

'You've lost it, Niall,' she whispered hoarsely.

At first I thought she was referring to the corpse. I crammed a few clothes, my penknife and binoculars into a rucksack, and grabbed a couple of tins, a carton of milk, half a loaf of bread, some cheese and the rest of the bottle of brandy from the kitchen. I was just about to leave when I realized I'd forgotten something. I ran back upstairs and picked up Riordan. She was weak from vomiting, and did not protest when I wrapped her up in a towel and tucked her down the front of my shirt. Riordan and I left that house by the sea for good, climbing in a most undignified fashion over the fence in the back garden.

I took a long detour round the village, resting frequently behind old stone walls and in tangled thickets. It was early evening by the time I arrived at the fallen-down cottage and the old greenhouse out past the scrubland. It was choked with brambles, the leaves coarse and flushed with port on the underside. I thought of Eddie, and how I'd taken her there one afternoon; we'd had sex against the old wooden bench, the pebbles I'd collected for her clinking in my pocket. I could almost smell the milky saltiness of her through the dank verdure. There had been daffodils growing here then. When I was eight my father had shown me the spring's first daffodil under a microscope. At first I stared down the lens at a kaleidoscope of yellows, but as I gradually adjusted the focus the colours crystallized into forms, became the crenellated ridges of petal valleys, a grand canyon of a trumpet exploding outwards as if shot by a bullet and frozen in time. The anthers were beaded with green-gold dew and the stamens, thickly dusted with pollen, were like alien time bombs, ticking with spikes.

Both the greenhouse and the cottage were too open, but nearby was a bunker; I'd almost fallen into it one day. It took me a while to find it, the entrance concealed by vegetation. Inside it was dark and damp and smelt of old fires. I left Riordan and my rucksack underground, and went back to cut some bracken: I made a bed out of the dead fox-red leaves, and piled fresh fronds on the top. They were dusty with spores which I knew were cancerous, but I was less interested in my long-term plans right then. I pulled the vegetation over the entrance as best I could and lit a couple of candles. I hadn't eaten since my dinner with Ruth. My hands were shaking slightly as I unwrapped the cheese and bread; I tore off great hunks which I washed down with milk. Riordan was still nearly lifeless, mummified in the tea towel and wedged into the bracken. I picked her up carefully and examined her. She opened one eye and gazed at me dopily. I was alarmed to see spots of blood dotted over her white chest feathers, but then realized it was my own – I must have cut myself when I was gathering the bracken. She opened her beak and made a soft babbling sound, her begging call. I tipped a few drops of brandy into the top of the bottle and dripped them into her throat. After a couple of minutes she started to look a little more perky. I soaked small pieces of bread in milk and fed them to her one by one until she turned her head away and refused to take any more. I looked at the tins I'd brought with me – flageolet beans and water chestnuts, just my sodding luck. We'd eaten half the bread, cheese and milk: food, I realized, was going to be a problem.

Halfway through the night, Riordan woke and squawked in alarm. I held her against my chest and kept her beak shut, but though I listened as intently as I could, I heard nothing. Maybe it was only a passing fox, or perhaps she was dreaming: the lithe black and white shapes of her siblings twisting before her sleeping eyes.

I slept fitfully through the rest of the night and the next day. Grey light seeped into the bunker and I woke often and fed Riordan small pieces of bread and milk. I drank the rest, and finished the bread and cheese. By the following evening I had a raging thirst. I decided to wait until it was dark before fetching some water. Riordan was a little more lively, though that could have had something to do with the frequent medicinal doses of brandy I'd been giving her. She lurched towards me. I let her land on my shoulder and preen my hair before putting her back down. There was a three-quarter moon, an indistinct thumb-smudge of light. I picked through the bracken carefully, anxious not to cut a great swathe that would boldly announce my presence. In the distance the sea murmured and broke on the shore, and the wood echoed with the low call of a nightjar. I found the small stream Eddie and I had crossed barely more than a couple of months ago and knelt down to drink from it. The water was cool and cold and the banks smelt of damp earth and the slightly sharp scent of wood sorrel. The edges of the stream were lined with drifts of nettle-like yellow archangel. I remembered Eddie telling me about Shakziel, angel of water insects, and Trgiaob, in charge of wild fowl and creeping things – both a far cry from the angels of war, and the archangels of wrath, and for an instant I had a vision of the man with the golden hair and the wings of a bird, glowing in the rain. I washed out the milk carton and filled it with water, then picked handfuls of sorrel and bittersweet leaves and stuffed them in my pockets. I was just about to go when I heard voices carried on the wind, cutting across the sound of the sea. I stepped behind a tree and waited. A shadow passed over the moon, and a couple of dogs began to bay.

I waited and the voices drew closer. There was an unpleasant smell of rank decay; I'd bruised the leaves of some hedge woundwort. Heading towards the bunker along the fringe of the beach were three men and two dogs. One of the men was much larger than the other two, and they were all carrying guns. It had to be Brendan and his cronies. I gripped the trunk of the tree tightly and felt the bark bite into my palms. A blackbird, startled from sleep, gave a staccato alarm call. The dogs were sniffing through the bracken and they turned towards me. The three men followed. I started to sweat and my muscles locked rigidly. The beating of my heart was vibrating in my throat and I could barely breathe. The dogs came within a couple of metres of the stream and cast about sniffing. I closed my eyes and waited for them to bound over to me, snarling and showing their teeth. After a few minutes they yapped and turned to their masters. One of the men seemed to stare right at me. He lit a cigarette and spat on the ground. The three started to walk upstream towards the cottage and the greenhouse. I licked my finger and held it up. By sheer accident I was downwind of the dogs, and crossing the stream must have confused them. It was too dark to read my tracks or else there is no doubt that Brendan would have seen where I had stopped to drink. Now I was worried they would find the bunker. They would certainly realize that I was nearby, and even worse, they would surely kill Riordan. There was little that I could do, though. I leant my head against the tree and listened to the small sounds of the wood, the creak of branches, the long drawn-out hoot of an owl, the tiny scrabblings of a vole in the undergrowth. It was so dark that purple afterimages flared in front of me as I tried to stare into the night and in my mind's eye I constantly saw the man with the golden hair and blue eyes lift his head to stare at me over the sharpened blade of his sword. After about an hour I risked moving. My neck and shoulders ached with tension. I walked carefully along by the stream, stopping to listen every time a branch snapped beneath my feet, or I slipped in the mud. Eventually I stopped opposite where I estimated the bunker to be. There was no sound and the bracken seemed to be undisturbed. I waited for what seemed like an eternity before crossing the stream and stepping into the open. I expected a bullet to sing past my head, or hands to grasp me by the throat. I crouched down and crawled through the bracken, following the well-worn trails left by rabbits. I couldn't find the entrance to the bunker, though, and started to panic, taking any path that crossed mine until I was thoroughly lost. In the end I risked sticking my head through the fronds to get my bearings. I was practically in front of the bunker. I edged a little way forward and found the entrance with its broken steps. I climbed down gingerly and stepped inside. There was a rustle and I thought my heart would stop. Cold air rushed towards me and something hit me in the face. I stifled a cry and dropped to the floor. Riordan landed in a tangle of wings and feathers on the stone floor and let out an indignant squawk. I clutched her to me and almost sobbed with relief. My matches were damp, but by the third attempt I managed to light one of the candles. The bunker seemed to be undisturbed. I poured some of the water into my cupped hands and let Riordan drink, then I opened the tins and mixed up the beans, water chestnuts, sorrel and bittersweet in the plastic bread bag and ate the resulting salad with my fingers.

Riordan perched on my knee with her head on one side and crooned.

'It's no food for a magpie, you wouldn't like it,' I assured her. 'I think it's pretty ghastly myself,' I added, but she continued to look at me hungrily.

I curled up in the bracken and she roosted on my arm, huddled into her feathers. I didn't feel well. The cold and damp had seeped into my bones, but my forehead was hot and tight, as if there were some pressure building up inside.

I woke to seagulls keening and thought I was in a field full of human bones, the tiny fragile skeletons of dead babies resting amongst unmarked stones. I sat up slowly and picked the bracken out of my hair. My face was rough with stubble and I ached all over. I drank a little brandy and the rest of the water before realizing with a sickening lurch that Riordan had gone. I stumbled to my feet, staggered up what remained of the steps and blinked at the brightness of the day. There was a single magpie down by the beach pecking busily through the short grass. It gave a shrill cry and flew towards me. I held out my arm for Riordan to alight on and stroked the feathers round her bill. She closed her eyes in pleasure. I let her go, and crawled back underground to wait for night to fall. I could row out to Skull Island, I thought, and hide there. No-one would find me. Ruth had a boat that I could borrow. When things calmed down, I could row further up the coast towards Belfast. Later on I could always tell Ruth where I'd left the boat; she'd understand.

In the middle of the night I tucked Riordan into my rucksack and headed back towards the village. I was weak with hunger and my head felt like a ripe watermelon: one tap with the blade of a knife and it would break open. Although the night was mild, I couldn't stop shivering. I drank the last of the brandy, and filled the bottle with water from the spring. As I walked I remembered the wrecked ship marooned on needlepoints of rock around Skull Island and realized how futile it would be to try to navigate a safe passage through the jagged teeth without smashing Ruth's boat. And the island itself was barren – there would be nowhere to hide, and little to eat. But Ruth had mentioned that she ripened the goats' cheese in the garage so I thought I'd pay her a visit anyway. I was unprepared for quite how well stocked her garage was when I broke into it. The stone had been painted white and it was lined with shelves. There were rows of bottled fruits, preserved vegetables, cheese wrapped in greaseproof paper, dark green wine bottles stacked on their side as well as spare rope, candles, matches, light bulbs and nails, and, for some reason, a jar of marbles. It was almost as if Ruth was preparing for a siege, for a time when she might need to hole up in her white house with her goats and her hens.

I was so hungry I ate a whole cheese there and then. Riordan hopped round the garage and pecked at brass tacks, fishing wire, and spare locks while I filled my ruck-sack with an assortment of bits and pieces I thought might come in useful and as much food as I could carry. Riordan proved difficult to catch; she flew from one side of the garage to the other with a five-inch nail clenched in her beak. In my efforts to trap her, I knocked a tray of eggs which fell to the floor and smashed, and the white dog started to bark. The magpie flew down to the mess and, dropping the nail, started to peck at the yolks. I attempted to scoop her up, but she squawked, grabbed the nail, and alighted on the top shelf in the garage where her wings hit a jar full of cherries. Fortunately it didn't fall, but as she shifted about on the shelf the jar moved nearer the edge. I cursed the whole damn species as I stood below my magpie, arms outstretched to catch the cherries. Above me a door opened. I grabbed my rucksack and ran out of the garage, leaving the door ajar. After a moment, I heard the sound of glass breaking on stone, and Riordan came flying after me, the nail glinting. I climbed over the stone wall into the goats' field. They started bleating and the hens clucked in alarm. Lights came on in the bedroom of the white house. I jumped over the far wall and half slid, half scrambled down to the sea; a surge of water rushed up to meet me as I fell to the beach. I swore, whistled for Riordan, and started to jog through the bitterly cold surf, sand and salt stinging my skin. The sand soon turned to uneven rocks and pebbles as I reached the beach below the Ismails' wood. I wasn't happy about crossing it to get to the bay on the far side; there was no telling whether Brendan and his cronies would be about, or if the strange ships that docked in the night might have anchored, but there was a far greater likelihood that I would be seen by Ruth, or the police if she called them, as long as I skirted the wood by walking along the road. There were no lights at sea or in the wood. It was difficult to see where I was going and I slid on the seaweed-encrusted rocks and twisted my ankles in the cracks between them. Riordan flew in front of me, her ghostly presence glimmering on a rock or the battlements of the walls as she waited for me to catch up. There was no sign of life in the small harbour, but the trussed-up yacht had disappeared. I continued as quickly as I could. Once we reached the bay, Riordan perched on my shoulder. I made her hide the nail in the top pocket of my coat; I didn't want her to poke it in my ear.

We finally reached our destination — the disused lighthouse that rose black and rugged and crumbling from the dark granite cliffs at the far end of the beach. I sat in the top of the tower and drank red wine, ate goats' cheese and apricots preserved in brandy while Riordan played with her nail. When I took out my penknife and started to sharpen the blade on a whetting stone I'd found in Ruth's garage, she tried to peck at the knife. I hadn't lit any candles, but there was just enough light from the moon to be able to see. The night was exceptionally clear; every star was visible. I'd completely disrupted the magpie's sleeping patterns. Very few creatures hunt by night compared to the day but there is a type of bird, the whip-poor-will, or goat-sucker, whose existence is regulated by the moon. This bird, a native of North America, is known as a 'sallying insectivore' because it sits and waits on perches before 'sallying' forth to snap at insects disturbed by other animals. As the height of the moon in the sky increases, the whip-poor-wills become more active, and their two-week breeding season is synchronized with the full moon. I could see the attraction in it, I thought, as I watched the moon sink, the sky turn to pearl and the sun begin to rise. As the sea glowed oyster in the dawn light, I saw a face reflected in the heavy glass pane of the lighthouse; a face that was half child, half man, the eyes bright blue, his reflection framed by a hint of wings.

I took my belongings, whistled to Riordan and climbed down one flight of the narrow stone staircase to the windowless room below to try to get some sleep. It must have been about midday when I woke. There were bells ringing, pealing out across the sea. I ran up to the top of the lighthouse and lay as flat as I could on the stone floor. From this height I could see the beach curving away from me, the Ismails' wood, the glint of blue that was its hidden lake, and also long lines of greenhouses that I had never seen before. On the far side of the wood, most of the village seemed to be in Main Street and the church bells were tolling. It was a funeral. I immediately assumed the worst: they must have found the body. I got out my binoculars and trained them on the coffin bearers.

Just then I felt a sharp jab in the ankle. I shook my leg and continued to focus the binoculars. There was another jab. I turned round in time to see Riordan about to peck my leg. When she saw me looking she crouched down, fluttered her wings and begged for food.

'Not now, you stupid creature. I'll sort you out in a minute. Here, go play with your nail.' I tossed it over to her.

There were calla lilies and ivy on the top of the coffin; directly behind it was a woman in black. I followed them to the doors of the church. As they were about to go in, she looked up. It was Mrs O'Malley. Of course, of course, it was starting to make sense now. It was William in the peat bog, William's body that I had uncovered, William with his soft, blank white face, dark shadows beneath his eyes, William who always sat hunched in the corner of the Spar, his hands twisted together. I thought of the face in the bog I had so fleetingly seen, and it seemed to me that it had indeed been William's.

It was hot in the top of the lighthouse. I finished off the rest of the wine and dozed in an alcoholic fug. I woke to find myself spreadeagled on the floor looking up into the night sky and for one long minute felt as if I could not move, as if I were that man who stared at another night's constellation, his body naked to the blight of sky, the cold earth next to his skin, iron stakes driven through his wrists and ankles as his life's blood ebbed into the soil. It was too exposed here. I finished the stale, warm water in my brandy bottle and ate the last of the food – a whole jar of roasted tomatoes preserved in oil – and felt the first taste of summer on my tongue.

Riordan followed me as I walked along the edge of the cliff until I managed to find a sheep path down from it. I put her in the top of my rucksack for safekeeping as I descended. About six metres below the top of the cliff, the path levelled out and ran along parallel to the shore. We were roughly fifteen metres above the sea; the occasional drop of water hit me. I was a little unsteady, my head ached and burned and I shivered with cold; I was also quite weak and every so often lost my footing and had to cling to the side of the cliff for support. It reminded me of the last expedition I went on to Venezuela, ostensibly to research the fauna and flora of the tepuy: enormous square-topped mountains with sheer cliff faces that towered hundreds of metres above the lush jungle below. High in the oxygen-thin air there was a completely different climate and unique species flourished that in their isolation had evolved into bizarre and quirky forms. On one mountain alone there might be twenty-seven kinds of lizard that had never been seen or recorded elsewhere. Likewise the five of us that went lived in complete isolation, eking out our food rations which had to last the full two months before a helicopter would return to airlift us to the nearest inhabited land at Canaima. It started well, we were enthusiastic, and we discovered a rare creatures and plants on a daily basis. They weren't brand new kinds, but they were weird variations of their sister species. The scenery was breathtaking – on a clear day you could see the Angel Falls, the highest waterfall in the world. Occasionally the hunting calls of indigenous tribes echoed through the forest. At night the temperature plunged to nearly zero, by midday it was stiflingly humid. Often the tepuy was shrouded in mist and we were marooned on our island in the sky. On days like that with no radio communication, no visibility and the imminent threat of death if one of us walked too close to the hidden cliff edges, I was reminded of that childhood feeling of isolation, of utter wordlessness, of the loss of language, and the loss, even, of the need for it. It was the same feeling I had when I walked on the beach in the mist, and out of the mist came Nadia and her horse, galloping silently towards me in dream-like slow motion, a feeling without a name before words were born.

Of course, I destroyed it all. I made wordless love to one of the girls, Karen. I took her by the hand, and took her amongst alien plants with strange, lip-like leaves, and orange-throated blue flowers, amongst succulents with fleshy spines, a bloom like a plum creeping over their skin, while the mist wrapped around us and took me back to that time when all was raw; a time when words had the power to scour the skin from a child. We carried on our clandestine affair even though she was on this expedition with her boyfriend, and at the time he was my best friend. But the words crept back in, and the betrayal, when it came, was bitter. He came back early one day and found us in his tent. They'd been together for five years. We had another two weeks of the expedition to go and they were probably the hardest of my life. The other three left us on our own, moving their share of the food and their tents to another part of the tepuy. Karen and I were left alone, and I found that when I had to speak to her, I had little to say. Our relationship dragged on when we got back to Britain; I felt it incumbent upon me to do no otherwise – after all, I thought there must be something to show for the ruin of a friendship, and the loss of any scientific credibility. She left me eventually, but only when she found out I was sleeping with someone else. Now she silently mails me dead roses.

I slipped again, and clung to the cliff face to steady myself. Small rocks scattered into the sea below and disappeared without trace. I could just about make out the white shapes of nesting kittiwakes, who stirred and cawed uneasily. I suppose, when I think about it, I was trying to follow in my father's footsteps, but at the same time forge something new for myself. I was so determined to fulfil the expectations of a long line of zoologists. My father turned from stuffing small Peruvian mammals to studying *Dracula bella*, a carnivorous orchid the colour and stench of rotting flesh that digests flies in acid. The mimicry is so perfect, the lips of the flowers are even shaped like a mushroom that grows on meat. The first species was discovered in 1872 by H. G. Reichenbach who named it *Masdevallia chimaera*. As he found more of these strange orchids, he gave them names referring to insects, bats, mythological creatures, dragons. In 1925, the Draculas were made a genus themselves – the name means 'little dragon' but obviously also refers to the legend of the vampire. I guess I was trying to prove that I too had the same versatility as my father, who swapped from animals to plants with ease, by leading an expedition that dealt with both flora and fauna. Maybe I thought that in this remote region unknown to all but the gods and angels, I would make my mark, even, perhaps, discover another member of the Dracula family to present gift-wrapped in moss to my father on my return. But I hadn't managed to accomplish any of those things.

That night Riordan and I camped in a cave that was

long and thin, but dry towards the back. When I'd walked over these cliffs in the daytime, I'd heard the boom of sea water resonating beneath me and suspected that they were honeycombed with caves. I found three that night, but this one was by far the best. I slept fitfully; it was uncomfortable lying on the ground without even the cushioning of bracken, and as the day dawned I woke aching in every limb, with a cramp in my neck and my head burning. The tide was out and the rocks below me stretched out to sea, oil-slick black, glowing like coal. I could believe I was the only person in the world: I could see nothing but the ocean and, to my right, the long curve of the cliff. Kittiwakes rose and fell around me, mewing and crying. But someone else was here; a small child clambered over the rocks near sea level. The sun shone brightly on his fair hair, and as I watched he turned towards me and held out his hand.

'Niall,' he called, 'Niall,' in a thin, reedy voice that was all but drowned by the swell of the sea.

I closed my eyes and rubbed my temples. The child had my father's eyes. When I looked again, he had gone. I stripped off all my clothes and ran over the rocks. The water was agonizingly cold. I made myself swim out to sea until I felt warmer and then returned to shore. Ruth had five white bars of Ponds cold cream soap in her garage and I'd taken one. I washed myself thoroughly in the shallows before clambering back up the rocks to my cave and pulling my clothes on over my still wet body. That morning I collected mussels, prising them from their holdfasts, and driftwood for a fire. I searched in rock pools as I had done as a child and caught a couple of sand gobies that were lurking in the darkest seaweed. I put them on the flattest part of the rock next to the pools from which they came.

The sun glinted from the iridescence on their scales as they drowned in air. By combing through tracts of bladder-wrack, I found small edible crabs, their shells flushed blue. I gathered dulse from the rock pools, a deep red seaweed that tasted of the essence of the ocean. I snapped the shells of the mussels, and scraped their pink and grey flesh into a small pan I'd taken from Ruth's garage. I chopped up the fish and the dulse and added them to the mussels, along with some fresh water from a thin stream that trickled and fell over the cliff edge.

Using loose stones I built a hearth and lit a fire. I put the pan on to cook, and baked the crabs directly on the hot stones. My stomach growled with hunger as the fish stew simmered. I sat at the entrance to the cave and looked out to sea. Riordan pecked through stranded kelp for insects, occasionally leaping back in an awkward flurry of wings as a stray wave came too close. A flock of dun-lin turned and wheeled with amazing precision, rustling over the sea, and I wondered idly how to model their behaviour, simulate it on a computer using simple laws. I thought about the cuckoo mafia and whether it would be possible to chart their behaviour using a computer pro-gram. I couldn't see how to do it, but I felt sure it could be done. It was an arms race of a sort between the mag-pies and the cuckoos. Now the cuckoos were trying to scare the magpies into submission. Would the magpies evolve a defence strategy, become birds that bred in groups, co-operatively fighting force with force? I thought of the cuckoo chick dwarfing the nest, its great beak gap-ing livid red and yellow, and how the cuckoo must have tossed out the magpie fledglings so that their lifeless and naked bodies lay spreadeagled on the ground below, their necks twisted, their embryonic wing bones broken. And almost immediately I had an image of myself and the fair-haired child of my dreams and nightmares: the child with my father's eyes. I'd seen pictures of my father when he was young and he'd been blond before his hair took on a sandy colour. My mother had light brown hair and she was small. They both had grey eyes. And me? Who was I? Taller and thinner than my father, I dwarfed my mother. My face was a different shape from theirs, my hair jet black, my eyes blue. Jacob Charles Eamonn Edwards. Could he be their child? Why did this five-year-old apparition haunt me with his thin voice, his boyish smile, his love of shells? Why did he drown in my waking dreams, weighed down with pockets full of stones, his breath crushed by the sea?

I snapped the legs from the crabs and peeled away the shell to get at the meat inside. Riordan returned, as if guided by some sixth sense, to pick at the scraps and share my fish stew. I felt a little better after I'd eaten, but I still couldn't stop shivering. I slept by the dying fire and dreamt of holding a bird in my cupped hands that became an embryo weeping blood through my interlaced fingers. I woke some time in the night and held my hands before my face, expecting them to be coated in a slick, congealing fluid. I drank water directly from the stream and retraced my footsteps back along the path. At my passing the kittiwakes murmured their discontent. It was a dark night, the moon almost completely obscured by clouds, and I progressed slowly, shivering and shaking, and fearful that I would fall into the boiling sea below. In the darkness afterimages swept across my gaze, of fiery-eyed men with burning souls and blazing swords, fair-haired Michael whose wings were green, Gabriel and Gadriel, and Uriel whose hands burnt and bled. From Eddie their names and faces had become familiar to me. I clung to the cliff face, and inched my way back up towards the top. Once the rock I was holding broke away in my hand and I staggered and fell to my knees before managing to grasp another ledge of stone. At the top of the cliff I sprawled face down in the grass, allowing the dew to seep into the cuts in my hands. I was trembling, and I could hardly see straight. The lights of the village smeared into one, and as I descended to the beach, I thought I saw lights out at sea; a small flotilla that bobbed like buoys.

I made my way towards Nadia Ismail's wood; at every step the sand sucked and dragged at my feet and I found it increasingly difficult to walk in a straight line, but I was determined to find out what lay in the heart of the wood. I had some half-baked idea that William's death was linked in some way to the Ismails. Instead of skirting round the trees and entering it from the beach side, I climbed directly over the wall and half jumped, half fell through the bushes on the other side. I disentangled myself and stood up. The wood was much darker than the night; the heavy canopy of leaves screened out the stars. I set off in the direction I thought I ought to take, but it was difficult to get my bearings. Like a sleepwalker, I held my arms in front of me until my eyes adjusted to the dark and I became more adept at avoiding overhanging branches. Fortunately this part of the wood was full of oak and beech trees, and little grew beneath their branches save a light covering of bracken and the occasional holly which I wandered into by mistake. Acorns and beech nuts crunched beneath my feet, but apart from my passage the wood was silent. Even the sound of the sea was muffled. I veered a little more to the left. I'd been walking for some time and was beginning to despair that I was ever going to get anywhere – I felt as if I were going round in circles – when the night seemed to close in. I was approaching what looked like a solid, black wall. I put out my hands and touched it. It was an evergreen hedge, almost impenetrable and about two metres tall. I walked round it, trailing my hand through the leaves. I rounded a corner, and had I not been touching the hedge I wouldn't have noticed the opening. I slipped through the narrow gap and turned to see what I had been searching for. It was a greenhouse lit dimly with soft blue lights. I pulled back the sliding door and stepped over the metal lintel. It was as warm as blood. There were no plants in this greenhouse. Light spilt from rows of boxes laid out on the wooden benches. I peered inside. They were full of straw. I pushed the straw covering away to reveal a row of perfectly smooth polished eggs. They were pale blue and faintly freckled. The rest of the boxes were full of eggs too, different shapes and sizes, but probably from ducks, moorhens and other waterbirds. At the far end of the greenhouse was an incubator. I didn't venture too near in case the ducklings – if that is what was inside – woke and started to cheep. Brendan had been right when he said they took the welfare of their birds seriously. Breeding the ducks intensively like this would mean there was always a steady supply of them to stock the lake, to shoot, eat, or sell. Beyond the greenhouse was another one. I closed the door behind me and walked round to the second greenhouse. This one was completely different from the first; it radiated a brilliant purple light and the glass was opaque with condensation. There was a padlocked chain round the door, but it was rusty and no longer locked properly. The first thing I noticed when I opened the door was the smell. It hit me right between the eyes. I shut the door and stared in amazement. The greenhouse with the ducks in was well hidden; it was also a useful front for this one, and for any others the Ismails might have. How easy it would be to explain the high electricity bills if you had a year-round hatchery. The electricity was being used for rather different purposes here – and not for heat. The place was lit with long tubes of UV light, and the plants that grew under these artificial conditions were thriving; their stems were dense and hairy, and their large five-fingered leaves were splayed to catch the light. Most of them practically touched the ceiling. They were giving off a heady, resinous scent. It was Skunk – a new variety of extra strong cannabis. I rubbed my eyes and stared down at my hands fluorescing in the purple glow. The smell was making me feel faint and I started to shiver. It had got much lighter and the sky above me was tinged with a faint wash of pink. I had to get out and back to my cave as quickly as I could. I didn't dare contemplate what Brendan would do if he found me here.

I remember very little after that. I woke about mid-morning, stiff and bruised. My mind was cluttered with images of eggs, and alien plants pulsating in a purple light; of walking at dawn through a forest full of dead trees whose limbs dripped lichen and whose torsos were encrusted with salt, of seagulls wheeling in from the night, their bellies lit by light so that they appeared like the souls of wounded sailors, spirits of the sea whose strength fades as the sun rises. I woke with words on my tongue: Jacob have I loved; the one refrain repeating endlessly in my restless mind . . . Jacob have I loved . . . Jacob have I loved . . . I woke clutching a bunch of leaves; their crushed stems smelt of tomato plants' hot odour and not like cannabis at all. I felt as if my insides were liquefying. I was gripped by fear: I could no longer distinguish between what was real and what was unreal, what I dreamt and what I remembered.

The only thing I had to hold on to was our survival, mine and Riordan's.

I climbed down to the narrow beach to salvage what driftwood the tide had thrown up in the night, and fetch more water from the spring. It tasted of copper and minerals. I couldn't see Riordan at first, although there was a pair of magpies a little further along the coast. The male was tree-topping – only the highest thing around was a low-growing shrub. The female was crouched just below him, quivering her wings and cooing. I looked more closely. It was Riordan. For a moment, I felt outraged, like a father who catches his daughter holding hands with some callow, greasy-haired youth. It was natural, after all. If she found a mate now, she'd stay with him throughout winter and they would breed the following year. Riordan saw me then and immediately came arrowing back and landed on my shoulder. She started to preen my hair and, putting her head on one side, flickered her white eyelids and gave a small, throaty call.

'Don't pretend it didn't happen,' I said, rubbing her throat, 'I saw you with him.'

It took me five hours to catch six small fish from the rock pools – two gobies, a blenny and three butterfish. I used the gobies as bait, feeding bits of them to Riordan and impaling the rest on a thin nail I'd fashioned into a hook attached to some fishing line. I crouched on one of the dark basalt rocks that overhung the sea and cast my line in. The gulls floating on the water below me barely stirred. A little way out to sea a cormorant shaped like a cross hung out its wings to dry. Beneath the rock the sea surged and boomed in underground caverns where seals would come to whelp; giant anemones bloomed and kelp unfurled as languorously as the unwrapping of Chinese scrolls. There was an irony in using fish to catch a fish; we are all cannibalistic upon one another; we are all programmed to fulfil our destiny. It made me think of a type of salamander which has a mutant strain. This strain is genetically different, its teeth are sharper, it grows faster, its taste is questionable: a kind of hopeless monster, it is born with a love of salamander flesh. It devours its siblings and, having eaten its kin, it turns on its own kind. A gene for cannibalism turns it into a killer.

The gulls and small fish nibbled my bait, but towards evening I caught a turbot, a round, ugly fish that fought for its life. I scraped my hands on the barnacles encrusting the rock, and sliced my palms on the fishing line, but managed to reel it in. I scraped off the scales and gutted it, throwing the intestines to the waiting seagulls. I chopped up the butterfish and the blenny with some wild celery and used the mixture to stuff the fish. By boiling a little sea water until the pan was dry, I was able to get enough salt to rub into the skin. Finally I wrapped the fish in several layers of large, flat celery leaves and tied it up like a parcel with fishing line before putting it to bake on flat stones in the embers of the fire. While I waited for the fish to cook, I broke the remaining driftwood into small fragments, and gradually fed the chips to the fire to prevent it from dying out completely.

William, I thought, must have seen something – perhaps he went too near the greenhouses, or maybe he wandered down by the Ismails' private harbour. And whoever had murdered him wanted it to look as if I'd done it – kill two birds with one stone – it was a convenient way of getting rid of a nosy biologist who trespassed too frequently. Which left the sword. Were Mike and John in on this too? Did they deliberately plant the sword on me first? Or was stealing my borrowed sword an afterthought on Brendan's part? The only thing that was certain was that William hadn't been killed with the sword. There had been no blood on his shirt. His heart had been speared after he'd died.

I cut the fishing line, and peeled off the outer layers of burnt celery. The inner leaves were still moist and green, and the fish, cooked to perfection, was sharp with celery juice. I kept back a little to use as bait the next day.

All the following morning I sat on the outcrop of rock in a waking dream and fished. The salt stung the cuts in my hands: childish hands sliced a child's hands until they ran with blood and wept bloodstained salt; I heard Jacob calling my name. Once I saw him drown before my eyes. I didn't know what was worse, his screams, or the harsh gasps for air torn from his heaving lungs before they filled with water. About midday I noticed that the brilliant aquamarine water below me was stained black. I glanced down and saw a naked woman floating in the sea, her blond hair tangled in the beds of kelp, clouds of blood drifting about her face.

By mid-afternoon I'd caught only two small fish. I decided to use one as bait and cut it into pieces. Hooking a lump of fish onto my nail, I cast it out to sea. As it fell towards the water, a herring gull swooped down and grabbed it. I cursed and jerked the line, but the gull was attached. The nail had pierced its beak. The gull screeched loudly and took off, and I found myself holding the end of a bizarre kite as the bird struggled frantically to free itself. I tried to reel it in, but it was a large bird and strong. In its panic, it dived and swooped and ducked, crying in pain. The fishing line caught on its wings and tangled round its legs. The more it struggled, the tighter the knots became. I dragged the stricken bird towards me.

Eventually it lay at the end of the rock, almost completely enmeshed in plastic. Its beak with its brilliant red spot gaped wide open, and it stared at me with one fierce yellow eye. I approached it cautiously. It attempted to move, but the line was bound so tight, it was virtually immobile. As I touched it, the bird tried to stab me with its vicious beak. I closed my hands around its neck and squeezed. The gull screamed until it couldn't draw another breath. Silently it stared up at me, its eyes harsh and cold. I felt the fragile bones in its neck crack. Wings fluttered above my head and I looked up in time to see Riordan taking off from a ledge on the cliff just outside our cave. She flew down the coast, parallel with the sea, before hitting a thermal that swept her over the edge of the cliff and out of sight. She did not return.

When I was sure the herring gull was dead, I cut the fishing line away, and started to pluck it. Night was falling by the time I'd finished and my hands were raw and bloody. I stoked up the fire to give me more light and sharpened my penknife on the edge of a rock. I cut off the wings and rubbed them with oil left over from the jar of tomatoes and laid them in the fire to roast. I hacked off the bird's head and feet, gutted the carcass and cleaned it in the sea. I was now faced with the problem of how to cook it as it was far too large to fit in the small pan I'd brought with me. In the end I decided to cut it into quarters, parboil each piece with wild kale and celery and then roast it, but that would be a chore for the following day – I'd need to gather more driftwood to make a larger fire, and right then I was almost too tired even to eat.

I still felt ill, my head throbbed and I often coughed and shivered, but the herring gull's gamy flesh made me worse.

When I became desperately hungry I ate part of the
breast, but was sick shortly afterwards. I shook uncontrol-
lably, my fever came back with a vengeance and I
vomited continually past the point when there was anything left to throw up. It was as much as I could do to
stagger to the stream and suck water from the rocks. I
could no longer tell day from night, warmth from cold,
and I drifted in and out of consciousness as if floating with
the tide, my body growing lighter as the ocean ebbed.
Some time in the darkness I climbed over the stones by the
sea and heard seals singing in caves beneath the cliffs; a
child's voice chanted in my ear, 'Down the great river to
the opening gulf, And there take root an island salt and
bare, The haunt of seals and orcs, and sea-mews' clang.'
I found an orchid in the moonlight growing out of the
rough black rock whose pure white petals exuded the
sweet smell of rotting flesh. I plucked the single flower and
its wounded stalk wept blood. When I presented it to my
father he turned his head away from me and said, 'I'll not
take it; you're no son of mine.' In his arms he held the
fair-haired boy who whispered my name and held out a
shell, purple-whorled, inlaid with ivory. As I sought to
take it from him, the shell burst into flames and became
a fiery sword. The boy grew wings as green as a peacock's tail, grew tall and strong, became Michael, the
angel of war and of chaos, whose face remained a child's.
On either side of him stood the other two angels of
war, Gabriel and Gadriel; next to them was Samael, the
poison angel, who flexed his pied wings, and, it is reputed,
can fly like a bird, and Camael, his sinuous body spotted as a leopard's, his eyes as red as Mars. By his side
stood Af, the angel of wrath, and Azriel, who was
destined to write and erase his writing in a great gilt and

250

leather-bound book: what he writes is the birth of a man, what he erases is that man's name at death; with a pen stroke he separates the soul from the body. I tried to see whose name he was writing, but his twin of darkness, Uriel, the rebel angel of destruction and vengeance, held the sword of God between his burning palms and whispered without words, 'On earth, Jacob is my name.'

I stared at these angels who glowed with an inner light so severe it hurt my eyes, and as I looked from one to the other and felt the cold heat from their burning swords and breasts, Michael bent towards me and said, 'Chance governs all . . .'

In the gritty light of dawn, I crawled from the cave to the spring and drank. The water was cold and refreshing and I splashed it over my face and rubbed it over my beard. The early morning wind seemed to whistle through my bones and I shuffled back to the cave and lay down by the dead ashes of the fire.

Once I looked up to see a pale reflection of myself sitting cross-legged at the far end of the cave: Eddie, her face in darkness, her translucent skin illuminated in one curve of light that ran like a brush stroke from temple to jaw. The sword, with its angel and its silver lilies, was balanced across her bleeding palms and as she held it out to me she said, 'Freely we serve, Because we freely love, as is our will, To love or not; in this we stand or fall.'

I tried to sit up, tried to speak to her, but she was gone, and the wind had blown the ashes so that the mouth of the cave was charcoal with the remains of dead trees and thin slivers of fish bone. I dreamt that Riordan returned to me; she flew back like a cross blazing against the morning's milk-white sky; and as she rose and fell in flight, a gun-shot shattered the still air and the magpie tumbled in a spinning ball of black and white, scattering feathers of pure metallic green.

Returning

I woke with a pain in my stomach and a bitter taste in my mouth. I sat up and light the colour of broken ivy turned to jelly and oozed through my skull. My whole body ached. I tried to sit up and was paralysed by fear. I was no longer in the cave but in a small darkened room. I waited for my vision to clear and fought my nausea. My first thought was that they had caught me and I was being held prisoner. Opposite me was a shelf of shells – top hats, periwinkles, cowries, pelican's foot, a giant whelk and several baby clams. There were white roses on my bedside table and old botanical prints on the walls. I was in my bedroom at home. I got up slowly and walked unsteadily downstairs.

'Niall!' My mother looked up in surprise when I went into the kitchen. 'Sit down, you shouldn't be wandering about like this.'

She directed me towards a chair and helped me into it as if I was old and infirm.

'How are you feeling, love? Do you want anything to eat?'

'Yeah,' I said, surprising myself, 'I'd like some beans on toast,' and then felt my throat constrict as I remembered the sinewy meat torn from the dead gull's bones.

'I'll make some tea,' my mother said. She filled the kettle.

Her face was drawn and she looked tired. 'You've been very ill,' she added, putting some bread in the toaster. 'You had food poisoning.'

'I don't remember,' I said. 'How did I get here?'

'Eddie found you. She said you were on the top of a cliff raving about magpies and angels, and then you collapsed. Eddie got help and flew back with you. I don't know what you were thinking of, Niall, you were practically naked, and you hadn't brushed your hair or shaved for what looked like weeks. I don't have any baked beans,' she said, peering in one of the cupboards. 'I'll go and get some.'

'No, Mother, it's all right. I'll have something else.'

'Are you sure, love? It's no trouble.'

I shook my head. 'No, it's fine, Mother, I'll have jam instead. Thanks for the tea.' I was starting to feel shaky.

'She's a very nice girl. So capable, getting you all the way back here, and you were in such a state. What a way to start your life in London. She said she'd never been here before.'

Eddie. I felt as if the bottom had fallen out of my life.

'Where is she? Is she still here?'

'No, dear, you've been ill for a week now. Eddie came to visit you once, but I don't suppose you'll remember. You were asleep most of the time, and when you weren't you were talking such nonsense. It was all garbled. We've all been so worried, Niall.'

'Well, where's she staying?'

'I don't know. She's a very independent young woman. She wouldn't even stay that first night when she brought you here. You can imagine how we felt when an ambulance turned up at the front door with you on a stretcher looking like John the Baptist.'

I had an image of angels; they smelt of burning oil and their faces smeared into a golden blur. I struggled to clear my head. Eventually I managed to ask, 'Did she leave an address?'

'No, she just said she was visiting friends, and that she'd come and see you.'

'When?'

'I don't know. She hasn't phoned since the last time she was here. I expect she's very busy, dear. She said she had a new job. Here's your toast, love.'

I suddenly thought about what I had lost. 'And Riordan? What about her?'

'I don't know who you mean. You mentioned her when you were talking in your sleep. Something about leaving you. Was she one of your friends?'

I remembered my dream of a magpie falling from the sky, blood and feathers pooling in the sea.

'Niall, why don't you go and lie down? You're still not well.'

'I have to find her, Mother.'

'When you're better. You've got to rest and get your strength back. She'll come and see you again, I'm sure.' She hugged me. 'Oh, Niall, how thin you are. Go on, go back to bed.'

Climbing up the stairs was such an effort I seriously contemplated sleeping on the landing halfway up, but for my mother's sake I waited until I reached my bedroom before collapsing.

Eddie didn't come, nor did she call. I was very tired and all my actions seemed to have slowed as if I was swimming through water at the bottom of a well. It felt as if my parents were tiptoeing around me; there was an unspoken agreement not to ask me anything.

The first day I got up my father put his hand on my shoulder and said, 'You're looking better, son. Come out to the greenhouse when you feel up to it. The Peruvian slipper orchids are in bloom.'

I nodded. 'How are the Draculas?'

'*Dracula amaliae* is in flower, but *Dracula woolwardii* is a little sickly. Good display this year overall. I've written a paper,' he added diffidently.

'I'd like to see it.'

'It needs more work. Bit more polishing.'

Late one morning there was a tap on the door of the study.

'Yeah?'

'Bloody hell, it's dark in here. Get some lights on, man.' It was David. He slapped me on the back. 'What you up to?'

I held out the book. 'My father's notebooks from his Peru trip. He seems to have spent most of his time looking at insects.'

'Most abundant genera on earth; God had an inordinate fondness for beetles.' David stretched his lean, rangy frame across two chairs and hooked his thumbs into the top of his tracksuit bottoms.

'How're you feeling?'

'I'm all right. I've slept a lot since I came back from Ireland, or so I've been told.'

'Coming back to Cambridge?'

'Shortly. There's something I've got to do first.'

'How's the data? Have you got enough?'

'Dunno yet. I should have. To tell you the truth, David, I haven't been thinking about it that much.'

'Yeah, understandable. But listen, don't leave it too long.

We've got to get a paper out on the cuckoo mafia, beat the competition.'

'Like they'll all be scooting off to Ireland as soon as they hear of it.'

'You know what Holland et al. are like – if they can go to Egypt at the drop of a hat to cut the tail feathers off swallows, and glue them back on again to see if females like males with big tails, then hopping over the Irish Sea won't be hard. And you know how quick these guys are when it comes to getting papers published. They're on the boards of all the best journals.'

'Yeah, I know. Honestly, couple of weeks or so and I'll be there. I'm still a little shaky.'

'Too shaky for a beer?'

'Well, now you mention it . . .'

'Then for God's sake get out of your dressing gown and stop acting like an invalid.'

As I was putting on my jeans, David leant against my bedroom door and said, 'And have you been thinking about the wrens? We need to come up with an experimental design to test my hypothesis – you know, numbers of nests as an indication of territory quality and male fitness.'

'David, I've been worried about saving my life, not thinking about your wretched wrens.'

'You've turned into a real drama queen, haven't you? Your mum said you were found on a cliff top spouting about angels. For Christ's sake, you're supposed to be a scientist, not a bloody prophet.'

'Do us both a favour, will you? Shut the fuck up.'

'I'm your boss. You can't talk to me like that.'

'Right now you're official drinks-buyer. Go on, get out of here.'

★   ★   ★

In the pub with David, and with my mother and father, I tried to hide the terrible emptiness I felt inside. It was as if I'd escaped from something that I had no right to escape from. The face in the peat bog haunted me. Some nights I pulled up a body with the face of a child who opened his wide blue lidless eyes, other times it was Michael, who unfurled his wings before me, water and dark earth cascading over the feathers. I tried to piece together what had happened, but the events and images were all jumbled up. Someone had killed William – presumably Brendan – because William had seen the Skunk plants in the Ismails' wood. And that was why Brendan was so down on me all the time. It wasn't just the magpies – he didn't want me to find out about the drugs whilst I was wandering around their property. I didn't know whether John or Mike was involved too; perhaps it was just a coincidence that Brendan found Mike's sword and used it to attempt to pin the blame on me. And that was why there were boats at night, coming in to that secret harbour – to ferry crate-loads of cannabis. But how had I got out of Ireland? Weren't they looking for me?

But then I remembered that no-one save me had seen the body in the bog, and who would believe evidence from a man who saw angels every night and hallucinated about small boys running along the seashore and women with bleeding wrists? And then there was that night in the cave when I visited the Ismails' wood. I'd woken up dreaming of dead trees with burnt salt for skin clutching a handful of leaves from a tomato plant. Not Skunk, not Skunk at all. I tried to think rationally. It was not beyond the bounds of possibility that one or even several of the Ismail brothers had been running some kind of trade in cannabis, though I couldn't imagine Mr Ismail being involved. What was frightening were the gaps in my knowledge; like a long night corroded by alcohol, some memories would remain forever corrupted. I felt as if there was a chasm opening up beneath me. I touched things: tablecloths, window sills potted plants, my own face, wondering what was solid, what I could count on that was real.

And in my waking hours, whenever I shut my eyes, I saw Eddie's face when she turned to me, her eyes dark with tears, Nadia and me on the TV behind her. It came to me when I was sitting in the kitchen one morning that Eddie was the human equivalent of my mother's gerberas: cartoon flowers with fleshy stems and big, brash, bright blooms. After a couple of days, those stems, which had seemed so sturdy, always drooped and the flowers wilted, crestfallen. And I realised that I had brought her from one state to the other; I had reduced her from independent and brave to miserable and insecure. I thought of how she asked me if I'd slept with Ruth, how she'd whispered that she loved me in the dark on those nights when her breath was sweet with wine, and the moon splintered on the sea's sharpest waves.

I looked up vegetarian restaurants in the phone book. There were hundreds of them. Of all the gin joints and all the cafés in the whole of London, how was I ever going to find the one she was working in? I made a list of all the areas I thought Eddie would think were trendy and exciting, borrowed my mother's A to Z and took the tube to the Barbican. It was a soulless place: acres of walkways cut across the remains of the original walls of London. The Barbican itself was a grey hulk, a termite tower block of shoe-box flats and car parks, ersatz greenery and regimental ponds. It seemed to take an eternity to get there, battling against slices of wind shaved from concrete corners;

in my mind a single phrase repeated endlessly: 'Bone of my bone, flesh of my flesh, my self Before me; woman is her name . . .'

I asked in the café and the restaurant, but no-one had heard of a black-haired girl called Eddie from Northern Ireland.

'Tall, thin, could almost be a bloke,' I added.

'No mate, no-one like that here,' said the waiter, and tossed more gloopy pasta into a wok full of tomato sauce, turned it over a few times and ladled it onto a plate for a middle-aged woman wearing a chiffon dress and a lilac-coloured velvet scarf.

I went to Butler's Wharf and peered through the windows of the restaurants whose steel-lined kitchens adjoined the narrow, cobbled street. There were chefs everywhere, leaning against the brick walls, smoking and chatting. The wind was laced with cinnamon and the rich smell of roast coffee from crumbling warehouses by the dock. I watched the chefs come and go while men in black delivered crates of lettuce, mackerel, plum tomatoes, yellow peppers and parma ham; gulls clustered on the edge of the Thames, skimming the surface for rotten fruit and live fish. There was no sign of Eddie.

I caught the district line to Embankment and walked down the Thames to the Oxo Tower. It was just starting to rain as I took a steel capsule from the ground floor to the top. The lobby was full of jars of olive oil and squid ink pasta, dried tomatoes and pickled capers with beautifully photographed labels from Harvey Nichols. From the bar I could see St Paul's, the Houses of Parliament and Big Ben. It was growing dark. I ordered a martini and asked the waitress if they had a chef there, tall, thin, black-haired and blue-eyed, a girl called Eddie from Northern Ireland?

She said she was new and she would check for me. I drank my martini and watched the violet light of the setting sun simmer and boil over the dome of the church as the bells pealed out a funeral march. There were bras dipped in wax and glitter pinned to the walls. I finished my drink, paid the extortionate fee, and left.

As I crossed the bridge to Charing Cross my footsteps, splashing through the puddles and echoing along the steel girders, rang out: 'One flesh, one heart, one soul.' She was my twin after all, my mirror image, my soulmate. How could she have left? And what had I been thinking of, letting her leave? I could imagine her saying, 'Oh, for Christ's sake, catch yourself on, Niall.' I realized belatedly that it wasn't quite that simple: it wasn't a question of her going or staying, or me allowing or preventing her from leaving. What I had done was force her into a position where she had no choice but to go. Single-handedly I had created that situation, undermined her love for me and destroyed our relationship. As if she were an angel I had taken away her free will, given her one choice and one choice only. How could I not have thought that my behaviour with Nadia, and even with Ruth, would not affect her or the two of us? Why could I not see the value of what I had when it was right there in front of me? Mostly, I thought, I never asked myself the right questions, and when I did, it was at the wrong time. In Leicester Square I allowed the throng of people to carry me into the centre. I wondered where I should go. Perhaps I should do a trawl of the Chinese restaurants? Go to Mildred's — Soho's battered vegetarian restaurant where nose rings and a zero concept of personal space were compulsory? Or maybe I ought to try the Swiss Centre? I stood in the rain and looked at the sky, now the colour of carrion. All around me neon signs blazed, trailing films I'd never heard of, much less seen; films that would live for an hour and die in a day. As rain poured over my upturned face I thought that all my life I'd never made any choices; I'd followed my impulses blindly, believing my behaviour to be the inevitable consequence of biology. If I'd wanted Nadia it was because I was meant to desire her; if I'd cheated on Karen it was excusable since I was a man. My masculinity was dictated by my genes, and as a zoologist who was I to argue against that? Science lent respectability to the way I wanted to live my life. I chose not to make choices; to drift and let life take its course, not realizing that that was a choice in itself. I never allowed anyone to become too close because to admit how one feels paves the way to pain. And intimacy coupled with chance – the chance loss of an unborn child; the chance of a car sliding into the sea; the chance of a single cell mutating; the chance of a young boy drowning – can lead only to a violation of the non-random way I thought I wished the world to be. I preferred to woo my women with piles of pebbles, give them gifts of small stones that could be counted and measured and set against other men's. And next year there would be more stones and other women. I remembered what Ruth had said the last time I'd seen her. It was something along the lines of 'no pain, no gain'. She'd said I could never have a loving relationship if I wasn't willing to allow people to become close to me. There always would be attractive women around, but I could choose not to pursue them. It was such an obvious revelation, but one I had never been prepared to observe before. I could choose commitment. I could choose intimacy. I could choose to make myself vulnerable. If I wanted to. I wiped the rain from my eyes. I was being totally ridiculous. Did I think I could just wander round London and ask a few chefs if they'd found what I had lost, a woman who was the other half of me? I walked back to Embankment and caught the train to Kew.

'We're leaving in half an hour.' My mother swept into the study borne on a cloud of perfume. 'Niall, you're not even half ready.'

'Ready for what? Where are you going?'

'It's our anniversary, dear. I *told* you, we're going out for a meal tonight.'

'Oh. Does Father know?'

'Of course he does. Go and put some nice trousers on.'

I looked through my clothes and immediately thought of Eddie, the day when she flung open the wardrobe door and there, for one day of her life, were four nearly identical outfits hanging neatly on their hangers. I didn't particularly want to go anywhere or do anything, least of all with my parents. I chose the cleanest jeans, and a shirt that still vaguely looked as if it had been ironed. When I slouched out of my bedroom, my father was knotting his tie in the hall mirror. He was wearing his tweed jacket, although it was the one that had intact elbows and no patches.

'Will Mother let you go out like that?'

'Why? What's wrong? I look all right, don't I?'

'Yeah, Dad,' I said, 'you look fine.' But I couldn't resist adding, 'Right down to the soles of your Clark's sensible shoes.'

'I've had these shoes for fifteen years,' my father said proudly. He looked at his watch. 'Your mother won't be ready for a while yet. Shall we . . .'

'No you are not going to go out to the greenhouse.' My

mother advanced down the hall putting on her earrings. 'And Charles, couldn't you . . ' She looked away in exasperation. Thirty years of marriage had taught her that there were some things in life you couldn't change. She turned on me instead. 'Niall, don't you have anything smarter?'

'My suit is in Cambridge. Anyway, you look good enough for both of us,' I said, kissing her on the cheek.

A smile twitched across her face.

'We're going by car?' I asked in surprise when my father opened the garage door. I'd thought we would be going to one of the local restaurants.

'We're going to Soho,' said my mother.

I raised an eyebrow. 'That's unusually adventuresome for you.'

'There's not many people who can claim they've been happily married for thirty years,' said my father. 'When I was in Peru, I met a man . . .'

I could have finished the rest of his sentence for him. '. . . who was married when he was a child. He's been with his wife for sixty years. And he said he loved her as much then as he did when they were children.'

But I didn't.

We parked in the NCP and stumbled after my mother as she determinedly wove through the crowds. She was wearing a red chiffon dress and we caught its flare and the bright flame of material as she swung round the bumpers of taxis, past the café culture on the sidewalk, over down-and-outs and between camera-heavy tourists.

At one point we lost her. I turned to my father who, in his Clark's sensibles and tweeds, was unperturbed by the whole affair and was merely treating the escapade as if he was wading through an Andean market in his khakis.

'Can't see her, can you?' I mouthed.

He cupped his hand to his ear, and promptly disappeared behind a strapping youth, six feet two of bronze muscle and black PVC. I started to feel supremely irritated. The thing that struck me most about London were the smells; you were forced to walk in the slipstream of other people's perfume. I hated being touched and jostled after months of space and light; days of seaweed and salt. I wanted to come home and find Eddie: she'd glance at me briefly as I walked in and then start to read me bits from her book on angels, punctuating her talk of wings and swords with new desserts and the decor of the restaurant she would open in London town. I felt like standing in the middle of Soho Square and howling like a dog. I finally noticed my mother waving frantically at me from the top of a short flight of steps.

'In there?' I asked incredulously, to no-one, it seemed.

My mother was whisked inside by a bouncer in a yellow mac and my father had started talking to one of the natives. I grabbed his elbow and ushered him in. We were caught up in a stream of people and flowed past a forest of bird-of-paradise flowers, Swiss cheese plants, Siamang orchids, red hot ginger, heliconia and palm leaves. A woman in an outfit the equivalent of Nineties power dressing meets Chinese peasant gestured towards a spiral staircase descending into the bowels of the building. We slipped on the smooth floor and clung to the polished aluminium banister. My mother casually continued in front of us, executing a perfect Norma Desmond. At the bottom of the stairs she was met by a transvestite in a white corset, feather boa and tiara with legs most men would have killed for on a woman, who offered her a packet of cigarettes from a box hung round his/her neck. My mother politely declined.

I wondered whether she had mixed up her restaurant reviews.

Another waiter in a shoulder-padded Chinese suit steered us to our places. We were in a hall full of beige tables, each with a single red gerbera in a blue fluted vase. The kitchens ran along one side of the hall, separated from us by no more than a thick sheet of glass. Behind the glass were acres of chrome and aluminium, and piles of raw vegetables. Huge vats of stock simmered on the hobs, and chefs darted between leaping flames and clouds of steam.

'One of his, you know, the man who designed Habitat,' said my mother as we sat down at our table.

That at least explained the gerberas if nothing else. My father gamely seized the menu in both hands, but it was quite obvious he didn't have a clue. When in Peru, choose anything that sounds remotely familiar. The starters arrived – he had ordered beetroot leaf, rocket and trevise salad, and he examined it carefully, but was still not fazed when the rocket turned out to be a kind of leaf. He looked at the midrib, and the petiole, then cut it into neat slices, chewed a small segment thoughtfully, and said he couldn't tell which bit was the beetroot leaf, and although he'd never considered eating beetroot leaves before, it did seem an economical and efficient way of utilizing the whole plant. He asked my mother whether one ever ate flowers, and suggested that a salad of beetroot flowers might be the next big thing in upmarket restaurants. After barely a pause to sort his trevise from his rocket, he said, 'Now, Niall, you seem very much better.' He glanced at my mother for help.

She leant forward and patted me on the arm. 'Why don't you tell us what happened?'

'This is supposed to be your anniversary, for goodness'

sake. Why don't you talk about something nice – Peru, or marriage, or, I don't know, what kind of orchid you'll give each other.'

'But you're the best thing we've done in our thirty years together. What could be better than talking about our son?'

'If I'm your son, how come I don't look like you?' I snarled. It was out. I shuddered at my clumsiness. There was complete silence. My father very deliberately wiped his mouth on his napkin and laid down his knife and fork. He looked across at my mother who stared at the table, frozen in the position she'd been in when she last spoke.

'Catherine,' said my father.

'Nonsense, dear.' My mother straightened her shoulders with an effort. 'You're just like us.'

'That's rubbish,' I cried. 'Look at me. Do either of you have black hair? Are either of you tall? Mother is positively tiny.'

'Of course you're our son,' said my mother a little more firmly.

My father picked up his cutlery again and prepared to finish off the rocket.

'Then who is Jacob?'

My mother blanched and my father turned away from us.

'Yes, that's right,' I said, getting angry now, 'Jacob Charles Eamonn Edwards. He has all the fucking family names, hasn't he? I found him. Buried in some godforsaken spot in the middle of fucking nowhere. He drowned, didn't he? He was your real son, and I'm some . . . some impostor. I must have been in an orphanage, a real hell-hole. I can't remember the first seven years of my life. But you know that, don't you? Don't you? It must have been so bad, I've repressed it all.'

'Niall,' said my father suddenly, and sternly. 'Jacob is not my son. To all intents and purposes, you are. And you did not spend a single minute of your life in an orphanage.'

'To all intents and purposes? Just what the fuck is that supposed to mean? Some kind of science-speak? It's now so ingrained you can't have a normal conversation with your so-called son?'

'I think you're getting a little carried away,' he said mildly.

'Niall, you're spoiling our meal,' said my mother. There were tears in her eyes. 'We can talk about it later.'

'I want to know now,' I said, realizing I sounded like a spoilt child.

My father looked up at me and I was struck for the first time how much he had aged. It wasn't the grey hair, it was the finer details – the way his skin had grown thin and transparent, how red veins had broken at his temples. The wrinkles round his eyes had deepened, and as I looked at the pale freckles that had appeared on his hands, I felt fear grip my heart and turn it cold. My father smiled faintly and said quietly, 'You are your mother's son. Now for her sake, please refrain from pursuing this subject.'

There was a lump in my throat and I couldn't eat another mouthful. Fortunately one of the waiters cleared our plates away and topped up our wine. There was an uneasy silence as we waited for our main course. My mother started to talk about the people at work. At first I felt angry – it was the way they had sidestepped the whole issue, and my mother's inane drivelling about the charity shop where she worked drove me insane. She was always talking about it and saying nothing. But for once I listened, and it struck me how interested she was in other people's lives. She knew all about the volunteers who worked there, all the people who regularly brought in clothes and gifts and made donations, and she befriended many of the customers. I'd always dismissed her job as the occupation of a bored housewife, and now I realized how unjust I'd been – she could easily be seen as someone who did something more worthwhile than either my father or me. Her words flowed like glue, seeping into the rift between us. All those years when I'd despised what I perceived as her shallowness, that was what she'd been doing, joining and holding us together. I looked at my shiny, white and empty plate and felt wretched.

My mother stopped speaking abruptly. 'Isn't that . . . yes, yes it is!'

I looked up wearily, thinking I was going to be introduced to another one of my mother's brittle society friends who would laugh the brittle laugh over my qualifications, and the quirkiness of my chosen subject.

My mother turned back to me. 'It's your friend,' she said triumphantly, 'Eddie.'

'Where?' I said, jumping up and looking round the room wildly.

'In the kitchen.'

'I can't see her.' Through all the steam and the white-coated chefs who seemed to have multiplied like amoebas, I could see no-one with black hair and blue eyes, tall, thin, Irish, slouching like a boy.

'There, Niall, look, do you see, right next to the second pan at the back.'

At first I thought she was wrong, but yet again I'd underestimated my mother. A woman was tossing something into a cast-iron skillet which spat and flared. She was dressed identically to all the other chefs, and there was no brace of knives hanging round her waist. She was wearing a cap, and the lick of hair that fell across her forehead was blond. But there was no mistaking her stance, the slightly awkward way she walked, her gauche gait and quick movements, her large hands and angular face. I pushed back my chair, squeezed through the narrow gaps between the tables, and elbowed my way past diners and waiters. I got to the glass wall and edged down it until there was a gap.

'Can I help you with anything?' asked the sous-chef. He was wiping flecks of gravy from the edge of a plate of lamb couscous artfully arranged with an intricate lattice of red peppers. I slid round a waiter balancing a large black tray as dexterously as a conjurer and past a rack of steel bowls.

'Customers aren't . . .' the chef shouted after me but his voice was drowned by the cacophony of frying, clattering and shouting.

I dodged two more chefs, a tureen of soup, a tray of filo pastry parcels, edged round a vat of stock, and skidded to a stop in front of Eddie. Her pale face was flushed red, the blood suffusing her clear skin, and her temples glistened with perspiration. I wanted to take her in my arms, but she was holding a carving knife in one hand and tossing flour-coated lumps into oil so hot it flickered into flame.

'Eddie.'

The head chef yelled, 'Main away,' at the same time and she didn't hear.

'Eddie,' I shouted and she looked up in surprise.

'Niall!' she mouthed. 'What are you doing here?'

'Eating,' I mimed, 'with my mother and father.'

'What?'

'Doesn't matter. I have to talk to you.'

'I'm working.' She swore and ladled out whatever was in the pan, rolled it deftly in kitchen paper to blot the grease and slid it onto a metal tray resting on top of the grill.

'I've been looking for you everywhere.'

'Martin sent me,' said a young man whose skin was white as tallow. 'Wants to know what's going on.'

'Tell him it's fine,' shouted Eddie. 'He's going now, so he is.' She turned and glared at me.

'I wanted to thank you.'

'Niall,' she said in exasperation, 'I'll lose my job if you don't leave me be.'

'When can I see you?'

'What?'

'When . . .'

'When I finish work, we can talk then. Twelve o'clock.' She turned back to the chopping board and brought the knife down with a swift and vicious motion.

'Eddie,' I said, horrified. 'It's meat. You're cooking meat.'

'I can see that,' she snapped, 'I'm not a fockin' eejit. You've got to get on in this world, Niall, and I'll not be going anywhere if I spend my time boiling carrots and lentils.'

'You never boiled carrots or lentils in your life. Your food was always so . . .'

'This is London, Niall, not some poky wee place in the back of beyond. If you want to be a top chef, you have to cook meat. You have to taste it. But I don't eat it at home. Now, will you get back to your ma and da.'

I watched her scarred hands for a moment longer as she rubbed chunks of flesh in flour before dropping them in the pan.

*   *   *

271

'I'm not coming back with you,' I said at the end of the meal. 'I want to speak to Eddie.'

'How will you get home?'

'I'll get a taxi. Don't worry about it.'

My father opened his wallet and peeled off a twenty-pound note.

'I don't need it, honestly.'

'For the taxi, go on, take it.'

'Thanks.' I pocketed the money.

I watched my parents leave, my mother darting between drunken clubbers, my father ambling along behind in his tweed jacket. I retired to the bar, competing with the foliage to get a seat. By midnight I'd worked my way through two double gins and a Scotch. The place was beginning to empty and there was still no sign of Eddie. I asked for another Scotch, but the barman shook his head.

'Sorry, mate, we're not serving any more.'

I put my glass down very carefully and half slid off the bar stool. I slouched out of the restaurant, past the bouncer in yellow who wished me goodnight, and stood on the pavement. Between the restaurant and its attached café was a tradesmen's entrance. I waited until someone came out, then slipped in before the door shut. Inside was a dingy corridor, the plaster peeling from the walls. It led into a changing room that looked and smelt like the locker rooms in a boys' school. I wandered between benches with wire mesh dividers. At the back of the room Eddie was standing in front of a mirror putting on lipstick. Her skin was back to its usual beautiful white, glowing with an inner luminance, and her hair was slicked back in a Twenties-style blond cap. She was more obviously made up than usual, with heavy black eyeliner, blue eyeshadow and pale brown lipstick. She caught me watching her in the mirror and put her make-up away.

'I thought you were stark staring mad fer sure,' she said. 'Whatever possessed you, Niall, to run away like that?'

I walked over to her. I had to ask, just to make sure. 'That body in the bog . . .'

'Och, you're not still going on about that, are you?'

'It was William.'

'Don't be so stupid. William died of meningitis. I went to his funeral.'

'Meningitis?'

'Aye. In the comfort of his own home. Certainly not out in the Ballyshannon bogs, though I'm surprised you didn't die of the cold yourself.'

She put her bag over her shoulder and started walking towards the door.

'Wait.' I grabbed her arm. 'There's just one more thing. You've got to tell me about the drugs.'

'What drugs? Your head's queer and turned. Look, I'm going to miss my bus, will you let go of me? Go home, will you, and get some rest.'

'Well, where did you get your stuff from?'

'From John. John said it was from Mexico, or was it Morocco? I forget. Why? What has that got to do with anything?'

'Nothing,' I mumbled.

'I'm sorry about your magpie, though. They were a bloody nuisance, so they were, but there was no need fer Brendan to shoot it. Still, you know how he felt about them. He had a personal bloody vendetta against the poor wee critters. It's not dead but.'

'Riordan's alive?'

'Riordan? I wasn't sure which one of them it was. They

273

all looked the same to me. Yeah – the bullet clipped her wing and broke some of the big feathers so she can't fly. John's looking after her and he thinks her feathers will grow back by next year.'

'How did you find her?'

'I was looking fer you, Niall. You had us worried. I found her out past the lighthouse – she came and begged me fer food. I couldn't find you anywhere and then I thought of the caves and how in your warped frame of mind you might be hiding in them. I'm not sure how hidden you were, but you were practically delirious. I had to get John to come and help me bring you back up the cliff.'

'And how did you get me home?'

'Ruth paid our air fares – I said you'd pay her back when you were better. And I thought I might as well kill two birds with one stone, drop you back where you belong and start my life in London. We doped you to the eyeballs so you wouldn't make a fuss, but you were so feverish – or maybe I got the dose wrong – you passed out at least a couple of times. So there you are. You're back home. I can't say you're looking fit as a fiddle, but you're a queer sight better than when I last saw you.'

'But. . .'

'I have to go now. I'll be seeing you.' She turned away.

I watched her walk away, and then ran after her.

'Now what?'

'I wanted to tell you that, well, that I'm sorry. I want to see you again.'

'Niall,' she turned to face me, 'when we lived together, you took very little notice of me. The most important thing to you was your magpies and your work. You went to Ireland to do your job and then you were planning to leave and that would be the end of it. Having a live-in lover was just an added bonus fer you. Now I'm here, and there's only one thing that matters to me, and that's to become a sous-chef. It's going to be tough for someone of my background, and it doesn't help to be a girl. I might be working in one of the best restaurants in town, but my job is badly paid, the hours are long, and when you think about it it's only one step up from washing dishes. I haven't got the time and the money to see you, not when you're going to be living in Cambridge. Niall, this is important to me, and you didn't treat me very well. So.' She stopped abruptly. She sighed and, leaning forward, kissed me on the cheek. 'I'll say goodbye.'

'But,' I said, 'but I love you.'

She remained with her face half averted from me. When she finally looked up, there were tears in her eyes. 'You're too late,' she said quietly.

I watched as she walked away. For once she wasn't wearing trousers and trainers; her low-heeled court shoes clicked on the pavement, and light from an all-night caff spilt over her legs. I watched until I could no longer pick out her purposeful stride from the small knots of people that surged from the pubs and clubs.

'Did you sleep well?' my mother asked me when I came downstairs the next morning. It was midday but there was not a trace of sarcasm in her voice.

'Yeah,' I mumbled, shuffling onto the gingham-upholstered bench. I noticed a sample of material pinned on the end, sage green and cream striped. No doubt our kitchen was currently in danger of going out of fashion.

She put a mug of tea in front of me and started making me some toast.

275

'I'm sorry about last night,' I said, and wondered when I'd be able to stop bloody apologizing to everyone.

She sat down opposite me and pushed a photo across the table.

'It was our fault, love. We should have talked about it before, but you seemed so much more balanced once you started speaking again. We didn't want to upset you.'

'What are you talking about, Mother?' I asked, looking at the picture. It was a black and white photo, thoroughly creased, but showing two small boys in shorts sitting on a wall, their arms wrapped round each other. The one on the left was me, and with a stomach-churning lurch I recognized the one on the right, a fair-haired child whose eyes, I knew, would be grey.

'Jacob,' I murmured.

'Yes,' said my mother matter-of-factly. 'After he died you didn't speak for two years. Actually, it was when his mother died that you suddenly went mute. We were so worried about you. We gave you all sorts of tests in case you'd gone deaf, or your vocal cords had seized up. The doctors said there was nothing physically wrong, it was, what did they say, psychosomatic. You started talking when you were seven, as if nothing had happened, and at the same time you insisted we spell your name the Irish way.

'I remember the first words you said: you came home from school, and you said, "Look, Mum, a camellia," and you'd drawn a picture of one – a big bush of pink flowers just like the one we had in Ireland. Then you said, "Mummy, why are you crying?"'

'When were we in Ireland?'

'We used to live there. We wondered, your father and I,

276

why you went back to Ireland. We didn't know whether you'd started remembering your childhood, whether this was some kind of rebuke.'

'Wait a minute, I don't understand any of this. Who is Jacob?'

'Your father had a sister called Sarah. She became pregnant when she was sixteen and came to live with us. No-one else would take her in. It was still a scandal then – there was no father. At least, I suspected who it was, but he wasn't someone who would have taken care of the child. We were living south of Newcastle in Northern Ireland at the time – your father had just come back from Peru and he took a job in Tollymore Forest Park as a groundsman. We needed the money and he wanted to do something that wasn't too taxing so he'd have time to preserve all his specimens and write up papers about the expedition. I was pregnant too – you and Jacob were born within days of each other, and right from the start you were inseparable. I suppose that was why it was such a shock when he died – well, it was a blow to us all.' She stopped speaking and put her head in her hands.

'Drowned,' I said, 'in the harbour.'

'Yes. You played on the beach on your own such a lot, we never thought you'd . . . well, no-one is to blame. You tried to save him even though you were only five. It was a miracle you didn't drown too.'

There was a strong acrid smell. I sniffed and my mother suddenly screamed, 'The toast!'

She ran across the room and pulled the plug out. The toast popped up, black as charcoal. Clouds of smoke filled the room. She threw open the window and the kitchen door and shut the door between the kitchen and living room.

'It's OK, Mother, I didn't want it anyway.'

When she sat down again, her eyes were red. She took a deep, juddering breath. 'Would you like anything else, love?'

'No. Tell me what happened next.'

'Well, Sarah took it very hard.'

'She committed suicide, didn't she?'

'Yes. You found her, unfortunately. In the bath.'

'She'd slit her wrists.' I thought of Sarah with her white waxen features, her lips tinged with mauve and her hair flowing like weed in the red, red water.

My mother nodded. 'And after that, we came back to England. Your father worked in the Natural History Museum for a while and then was offered a job at Kew. Things were a bit better once we were in England – apart from the fact that we had a small, silent child whom teachers branded educationally subnormal for two years.'

I leant back against the wall and thought for a moment, and then said quietly, 'But I'm not his child, am I?'

She sighed. 'No, dear, you're not. To his eternal credit he's always treated you like his son, but no, you're not. It's been hard on your father – though he's never shown it – because you've grown to look more and more like your real father as you got older. You're the same age now as he was when I first met him,' she added wistfully. 'I'll make some more tea.'

I held back from saying anything, but waited as patiently as I could for her to boil the kettle and make us both another cup.

'The camellia, of course, is doing so well,' she said, as if addressing someone other than me. 'Sarah planted it in our garden in Newcastle. It was originally a cutting from

278

Tollymore. I brought a leaf of it over in my handbag when we left Ireland.'

'Amazing that such a huge bush could grow from only one leaf,' I said, following the direction of her gaze to where the camellia in question was in full bloom.

'It might be the heat from the greenhouse that helped it. Certainly Ireland is milder than it is here,' she said, continuing to speak in non-sequiturs. She came and sat down again.

'So who is my real father?'

'He was utterly charming. I met him when I was nineteen and fell head over heels, as they say. I knew your father too at the time, I mean Charles. But somehow I didn't feel, I don't know . . .'

'Passionate?'

'Yes, passionate about him. But then passion can be short-lived. In the long run it's companionship that will see you through to the end. No-one tells you that when you're in love, Niall, no-one says you will have to see the same face day in and day out over the breakfast table, no-one ever tells you that ten years down the line you might be thoroughly bored of that face, or that you . . .' She stopped speaking and looked flustered, and then said, 'We planned to have a June wedding, you real father and I. But I cancelled it. I remember it was the third of May. I was in the garden at the time. There were bluebells and apple blossom out and I thought vaguely, I'll miss all this when I'm away. You see, his family owned a tea company and on his twenty-first birthday he was made manager of one of the plantations in Sri Lanka. And then it dawned on me that I couldn't go. I couldn't leave. I didn't want to spend my life in a foreign country surrounded by people with whom I could have no real contact or connection. I love the countryside here, and there was something about the heat and the alienness of the landscape out there that appalled me. And any children that we had would have to be sent back to England and put in public schools. But of course, if I didn't go with him, I'd be on my own for long periods of time while he was away. I wanted a husband who would always be with me, who would come home from work every day and his face would light up when he saw me.' She looked unbearably sad. I held her hand.

'Your father was kind enough to marry me even when I found out I was pregnant. And Jacob,' she said suddenly, bitterly, 'was not just your cousin by marriage, he was your half-brother.' She wiped away a tear. 'I suppose your father wanted to hurt me – and Charles, when it became apparent that I was going to marry Charles. Or maybe it wasn't deliberate, Sarah was such a sweet, pretty little thing. She could have turned any man's head.'

It was as if I'd known it all my life: I'd been carrying round the death of my brother like some kind of albatross, weighing me down and preventing me from ever getting close to anyone else in case I lost them too. Every day when my father looked at me he must have been reminded of my mother's betrayal; every day when my mother looked at Jacob she must have thought of her lover's infidelity. Jacob and I. Twins of pain. No wonder when he left me I had no words with which to shape the world. The way my mind had been moulded no longer matched the names the adults named us. Words have the power to cut both ways and I was not strong enough to wield them, nor agile enough to dodge those that fell as soft as stones and slid into my skin like scalpel blades. It was not surprising I lost language and emerged as stunted as the crippled chicken child whose life

280

had been filled with the calls of birds and who awoke in an alien place where humans spoke in tongues.

I offered my mother a hanky.

'Niall! That's disgusting! How long have you had that in your pocket? Put it in the wash at once. And put on a clean shirt, you haven't had that one off your back since you got home.' She looked at her watch. 'I'm horribly late. I'm supposed to be at the shop this afternoon.' She hurried out of the kitchen still talking to me. 'Is there anything you want from the shops, love?'

I shook my head even though she couldn't possibly see me. The front door bell rang. 'I'll get it,' I yelled upstairs to my mother.

It was delivery man with a thin, white box. 'For Mr N. Edwards. Sign here.'

I signed. Inside the box was a single white rose and a piece torn from a magazine. I smoothed it flat. It was an article from the *Independent on Sunday* about a Tintoretto exhibition. The picture was of an angel with a child's face swathed in orange damask. The details of where the exhibition was held were ringed in black biro, and in Eddie's unmistakable round-lettered handwriting, it said, '2.30 Sunday. Be there.'

I ran up the stairs two at a time. 'From Eddie,' I said, with a childish grin, showing my mother the flower. She put her head on one side and smiled at me.

'Oh, I'm so pleased, Niall,' she said, kissing me, and I felt like that lost child who'd just discovered language showing his mother the camellia.

I went and sat outside in the greenhouse, perched on one of the benches as I'd done from the age of seven – or was it before then? I read the article thoroughly, and then re-read it. I even considered going to the library and getting

281

out some books on Tintoretto. I didn't want to screw things up this time. Nothing, I thought, should be left to chance.

In fact, I did go to the local library, but I didn't read about painters. The weak London sunshine percolated through the library's tall, thin and grimy windows and I sat with books on the desk in front of me and on my lap, but I read very little and what I did read was what the finest minds of our time had to say about biology. For the three days before I was due to meet Eddie, I seemed to exist in a timeless dimension, like an insect trapped in tree sap, turning and turning in the sticky, gold light before the sap solidifies into amber. If my father was not my father, then who was I? In some ways it was strangely liberating to think that I didn't have to be a zoologist, that I had not descended from a long line of eminent biologists; my son would not have to decipher my journals and read my papers and I no longer had to dream up mad expeditions to foreign parts, places where the inhabitants' speech and the songs of the birds were equally indecipherable; places locked into the clouds where new orchids unknown to science sucked the lifeblood from other flowers. I could escape from the terrible pressure to be like my father and follow in his footsteps. No-one, I thought, would be able to compare me to him, and his father's father, right down through the generations, and find me wanting. I could, I thought, in the cold, yellow light, be anyone and do anything. But when I asked myself what I wanted to be and do, there was no answer, only a stillness and a clarity. On the last day I found a paragraph in one of the books I'd been idly flicking through. I photocopied it, blowing it up to three times the size. I rolled the piece of paper into a scroll and left the library. It said that perhaps there was a gene for free will – a gene that determined whether we were capable of making choices. It was, I reflected on the train back to Kew, one of life's great ironies: a biological blueprint for the determinism of the indeterminable. I would show it to my father, I thought. It would make him smile.

THE END

THEORY OF MIND
Sanjida O'Connell

'TAUT, COMPLEX AND HIGHLY ORIGINAL'
The Times

A thriller, a love story, an exploration of the human heart

Sandra is caught in the complex web of a relationship with Corin.
His energy stimulates her; his passion for her excites her; his work
as a TV producer fascinates her. But does he have real feelings
for her, or does he just want to control her?

Feelings preoccupy Sandra as she carries out her research into the
emotions of chimps. Do they 'care' about other chimps? Do they,
in fact, have 'theory of mind'? During her daily visits to the zoo,
Sandra meets a strange and isolated child, Paul, son of one of the
keepers. What is he doing when he disappears for hours on end?
She also worries about her exotic, brilliant friend, Kim, a
scientist who has built the killing instinct into her predator
robots. Something, or, someone, in Kim's past is making
her unpredictable and aggressive.

As *Theory of Mind* races to its shocking and terrifying conclusion,
much more than Sandra's emotions are at risk. Richly observed,
powerfully written, this extraordinary and thought-provoking
first novel introduces a compelling new talent.

'STARTLINGLY ORIGINAL'
Good Book Guide

'UNSETTLING'
Independent

0 552 99709 9

BLACK SWAN

KNOWLEDGE OF ANGELS
Jill Paton Walsh

SHORTLISTED FOR THE BOOKER PRIZE 1994

'AN IRRESISTIBLE BLEND OF INTELLECT AND PASSION
. . . NOVELS OF IDEAS COME NO BETTER THAN THIS
SENSUAL EXAMPLE'
Mail on Sunday

It is, perhaps, the fifteenth century and the ordered tranquillity of
a Mediterranean island is about to be shattered by the appearance
of two outsiders: one, a castaway, plucked from the sea by fisher-
men, whose beliefs represent a challenge to the established order;
the other, a child abandoned by her mother and suckled by
wolves, who knows nothing of the precarious relationship between
church and state but whose innocence will become the subject
of a dangerous experiment.

But the arrival of the Inquisition on the island creates a darker,
more threatening force which will transform what has been a
philosophical game of chess into a matter of life and death . . .

'A COMPELLING MEDIEVAL FABLE, WRITTEN FROM THE
HEART AND MELDED TO A DRIVING NARRATIVE
WHICH NEVER ONCE LOSES ITS TREMENDOUS PACE'
Guardian

'THIS REMARKABLE NOVEL RESEMBLES AN
ILLUMINATED MANUSCRIPT MAPPED WITH ANGELS
AND MOUNTAINS AND SIGNPOSTS, AN ALLEGORY FOR
TODAY AND YESTERDAY TOO. A BEAUTIFUL, UNSET-
TLING MORAL FICTION ABOUT VIRTUE AND
INTOLERANCE'
Observer

'REMARKABLE . . . UTTERLY ABSORBING . . . A RICHLY
DETAILED AND FINELY IMAGINED FICTIONAL NARRATIVE
Sunday Telegraph

0 552 99780 3

BLACK SWAN

HUMAN CROQUET
Kate Atkinson

'VIVID AND INTRIGUING . . . FIZZLES AND CRACKLES
ALONG . . . A COMPELLING STORY WITH EXCURSIONS
INTO FANTASY, EXPERIMENT AND OUTRAGEOUS GRAND
GUIGNOL . . . A *TOUR DE FORCE*'
Penelope Lively, *Independent*

Once it had been the great forest of Lythe – a vast and impenetrable
thicket of green with a mystery in the very heart of the trees. And
here, in the beginning, lived the Fairfaxes, grandly, at Fairfax Manor,
visited once by the great Gloriana herself.

But over the centuries the forest had been destroyed, replaced
by Streets of Trees. The Fairfaxes had dwindled too; now they lived in
'Arden' at the end of Hawthorne Close and were hardly a family at
all.

There was Vinny (the Aunt from Hell) – with her cats and her crab-
apple face. And Gordon, who had forgotten them for seven years and,
when he remembered, came back with fat Debbie, who shared her
one brain cell with a poodle. And then there were Charles and Isobel,
the children. Charles, the acne-scarred Lost Boy, passed his life
awaiting visits from aliens and the return of his mother. But it is Isobel
to whom the story belongs – Isobel, born on the Streets of Trees, who
drops into pockets of time and out again. Isobel is sixteen and she too
is waiting for the return of her mother – the thin, dangerous Eliza
with her scent of nicotine, Arpège and sex, whose disappearance is
part of the mystery that still remains at the heart of the forest.

'READS LIKE A DARKER SHENA MACKAY OR A FUNNIER,
MORE LITERARY BARBARA VINE. VIVID, RICHLY
IMAGINATIVE, HILARIOUS AND FRIGHTENING BY TURNS'
Cressida Connolly, *Observer*

0 552 99619 X

BLACK SWAN

THE GREAT DIVORCE
Valerie Martin

'UTTERLY COMPELLING'
New York Times

The Great Divorce is a novel about three women, each of whom has a special bond with a great cat. First there is Ellen, a veterinarian at the New Orleans Zoo, who is trying to contain an infectious disease that threatens the zoo's animals, including Magda, the black leopard. At the same time she is trying to come to terms with her crumbling marriage to Paul. Then there is Camille, a disturbed young woman who is a keeper at the zoo, and who finds herself caught in terrifyingly real fantasies about metamorphosing into a big cat. Finally, there is Elisabeth, 'The Catwoman of St Francisville', whose life is being researched by Paul. She was hanged in 1845 for murdering her bullying husband by tearing out his throat with her teeth.

Valerie Martin blends these interweaving stories into a powerful and resonant narrative which grippingly portrays the inner lives of Ellen, Camille and Elisabeth, and their relationships with men, civilized as well as feral. It also conjures up larger themes – in particular the great division between the human species and the rest of nature, and our struggle with that untamed part of ourselves that calls us back to the wild.

'SHE'S MORE CONVINCING, AND OFTEN EROTIC, IN HER DESCRIPTIONS OF SEX THAN MANY WRITERS BETTER KNOWN FOR IT. A RICHLY ENJOYABLE, THOUGHT-PROVOKING BOOK'
Lisa Tuttle, *Time Out*

'A CAREFULLY CALIBRATED BLEND OF GOTHIC HORROR AND PSYCHOLOGICAL DRAMA, THIS IS AN EXTRAORDINARY, AND ENDLESSLY MYSTERIOUS, WORK OF FICTION'
Tom De Haven, *Entertainment Weekly*

'AT TURNS EERIE, DISTURBING, PAINFUL AND PASSIONATE, ALL THE WHILE HONEST AND COMPELLING . . . MARTIN'S MOST PROVOCATIVE AND RESONANT WORK'
San Francisco Chronicle

0 552 99392 1

BLACK SWAN

A SELECTED LIST OF FINE WRITING AVAILABLE FROM BLACK SWAN

THE PRICES SHOWN BELOW WERE CORRECT AT THE TIME OF GOING TO PRESS. HOWEVER TRANSWORLD PUBLISHERS RESERVE THE RIGHT TO SHOW NEW RETAIL PRICES ON COVERS WHICH MAY DIFFER FROM THOSE PREVIOUSLY ADVERTISED IN THE TEXT OR ELSEWHERE.

99313 1	OF LOVE AND SHADOWS	Isabel Allende	£6.99
99619 X	HUMAN CROQUET	Kate Atkinson	£6.99
99532 0	SOPHIE	Guy Burt	£5.99
99686 6	BEACH MUSIC	Pat Conroy	£7.99
99670 X	THE MISTRESS OF SPICES	Chitra Banerjee Divakaruni	£6.99
99587 8	LIKE WATER FOR CHOCOLATE	Laura Esquivel	£6.99
99602 5	THE LAST GIRL	Penelope Evans	£5.99
99721 8	BEFORE WOMEN HAD WINGS	Connie May Fowler	£6.99
99616 5	SIMPLE PRAYERS	Michael Golding	£5.99
99656 4	THE TEN O'CLOCK HORSES	Laurie Graham	£5.99
99681 5	A MAP OF THE WORLD	Jane Hamilton	£6.99
99677 7	THE INFLUENCING ENGINE	Richard Hayden	£6.99
99668 8	MYSTERIOUS SKIN	Scott Heim	£6.99
99605 X	A SON OF THE CIRCUS	John Irving	£7.99
99708 0	METHODS OF CONFINEMENT	Simon Maginn	£6.99
99392 1	THE GREAT DIVORCE	Valerie Martin	£6.99
99711 0	THE VILLA MARINI	Gloria Montero	£6.99
99709 9	THEORY OF MIND	Sanjida O'Connell	£6.99
99718 8	IN A LAND OF PLENTY	Tim Pears	£6.99
99667 X	GHOSTING	John Preston	£6.99
99783 8	DAY OF ATONEMENT	Jay Rayner	£6.99
99777 3	THE SPARROW	Mary Doria Russell	£6.99
99749 8	PORTOFINO	Frank Schaeffer	£6.99
99780 3	KNOWLEDGE OF ANGELS	Jill Paton Walsh	£6.99
99366 2	THE ELECTRIC KOOL AID ACID TEST	Tom Wolfe	£7.99
99726 9	DR NERUDA'S CURE FOR EVIL	Rafael Yglesias	£7.99

Transworld titles are available by post from:

Book Service By Post, PO Box 29, Douglas, Isle of Man, IM99 1BQ

Credit cards accepted. Please telephone 01624 675137
fax 01624 670923, Internet http://www.bookpost.co.uk
or e-mail: bookshop@enterprise.net for details

Free postage and packing in the UK. Overseas customers: allow £1 per book (paperbacks) and £3 per book (hardbacks)